Merrick eased back a touch and opened his eyes, noting at last that Louisa's height had increased in the interval since he'd last spoken to her and her normally passionate responses remained subdued. In the low light, even his vision played tricks. Louisa looked nothing like Lady Farnsworth. They were as different as night and day. He shook his head to clear it, yet Arabella still stood there.

He drew back, resting one hand at the side of the woman's head and the other at her hip.

Arabella stared back, full lips slightly parted, chest heaving. He ran his hand down the length of her sleeve and found the tassel adorning the edge that proved it was indeed Arabella and not Louisa in his arms.

Her brow furrowed suddenly as shock likely gave way to outrage. "What are you doing here?"

Heather Boyd

BESTSELLING AUTHOR

An Accidental Affair

Distinguished Rogues

4

DISTINGUISHED ROGUES SERIES

BOOK 1: CHILLS (JACK AND CONSTANCE)
BOOK 2: BROKEN (GILES AND LILLIAN)
BOOK 3: CHARITY (OSCAR AND AGATHA)

BOOK 4: AN ACCIDENTAL AFFAIR (MERRICK AND ARABELLA)
BOOK 5: KEEPSAKE (KIT AND MIRANDA)
BOOK 6: AN IMPROPER PROPOSAL (MARTIN AND IRIS)

BOOK 7: REASON TO WED (RICHARD AND ESME)
BOOK 8: THE TROUBLE WITH LOVE (EVERETT AND WHITNEY)
BOOK 9: MARRIED BY MOONLIGHT (GILBERT AND ANNA)

BOOK 10: LORD OF SIN (JULIAN AND PORTIA)
BOOK 11: THE DUKE'S HEART (SINCLAIR AND KITTY)

AN ACCIDENTAL AFFAIR

Edited by Anne Victory

Dedication

For Crystal.
Because you made me want to write this story so very badly.
Thank you for your continued support and generosity.

Chapter One

Being good was a damned nuisance. Merrick Bishop, Lord Rothwell, steered Lady Harrison away from curious onlookers for a moment's privacy.

When they were alone and safe from prying eyes, Louisa's lit up with mischief. "I thought you came to my ball to further your search for a wife, Rothwell?"

"I did." He sighed at her suggestion that he was after more than just information from her tonight. Louisa might be very lovely and have curves enough to tempt a man away from honorable intentions, but she had connections he needed to make use of first. Merrick wanted a wife this season, not a potential scandal. He'd put the decision off long enough. He was thirty and at an age when the future, not just his but others, preyed on his mind. "There is still much you can tell me about my quarry. What did you discover?"

She smiled at him fondly and ran her hands over his forearms. "A pity it must be so, but I agree it is high time you married. With your connections and wealth you should have had even the most cautious of fathers lining up to offer up their daughters for marriage to you by now."

He frowned. "That has *not* been my experience. I only need one." If he wanted to find himself the right sort of wife, then he needed access to information about the candidates and their families before he approached them. Louisa had her ear in the right circles, and the wrong ones too. Merrick cast an anxious glance along the hall, hoping no one was lingering close enough to overhear their conversation. He didn't want to ruin what he'd started before he'd truly begun. "Where is your husband tonight?"

"Oh, the card room, I imagine. You know how he is when there are high stakes involved. Except"—her brow furrowed and her head turned toward the hall door—"he did seem rather interested in the guest list, so I think he may have his eye on someone I invited tonight. I do hope it's not one of your possibilities."

Merrick studied her face, wondering if Louisa had it in her to be the least bit jealous of another woman. "Does that disturb you? That he might be meeting with a lover of his own even now?"

She made a face and then laughed. "Only if he chooses someone I dislike. I do not like to share with my enemies."

He laughed along with her, but he wasn't the least bit amused. Marriage was a serious business. When he found the right woman, Merrick would not share. He knew his own mind well enough to believe that when he found a woman who matched his criteria and married her, he would be entirely possessive about her company. "Tell me."

Louisa's gaze softened. "It is as you feared."

He cursed under his breath. "Why?"

"I'm not entirely sure." She frowned. "The old rumors about your father's frequent dalliances are circulating again, as well as whispers of your own more recent affair with that dreadful actress. I warned you anyone who named herself after fruit would be trouble. But she has cried so convincingly over the loss of your affection and everyone thinks you were a monster to her."

Merrick scowled at the memory of his last affair with Josephine Peach. He was not sorry to have ended things as abruptly as he had. "I found her in bed with not one but two grubby stage hands when she'd claimed to be indisposed for dinner. I brought her flowers for heavens sake to brighten her bloody room."

"Well, she is an actress and they do lie for a living." Louisa shrugged. "Couple that with your new interest in balls and even attending the odd picnic, and your behavior has taken on a wholly different light than what you wished for. I imagine every father with a daughter fresh to the marriage mart is watching you closely, and they don't believe you intend to marry. It's no wonder there's a chill greeting you."

Merrick slumped against the wall. "I'm nothing like my father."

"I know. We've been friends a long time and that is why you have me on your side. I'll help ease your way into their good graces, though I'm not sure how much good it will do. You'll have to prove you have honorable intentions, at least for a while." Lady Harrison eased closer, her hands caressing his chest fleetingly. "So, the Howard chit is rumored to prefer books to balls, and there is Lady Cecily, who seems meek and mild at first glance, but she has more spirit than most beneath the well-polished exterior."

She paused for a moment, thinking. "You also asked about Miss Milne's family. Her father has built a reputation as a shrewd businessman, thanks in no small part to the weight of his pocketbook, though that also makes her less appealing when compared to other young ladies coming out this year. The girl is quiet but always the first to supper. Nerves, I expect. Some women eat when they are anxious. She will regret that later in life, I believe."

Merrick nodded. "The Howard girl clings to her mama's skirts at balls and will not leave her side, so we have not spoken more than a few words." He would never consider Lady Cecily, though he did not mention that to Lady Harrison because he didn't care to fuel the gossips as to his reasons. Miss Milne was a possibility, though with her background and lesser connections, she had not been invited to tonight's ball. Louisa's remarks about her appetite did explain why he could never find her at other events she attended though. He'd avoided the supper room in the hopes of striking up conversation away from prying eyes. He wasn't keen to single out any one woman yet, but if he wanted to speak with Miss Milne, he was looking for her in the wrong places. "Thank you for the information."

"It must be rather tedious to court a proper girl, given your past preference for naughtiness. Everyone expects you to continue as you always have, and there have been more than a few long faces this season, I can tell you." Louisa's gloved fingers curled around his. "You should stick to your own kind, Rothwell. You want a wife with an adventurous manner, not a frumpy mouse who'll clear the sideboard in one sitting. I think Lady Cecily deserves a longer look. She has come into her own in terms of fashion, thanks to her aunt's excellent influence. If you would simply tell me your exact requirements the pain might be done already. You're holding back something, I can tell. If I knew all it might make finding the right wife for you easier. I hate to see you unhappy and I know just the way to make you smile again."

Her hand slipped lower to brush across his groin, tempting him away from his plans for the night. A romp with Louisa would do his body good, though getting caught in an affair, no matter how fleeting, was the surest way to lose ground. The ball underway was in part a way to help him find a wife. He had spoken with Lady Mary tonight, though he still had doubts they would suit. Her mother and father had seemed ill at ease when he joined them, almost frightened, which he found utterly ridiculous. He did not make a habit of seducing virgins, though it was highly likely he would end up married to one. Observing Miss Milne's behavior around others would require planning on his part and would await another evening.

"What I want precisely is my business to know." Merrick eased back from Louisa, offering an apologetic smile. "I do appreciate whatever advice you can offer, my dear."

She pouted. "Whoever you marry had better deserve your skills in the bedchamber. You will find you sacrifice much freedom in a marriage."

"That is true." And it was also not. The lady he married would be the one to sacrifice much. The rumors of his father's misdeeds had plagued Merrick his entire life. His mother had fled society eventually, humiliated and hurt because it was all too true. Once Merrick married, he feared that his wife could be subject to the same sort of horrid speculation.

Yet he needed a son—a legitimate heir to take responsibility for the estate and all those who depended on him.

So in return for taking him on, and the burden of his father's legacy, Merrick would make his own pledge. *Fidelity.* His wife would be the only one to bear his children. There would never be a bastard child bearing his likeness. He would not cause the same pain as he had witnessed in his parents' marriage. He had told no one of his thoughts on the subject because in truth, he expected to be disbelieved. However, he had come to the decision that the woman bound to him for the rest of her life deserved the best from him. "I should return to the ball."

"A pity." Louisa's gaze searched his, and then she smiled, proving there were no lingering hard feelings about his unavailability for a romp in the foreseeable future. "There is a dinner at Lady Berry's this week. I shall endeavor to have you invited so you might meet Miss Milne in simpler surroundings. Her parents will be guarding her as carefully as usual, which would get in the way of any seduction, but I am sure your charm alone will win her over the dinner table." She looked up at him from under her lashes. "And if you change your mind and want my company in private, I'm only too happy to oblige."

"Thank you." Miss Milne was at the top of a short list. There were still questions in his mind about her nature to be satisfied, and although she stirred no great passion in him now, Merrick had no doubts he could bed her successfully if they married. He had scant enough new information for tonight, but what he had would have to do.

Louisa flicked her fingers in an intimate wave and departed, leaving Merrick to make his way slowly back to the ballroom. As he returned, he mused at the gamble he was taking in confiding in Lady Harrison and placing so much faith in the reliability of her information. The one thing in her favor was that she was no friend to his wider family, having locked horns with his aunt, Lady Penelope Ford, on several notable occasions.

Louisa was also very critical. She frowned upon indiscretions in the very young and unmarried set, an amusing contradiction for a woman whose dalliances were as scandalous as any he'd heard. But not for the first time did he fear that the names she'd supplied him were what she might want in his wife and not what he needed. It was clear she expected him to continue their assignations once he was married. It was altogether likely the names she'd provided were for women whose morals would bend to match hers and who would turn a blind eye to indiscretions.

He caught the eye of a servant and secured a cup of punch. Not his favorite beverage, but his aim was to appear innocuous and no threat to a good woman's virtue. As always when he thought of a good woman, his eyes turned to one in particular. Tall, slim, and perfectly poised. Arabella, Lady Farnsworth, stood well above those around her, wrapped in pink, tasseled muslin and a feathered turban hiding her pale hair. He had a slight acquaintance with her through a mutual friend, but while he knew much about her from shared confidences, he had actually spoken very little to the lady. Arabella might be a widow, but she wasn't the kind to invite a gentleman to get to know her better. She was much too straightlaced to give him more than a cursory glance when they met. Judging by her frequent high color, his reputation with the ladies made her distinctly uncomfortable. She would never give him the time of day, so Merrick kept a distance and enjoyed the view from afar.

He frowned now though, his eyes flickering to her unexpected companion. What the devil was she doing in Lord Parker's company again? Her niece, Lady Cecily, a debutante whose behavior bordered unacceptable, wasn't even there to be paraded before the man. Parker, an older bachelor like himself, might have the distinction of being received everywhere, but there was something about him that didn't sit well with Merrick. He wasn't worthy of standing so close to the very respectable Lady Farnsworth, but Merrick couldn't pinpoint why.

"Ah, Rothwell." A pleasant male voice interrupted his musing. "Are you making the rounds again tonight?"

He turned to find Lord Louth, an earl he'd not spoken to in close to a year, looming beside him. Louth was extremely tall and broad and well-muscled. He dwarfed most gentlemen and tended to keep to himself. Merrick shook hands with him. "I seem to be. I'm surprised to see you here tonight."

An unhappy grumble left Louth. "Keeping up with recent events."

Merrick glanced at his face and laughed. "Your cousin's suggestion?"

"Something like that." His gaze scanned the room slowly, as

if looking for someone. His next words confirmed he was. "Have you seen Taverham of late?"

"Last week, I think. Passed him on Bond Street. Why?"

"Was he with anyone?"

"Only Lord Acton and his widowed sister. They're thick of late, and I wouldn't be surprised if Taverham is ready to give up on his wife's return and find a new one."

"That's what I heard, too." Louth smiled grimly. "Well, so good to see you again. My thanks again for the lease of your Yorkshire property."

"My pleasure." Merrick grinned. "Did you and your lady friend enjoy the winter there? I'm told it's quite lovely if one doesn't leave the bedroom."

"I don't know." Louth scowled. "The lady threw me out in a fit of temper the very first night."

He hurried off, leaving Merrick to puzzle over that final remark. After all the trouble Louth had gone to in leasing the property and practically begging for absolute discretion, he must have blundered quite badly to not spend even a single night with the woman.

He faced Arabella again and froze as Lord Parker, being taller than the lady by several inches, cast a lascivious eye over Arabella's perfect breasts. The man was practically drooling over her. In fact, as Merrick watched on, Parker's hand rose to play with the tassel hanging from her loose-fitting sleeves. The touch was protracted, and yet Lady Farnsworth did not slap his hand away.

Merrick took a moment to suppress his surprise and then checked the room to see if anyone else had noticed the proper Lady Farnsworth being seduced so publicly. Unfortunately, Louisa had noticed. Her little fists were clenched tightly at her sides, her eyes narrowed. Louisa certainly wasn't the sort to guard the virtue of another lady, so he was convinced she wasn't outraged on Lady Farnsworth's behalf. Was she engaged in an affair with Lord Parker too?

A cunning smile flittered across Louisa's face, and it seemed a distinct possibility she was engaged to some degree with Lord Parker. When she glided slowly toward Arabella and Parker via a circuitous route, Merrick moved to better view the encounter, heart sinking with dismay. Louisa clearly had no love for the situation and Lady Farnsworth seemed unaware she was in the line of fire. It wasn't in Louisa's nature to make a public spectacle of herself, but as she had told him on more than one occasion, there was always a first time for everything.

However, when Louisa insinuated herself into the conversation, Arabella engaged her in a protracted conversation, leaving Parker at a distance from the pair and largely out of the conversation. Indeed, they spoke so exclusively together that when Parker went on his way, neither paid much attention except to bid him farewell. Perhaps he'd been wrong about Louisa and Lord Parker. But whatever the situation might be, it seemed Arabella's knack for avoiding awkwardness with other women was as strong as ever. Her ability to appease others was a skill she employed effortlessly. No matter what happened around her, Lady Farnsworth continued on as if any untoward behavior had never happened.

Chapter Two

At the age of eight and twenty Arabella Lawson, Lady Farnsworth, was not the kind of woman to incite great passion in the gentleman she met. In truth, she did not believe she had ever stirred the slightest rush of desire in her entire life. Nevertheless, she would not be deterred from her mission this night as she had been on so many others. She wanted a lover this season. At long last. Someone who would not laugh at her inexperience. Someone who would show her what her marriage had lacked without thinking there was something wrong with her.

Around her, the most handsome, witty, and downright dangerous lords of society strolled the throng, taking their pick from any number of willing widows. Arabella was both a widow and exceedingly willing. It was simply a matter of catching the right gentleman's eye and praying he understood her intentions. Thanks to a friend's explicit advice, she was as prepared now as she'd ever been. Rosemary Randall, now Lady Grayling, had shared many intimate details of how one might spend a night in a lover's arms, though Arabella had not had the opportunity to put any of that into practice.

So far a lover hadn't fallen into her lap, and the more time passed, the more nervous about the matter she became. She had allowed the need to prepare her niece for the season in London as a reason to set the issue aside until tonight, and that had been a mistake.

What she wouldn't give to have Rosemary at her side now, promising again that all would be well. It was so unfair. If only Arabella's husband had loved her a little, she'd never have been in this predicament. They had married for different reasons, reasons Arabella had not fully understood when she'd made her vow, and she had promised herself to never assume happiness couldn't be hers again. She would never remarry, but that did not mean she had to be lonely. Once the small matter of her virginity was put behind her, she would be content to grow old alone.

She darted a discreet gaze around the room in search of likely candidates for a lover and found no new faces. *Drat.* Even the unexciting Lord Parker was nowhere in sight, likely discouraged by her talk of fashion with Lady Harrison. Lady Harrison had latched on to the topic of riding habits and confessed she collected riding crops to match them. She could never get enough apparently and had a vast array upstairs. The topic had sent Lord Parker on his way in a hurry, his face flushed red.

Lady Harrison winked. "Do excuse me, won't you my dear Lady Farnsworth? A hostess must not neglect her guests, and I see a gentleman over there desperately trying to catch my eye."

"Yes, of course," Arabella said quickly, not in the least concerned to be abandoned so soon. "I do understand. It is so easy to ruffle the feathers of an overlooked acquaintance when hosting a ball. Your events are always so well attended."

Lady Harrison gave her an odd look, then sauntered away in a swish of red silk. Arabella envied her assurance as she moved through the crowd, throwing teasing smiles at the gentlemen she met. Unfortunately, such behavior was beyond Arabella's skills. She wished she only had to look at a man for him to know what she was thinking, but so far interesting things only seemed to happen to other ladies.

The last time she'd tried fluttering her lashes, Lord Louth had asked her if she was ill.

Across the room, Lady Harrison paused to speak to Lord Rothwell, and a devilish smile flittered across his lips before he whispered something in her ear. Tall, dark, and sleek as a caged leopard at Wombwell's traveling menagerie in his dark coat, breeches, and gold-and-white-striped waistcoat, Rothwell could have any woman he wanted and, according to London's finest gossips, frequently did many times over. Was she witnessing an assignation?

More than likely, given his eager nod of agreement and Lady Harrison's pleased, secretive smile. At least that is what Arabella had to assume. Having never been in the same situation, she could only guess what one might say to make that man smile so wickedly.

Arabella put her speculation aside and reluctantly returned to her brother-in-law's company. She smiled at the few friends standing about him, but was astonished to find her niece Cecily was not amongst them anymore. After a discreet check among the couples gathered on the dance floor for the quadrille, Arabella groaned under her breath. Cecily had vanished. Again. She tightened her grip on her fan. Cecily had promised no more disappearances, yet the minute Arabella's back was turned the girl flitted away. Chaperoning her was proving to be a nightmare.

A hot breath against her ear made her jump. "Go find her this instant and bring her back to me."

The demand from her brother-in-law was not unexpected. He'd made it very plain that Cecily's behavior and her failure so far to snare the right husband was entirely Arabella's fault, and to a degree he was right. Yet she'd spent little time with the girl as she was growing up, and Cecily already had firm opinions on what she would do and would not do. She could hardly be blamed if the girl refused to heed her words. When they clashed, Cecily was always quick to point out that Arabella should have had a daughter of her own to mother by now.

"She won't be far," Arabella said quickly, eager to appease Farnsworth before anyone noticed the steam billowing from his ears. She didn't have the faintest idea where her niece had disappeared to in this crowd, but if Arabella didn't make a start on finding the girl then everyone around them would soon know Cecily was unchaperoned yet again.

Her brother-in-law elbowed her arm hard enough to sting. "The minute you discover her location, we are leaving this madhouse," he said. "Tomorrow I'll decide whether remaining in London another month is worth the expense of having come at all."

Arabella's heart soared. Once she was done chaperoning Cecily, she could return to Winslette, her home in Wiltshire, and the company of her closest friends. Because of Farnsworth's demands and assurances that his daughter's needs came first, she'd missed two of the most important weddings of the season. The first was the Duchess of Romsey's and the second was of her friend and neighbor Lord Grayling to Miss Rosemary Randall. She was very sorry to have missed the latter as she'd had a hand in matching the pair together. Farnsworth had refused her leave to go, citing that his daughter's needs took precedence over everything she'd wanted.

Since Farnsworth had become the earl, he'd developed the most penny-pinching and demanding habits. Not that any of the Farnsworth men had ever been reasonable creatures. It was uncharitable of her to think ill of the dead, but her husband and his son, short though the latter's life had been, had not been easy people to make happy.

Her husband had married her to run his homes and promptly ignored her in favor of his own amusements. Since his death, it had become clear the most recent Lord Farnsworth had little patience for either the social whirl or the expense and fuss of his daughter's first season.

Arabella squared her shoulders and set off in pursuit of Cecily with a heavy heart.

Mending fences when Farnsworth was rude to their hosts gave her a nightly megrim she could easily do without.

Farnsworth's dislike of London and the season's frivolous entertainments ran counter to his expectations for being here. If he wanted his daughter to make an advantageous match, then at least he could expend some effort to get the girl successfully married off.

She studied the men around her as she moved through the crowd in search of Cecily and contented herself yet again with inspecting the lords present. Arabella was tall herself, so her eye was drawn to the men of equal or greater height more often than not.

When it came to choosing a lover, Arabella also had a short

list of requirements: Cleanliness was essential, though not the suggestion of it that came from heavy-handed application of perfumes. Unmarried and unattached by affection for the season was her main requirement, however. She could not contemplate usurping another woman's place. What she wanted was someone to be hers alone when they started, someone who did not mind that one short affair might be enough but would not be averse to a repeat meeting if their tryst proved enjoyable. Arabella blushed as she gained the entrance hall and looked around. She didn't have the first idea under what circumstances that might be possible. She only had the guidance of a distant friend's confidences to rely upon that the sexual act was both pleasant and worth repeating.

As she traveled through the card room and came up empty-handed, she marveled that there were so many widows in London for the season, many of whom already seemed in the company of unattached men. She envied them their confidence. Arabella couldn't look at a certain well-known rake with whom she was acquainted without a blush heating her cheeks. But from all she'd heard, Lord Rothwell had a similar effect on every woman he met.

She fanned her face quickly, then snapped the fan shut. Now was not the time to dwell on her own interests. She had a niece to find before society noticed her absence and scandal caught them. She was almost satisfied she would survive one more night without incident until she ventured to the retiring room. Cecily was not there either, and Arabella retraced her steps, hoping they had passed each other unseen.

As she regained the ballroom and looked around for her niece, an elegant, silver-haired matron caught her eye. Lady Penelope Ford, society's most intimidating stickler when it came to propriety, met her gaze steadily as she drew closer. Arabella straightened her spine instantly, even while concentrating on appearing as unperturbed as possible.

"Good evening, Lady Farnsworth," Lady Penelope Ford murmured as she drew near.

"Good evening, Lady Penelope. A pleasure to see you again."

After a long, uncomfortable moment, Lady Penelope nodded regally and returned to her own party, a half dozen members of the Ford family by their looks. Arabella continued on with as much calm grace as she could manage, but her heart was pounding. Quite frankly, Lady Penelope's scrutiny terrified her. It always had. One curt word from that lady would ruin Cecily's chances of making a good match and put the family out of favor with those who mattered.

She glanced behind her self-consciously and shuddered. Every time she crossed paths with the Fords, Arabella developed an uneasy feeling in the pit of her stomach. Society called them the *Fighting Fords* for a reason. Navy men, every last one, and with tempers little suited to conforming to society's expectations. No one doubted their loyalty to king and country, but they were said to fight as much amongst themselves as against the French.

A prickle of awareness caressed her neck. She turned her head a fraction, startled to meet the Earl of Rothwell's intense stare. Lady Penelope Ford's wayward nephew was known to her through a neighbor and friend in Wiltshire, so she smiled kindly.

His attention did not waver when dancers formed lines between them, and he did not smile at her as he had done with Lady Harrison. Heat swept up her neck and cheeks, making her wish her discomfort wouldn't be obvious should she reach for her fan and beat it furiously before her face.

Arabella returned her gaze to the path ahead, determined not to appear as virginal as she felt at that moment. Rothwell's scrutiny, even from across a crowded ballroom, was worse than his aunt's. He had the most remarkable effect on her nerves, sending them in all directions at once. Yet when she peeked in his direction again, Rothwell had vanished, leaving her to sadly conclude that *he'd* certainly had no trouble forgetting her as soon as his gaze moved on.

Chapter Three

Merrick stood alone in the darkened chamber, waiting for Louisa to join him and deliver whatever urgent news she had whispered to him in the ballroom earlier. Her entreaty to meet with her within twenty minutes puzzled him at first, but he soon discovered he was eager to avoid the ballroom and the irritation certain parties presented.

His family, Ford cousins, were present and again eager to return him to the fold.

He didn't want anything to do with that side of the family.

Then there was Lady Farnsworth, dressed in beguiling pink silk and likely being pursued by a man far too old for her. He shouldn't feel protective of her. She'd barely spared a glance his way, yet there was something so innocent about her that he regretted they were not better acquainted so he might advise against the connection.

He leaned his head back against the paneled wood wall as irritation filled him. He had his own affairs to arrange, and it was going poorly. A proper courtship. A marriage and then years of wedded bliss seemed well beyond his reach after months in London. The last two ladies he'd smiled at had disappeared behind fans and rushed off together. It wasn't the first time such an event had happened, but his patience for nonsense was wearing thin. A score of fathers and guardians had followed his progress through the ballroom, and he could still feel their disapproval now in this very room.

Was being good all for nothing? If he denied himself any pleasure at all, would it make a scrap of difference in how society viewed him? It didn't seem likely.

Maybe he and Louisa could come to an arrangement, one that could be ended at a moment's notice should he find a woman he wanted to marry and that would cause no hard feelings between them. It was not as if they hadn't slept together before. Louisa was always eager for bed play and she was very, very good at making a man lose track of time.

She'd been dropping hints all season that they could be together whenever he wanted. He'd be using her, but then again, she'd be using him too. He considered a moment longer. What harm could there possibly be?

He was dazzled momentarily as the door creaked open, and as soon as Louisa closed it, Merrick pulled her into his arms. He allowed a brief squeak of protest at his urgency before he sealed his lips to hers. He closed his eyes as Louisa's hands fluttered by his shoulders like frightened butterflies before settling lightly on his upper arms.

Merrick crowded her against the door and kissed the woman fiercely. Although restrained at first, she didn't stop him but played at seeming inexperienced. Merrick loosened his grip and skimmed his hands down her sides, ending his exploration at her delightful derrière. She squirmed in his arms, her hands clutching then releasing his coat as if she didn't know quite what to do with them. The thought plagued him until he forced himself to pay greater attention. The light embrace tightened, arms rose to loop around his neck, gloved fingers teased the back of his hair and encouraged him to continue.

Yet her kiss was wrong. This wasn't Louisa. Not even his imagination could conjure up a less-experienced version of that woman.

He eased back a touch and opened his eyes, noting at last that Louisa's height had increased in the interval since he'd last spoken to her and her normally passionate responses remained subdued. In the low light, even his vision played tricks. Louisa looked nothing like Lady Farnsworth. They were as different as night and day. He shook his head to clear it, yet Arabella still stood there.

He drew back, resting one hand at the side of the woman's head and the other at her hip.

Arabella stared back, full lips slightly parted, chest heaving. He ran his hand down the length of her sleeve and found the tassel adorning the edge that proved it was indeed Arabella and not Louisa in his arms.

Her brow furrowed suddenly as shock likely gave way to outrage. "What are you doing here?"

"I do beg forgiveness." He swallowed quickly. "I was expecting someone."

Her brows rose in surprise. "Me?"

Merrick winced. "No, of course not."

"Oh." Arabella sighed as her gaze lowered to his waistcoat, and to his astonishment, she smoothed it. "I suppose you wouldn't be really, would you? You clearly meant to meet another. Of course, of course. Do forgive my mistake."

Merrick frowned at her rambling, but her touch was driving him wild. She should be angry at the very least, not apologizing, but she appeared more concerned with setting him to rights than beating him with her fan. The fact that she assumed he was meeting with someone alarmed him too. Was he so transparent to others? "What are you doing here?"

She grimaced again and her eyes darted around him. "Searching for my niece. I don't suppose you have her?"

"She would not be with me. Never with me."

"Oh." Her expression brightened as she met his gaze. "Oh, that is good. Really. I could not imagine. What would she have said? Oh, never mind what I might imagine. I'm so sorry to have interrupted."

Merrick grinned at Arabella's confusing babble. He'd muddled her well with his kisses, and he was tempted to confuse her even more. He would be much better for her than Parker. Their ages were closer as was their height. He eased closer, delighted when her hands caressed his waistcoat again. He tilted his head to the side, catching her eye as he leaned closer still. Their lips hovered an inch apart, and he thought he might just have the opportunity to kiss her again. She didn't appear too upset about his mistake. In fact, he believed she might be agreeable to another kiss, as she never pushed him back or moved away. The idea of kissing her again was so terribly tempting.

Her soft breath rushed across his lips, but just when he would have kissed her again the door they leaned upon bucked. Merrick threw his and Arabella's weight against it to keep it closed. He quietly turned the key in the lock to ensure they wouldn't be disturbed.

Wedged between him and discovery, Arabella remained still and very quiet in his arms. After a time, when Merrick was sure whoever it was had gone away, he glanced at his companion's face. Her eyes were closed, her body resting snugly against his. As she took a deep breath, her firm, high breasts brushed against his chest. He cursed his luck that they were not both naked at that moment. All he could think of was her long, silky smooth limbs entwined with his and her passionate sighs filling his ears.

But with the ball outside and her niece being searched for, he didn't like his chances to experience any of that.

He stood back, folding his arms across his chest to stop himself from hauling Lady Arabella back against him to finish the night as he'd prefer. Naked and writhing with him in a bed unfortunately seemed a vast improvement on finding a bride.

Arabella pressed her hand to her cheek and then covered her lips. After a long moment, her hand fell away and she glanced at the door. Her fingers clenched together at her waist. "I'm sorry for disturbing you. I hope I haven't ruined anything important. I suspect you were awaiting Lady Harrison, and she's likely gone back to her guests."

He was stunned that she'd correctly guessed who he was waiting for. Merrick hadn't thought she ever paid attention to him. A meeting with Lady Harrison mattered little when compared to merely kissing Arabella. "I will find her later."

"She might have retired upstairs for a short time," Arabella said. "She's rather proud of her riding-crop collection and invited Lord Parker to view it. I did consider asking to go along with them, but my interest in horses is fleeting at best. Have you seen them?"

Merrick gaped at the primmest woman he knew. Had Arabella really believed that Louisa was speaking of riding *actual* horses? She couldn't be that naive. He chose his next words with care just to see how she answered. "I've no interest in inflicting pain on my mounts."

Her face twisted into a puzzled frown. "But you ride every day. I have seen you at it and always with a riding crop in your hand."

Oh, dear God. He rubbed a hand across his face to hide his astonishment. She truly had no idea what the conversation had been about. "Not like that."

"Oh," she said at last, but Merrick wasn't at all convinced that she had the faintest idea how and where Louisa applied her riding crops. He certainly wasn't going to tell her that Louisa liked to dominate her lovers in the bedroom. That was not a conversation he wanted to have with Arabella on any day. He might have to explain then how he knew and why, on occasion, the experience to be on the receiving end could be thrilling.

She fiddled with the tassel on her sleeve. "I should go and find my niece. I would appreciate you refraining from mentioning I was in search of her."

"Yes, your troublesome niece." Merrick was not at all impressed with the way that girl behaved when unchaperoned, which appeared to be every chance she could get. "Of course. I'm not one for adding to gossip. Go find her before she truly gets into trouble."

Lady Cecily was swiftly building her own reputation as a hoyden. She would ruin herself if she didn't exercise more care, and she would drag Lady Farnsworth's good name down with her.

"She's really very lovely," Arabella said firmly, although Merrick thought her words lacked a degree of conviction, as if they were well rehearsed.

He didn't answer but raised a brow, daring her to say something unflattering. It would be the first time ever to his knowledge.

When Arabella instead turned decisively for the key in the door, Merrick pressed his hand back to the door to hold it closed a little longer. He eased close to her one last time and inhaled the subtle fragrance that clung to her. Roses had never smelled as sweet. "Thank you for the kiss."

Her eyes met his over her shoulder, her expression one of utter astonishment. "Oh, no. Thank you, Rothwell. Thank you very much."

Arabella stumbled into the hall on legs of wet clay and attempted to appear unruffled by her private encounter with Lord Rothwell. The man could kiss a woman so well she practically melted into a puddle at his feet. Arabella desperately needed a moment to gather her thoughts and to understand what had just happened between them. How could that man kiss her so soundly and yet have been waiting for Lady Harrison to join him instead?

And he'd thanked her for one kiss!

She snapped her fan open and created a cooling breeze across her face. She was sure her cheeks must be bright red from the excitement and delightful shock of his attention. Part of her wished she could go back and let him continue with everything else that kiss had promised. Yet the other half, the sensible and rational half, whispered its terror that she might never get enough and would make a fool of herself over the rogue.

If not for Cecily needing to be found, she might still be in Rothwell's arms and happy to remain there. If that was how most men behaved when alone with a widow, she was terrified of what the somewhat bolder Cecily might allow when faced with another man of similar skill. That girl had no idea how close to scandal she skirted or what that would mean for others if she were ruined and discarded. It would be a catastrophe.

Properly panicked by how easily she'd forgotten her responsibilities while in Rothwell's arms, Arabella glided back into the ballroom, hoping to appear unruffled, and glanced around carefully. The whole room wasn't staring at her, but she feared at any moment they would turn and ask her if she agreed with the gossip about Rothwell's appeal to women. There was no way she could deny it now.

She followed a footman through the crowd, skirting along the side bordering the terrace door in search of a cooling breeze along with her niece. She caught her gown in her hands as she spied the exact color of Cecily's peach muslin gown flittering away from her. She followed Cecily as quickly as she could, rather glad that the direction would take her away from Lord Rothwell. After experiencing his kiss, his presence would be unbearable now.

She inched through the crowded ballroom, apologizing profusely as she squeezed past revelers; however, there was no sign of Cecily on the dance floor or trapped near the wall by one of the groups milling about, which meant that her niece had *successfully* slipped out of the ballroom, most likely through the open terrace door ahead. Farnsworth would be livid when he found out she'd courted scandal and would likely blame Arabella yet again for his daughter's exasperating behavior.

Arabella gained the terrace and peered into the darkened corners in search of Cecily. Not a shape could be seen in the shadows of the garden's shrubbery, which was lit by the waning moon above. But then she caught a whispered word, just beneath the volume of the ball taking place behind her. A trickle of dread caressed her spine and she eased further along the terrace until she'd left the safety of candlelight spilling from the ballroom. She stopped in a patch of deep shadow with her breath held and waited.

When her eyes had adjusted to the gloom, she detected a couple, a tall man and a woman of slight build, standing below her on the lawn beside a garden statue. The couple also appeared to be kissing very passionately.

She squinted at them, praying her first suspicion was wrong. Her niece would not be so easily led astray, yet it might just be Cecily. Although the fellow below needed to bend considerably to kiss the woman, he was very tall, lean, and the gold buttons of his coat shone brightly. He reminded Arabella of a stork. She groaned. Lieutenant Laurence Ford, one of Rothwell's cousins, in fact, fit that description and had been flirting with Cecily since they'd first met nearly two months ago.

Arabella drew in a deep breath, ready to descend and break the would-be lovers apart, but a firm hand curled over her arm and held her still.

"Stay here," Lord Rothwell said quietly, appearing at her side as if from thin air. His touch slid down her arm in a slow caress and he squeezed her hand briefly. "I'll send her back to you immediately."

At a loss for words, Arabella stared at him. The sensations he'd stirred in her during their kiss returned, but gaining Lord Rothwell's assistance to avoid scandal was the last thing she'd counted on. Before she could assure him that assistance was unnecessary, he was gone, rushing down the stairs, separating the lovers by force, speaking harshly to them both. Although she strained, she could hear none of Rothwell's remarks clearly. But given the tone and the way the lieutenant drew back, Rothwell had clearly made a good argument for a return to decorum.

Cecily persisted, however, and stepped toward Lieutenant Ford again. The young man shook his head and backed up several steps.

"Return to your aunt before you cause her even more embarrassment than your current behavior has," Rothwell urged in a louder, clearer voice. He turned on his cousin. "And you, Aunt Pen is here, you fool. Do you really want everyone to hear her opinion on your behavior tonight?"

Lieutenant Ford's shoulders sagged in defeat. It seemed there were more people besides Arabella eager to remain on Lady Penelope Ford's good side. Even grown members of her family seemed intimidated. Arabella thought Lieutenant Ford very sensible at that moment.

For a few perilous seconds, Cecily held her ground, but then her niece fled back toward the terrace where Arabella waited. Cecily's face was a mask of mutinous fury, jaw clenched, eyes narrowed. The girl stopped a few paces away. "Do you have any idea what your meddling has ruined?"

"Cecily, please. Your father demands…"

"Don't you dare speak to me again tonight. You're just like Father. I will never get to have any fun or have a say in my life if you support him and not me. It isn't fair." Then, with a noticeable effort, Arabella's niece drew in a shuddering breath and calmed her temper. Cecily smiled serenely, turned on her heel, and strolled to the ballroom, pausing in the doorway a moment before gliding through as if she had not just been caught acting inappropriately.

Arabella glanced at Rothwell where he stood with Lieutenant Ford on the lawn and remembered their earlier conversation. Rothwell had been adamant that Cecily would never be with him, which Arabella feared meant he knew something unpleasant about the girl and meant to avoid being linked to Cecily at all costs. She winced. She didn't know what to do about her niece's shocking behavior. She seemed completely without remorse for the scandal she was courting.

Arabella wanted to give Cecily the benefit of the doubt, hoping she'd misjudged the girl's nature. She would pay more attention to the girl and relegate her own hopes for a lover this season to a date well past Cecily's wedding. The girl desperately needed her guidance and a firmer hand if she wanted to make a good match.

Curiosity propelled her down the steps toward Lieutenant Ford and Lord Rothwell. She needed to know how bad her niece's behavior had become in order to correct it. Arabella wanted to know just how many times Lieutenant Ford had snuck away with Cecily to be so enamored of the girl.

Chapter Four

Merrick set his hands to his hips and glared at his young cousin. "Touch her again without having spoken to her father first about a marriage and we will not meet so civilly again. You cannot behave in such a manner without considering the consequences for both of you."

"I love her," Laurence protested passionately.

He took his cousin's measure. His time at sea, exposed to the elements and a harsher way of living, had hardened Laurence's features somewhat. But given his protestation of devotion to Lady Cecily, he was still an exuberant young man and had much to learn about thinking before acting on his passions. "You're the right age to spout that nonsense and yet still too foolish to understand what it means. Go back inside, stay away from the girl, and do not dishonor her family or yours with this nonsense until you're at least a half dozen years older." Merrick scrubbed a hand through his hair. He had little patience for the Fords right now.

Laurence glanced toward the terrace with an expression reminiscent of a scolded puppy, wide brown eyes pleading to be forgiven. Merrick turned his head and saw Arabella had remained. Laurence made to approach her, yet Merrick could not allow that. He pushed his cousin toward the side of the house. "Go that way, you fool, and do not be seen returning to the ball."

The puppyish eyes turned on him. "Please, coz. Let me explain myself."

He'd had some idea that Lady Farnsworth's niece and his cousin were moving beyond harmless flirtation before tonight and had meant to warn off his cousin from making a foolish choice. If he hadn't followed Arabella discreetly, he would never have stumbled upon the truth of just how far Laurence had fallen under the minx's spell. He'd placed his commission in jeopardy with this foolishness. Given what Merrick had discovered of Cecily, the family would never support a match to such a girl.

"Not a chance." He gave his cousin a harder shove that sent him on his way to the side door. "Now off with you."

Once Laurence was out of sight, Merrick faced with trepidation the dazzling beauty waiting at the base of the steps. Damn the Fords and their troublesome natures. Coming so soon on the heels of their accidental kiss, he wasn't sure what Arabella would say to him. She would have every right to be furious if the girl was ruined and no marriage proposal came of it.

Yet when he had determined her intent to break up the lovers, he had not been able to abandon her to the task alone. That ungrateful niece of hers might pretend to be proper when society was watching, but she was beyond the pale when it came to men. Lady Cecily was hell-bent on her wild rebellion. He didn't know what Laurence was thinking to court such a scandal-loving girl. He supposed it was for the money to be found in her dowry. Little could be said for her connections, save for the pleasure of Arabella's company.

Merrick started back the way he'd come, fighting to return his pulse to normal before he spoke with Arabella. Laurence was a fool. A man in love did not maul an innocent girl in a dark garden, even if stridently encouraged to do so. He treated her as if she were precious and with the utmost respect. The girl was encouraging her own ruin and Laurence was likely a means to an end.

He stopped three steps away from Arabella, maintaining a discreet, respectable distance. She was so beautiful that his heart skipped a beat. He barely believed she'd been in his arms, even unwittingly. He was ashamed to have acted so rashly. "He won't bother her again, I give you my word."

The pale wisps of hair peeking from beneath her turban appeared as a glow about her soft skin like a halo of an ethereal siren. "Thank you. I am very much obliged to you."

"My pleasure, my lady." After a long moment of silence, he wrenched his gaze from her and checked the terrace to see that they remained observed together. Thankfully there was no harm done so far. "You should return to the ballroom," he murmured gently.

"Wait." She moved closer a step. When she stopped, he found it pleasant, despite the frown that had appeared, to look into a face that matched his in height. Arabella was quite tall compared to most women and very lovely. It was a shame his rash act had revealed he was still the rogue society thought him to be.

"I am sorry for any trouble my niece may cause between you and your cousin," she said suddenly.

He shrugged away her concern, noticing she didn't appear at all put out with him. "Hardly a day goes by when someone in the family isn't irritated with the other. The difficulty will amount to nothing. Laurence is to return to his ship next week and will likely return to action soon after. I'm sure if their affections are merely infatuation, they will fade soon enough."

"So soon? I will pray for his safe return," she whispered.

Merrick drank in her beauty and good nature for a long, selfish moment. A woman of her character would not choose to be with him unless forced to. If anyone learned of their kiss, she would be cast in an altogether unflattering light. She likely knew being in his company for any length of time might tarnish her reputation and should draw away, but for the moment it seemed she had forgotten. It was nice to stand before a proper woman without caution shadowing her eyes.

But the moment could only be fleeting. The impulses of youthful exuberance and excess of living were a part of his history that he could never shake. Everyone had expected him to live up to his father's reputation as a scoundrel, and he had to a small degree. Only now was he regretting that his behavior made it likely he would never have a chance with a woman like Arabella. He steeled himself to return to his admiration from afar and think of her reputation first. "After you. Please."

She stared at him a long moment before she dipped a perfect curtsey and then hurried up the steps and disappeared into the ballroom without a backward glance. Her poise was something he admired, along with the sway of her long body when she moved. Quite mesmerizing, really. The woman had to be almost as tall as he was—her legs would likely go on forever. He halted at the railing and faced the dark gardens, struggling to reorder his thoughts and baser impulses. Thinking of her like that was hopeless. He would wait a decently long time before he rejoined the ball, long enough that his return might never be linked to hers.

"There you are." The exasperated admonishment broke the quiet and got his hackles up. If he was not mistaken, his aunt, Lady Penelope Ford, had come to deliver her usual scold. "What are you doing out here, young man?"

He glanced over his shoulder as anger swept through him. His Aunt Pen saw everything but rarely understood, and would not miss a chance to meddle in his affairs. Thank God she knew nothing of his plans to secure a wife. If she did, she would not hesitate to push any and every properly connected, buttoned-up debutante in his direction with the hopes of reforming him completely. That wasn't the sort of wife Merrick had in mind. He didn't want to change *that* much when he married. "Enjoying the fresh air in solitude until now. You?"

Her lips turned up, but he knew better than to trust her smiles. "I thought to ensure scandal might be avoided, but I see my fears were unnecessary."

He tensed at her words. Could a man ever spend one night in society without even his family thinking the worst of him? It was too much. She would never believe he was out here to prevent Laurence, the baby of the Ford family, from being foolish. "Is that so?"

Her smile dimmed at his clipped response. Once, they had been on intimate terms: Aunty Pen and little Merrick. But that was many years ago, and he was no longer a child and ignorant of his aunt's manipulative nature.

"You can cease your ridiculous coldness." Her gloved fingers slid over his arm and squeezed. "We are family, whether you wish to acknowledge it or not, and that makes your happiness my concern."

He stared at her hand and when she didn't release him, he dug deep for an insult sure to send her away. Merrick would prefer to deliver an original barb than rehash a previous accusation, but unfortunately, his mind was blank. His aunt was as unfeeling as one could be and still breathe. She hadn't a shred of compassion in her blood, but he'd accused her of that many times in many different ways. "I would prefer you stay out of my life altogether. What I do, or do not do, is my business."

Her hand didn't move. "You risk much with your actions."

"I risk nothing." Merrick stepped back so she couldn't touch him anymore. "Do enjoy your evening. Perhaps one of your other nephews will make a scandal for you to halt before the night is through. That should keep you amply entertained and happy to be in the thick of it. Go find one of them to reform tonight."

She said his given name, *Merrick*, exasperation tingeing her tone with annoyance, but he turned away, eager to catch one last glimpse of Arabella before he returned to the frustrating task of wading through society, searching for the one woman who could stimulate him in mind and body. Someone he could imagine sitting across from at breakfast every day for the rest of his life. To find someone who might come to care for him as he was and not want others so he might do the same.

As he entered the ballroom from the terrace, he caught sight of Lord Farnsworth and his daughter Cecily sweeping out toward the entrance hall. They were leaving and not a moment too soon in his opinion. Arabella followed after, speaking quickly to a few women of her acquaintance on her way out. She didn't notice his return.

He glanced over the room but found his view no different than earlier in the evening. Lady Mary held court with several gentlemen all trying to gain her favor. Since he was not inclined to take the part of a fool to acquire a wife, he stayed where he was. Unfortunately, none of his other possibilities were here. Perhaps it was time to move on to another party in his endless search for the right spouse.

Although, after kissing Arabella, he had to conclude his heart was no longer as keen on the others as it had been earlier. Their kiss intrigued him. Perhaps he'd been too hasty in thinking her disinterested.

Although Louisa attempted to catch his eye, he decided to forget their meeting. He had new information to pursue where Miss Milne was concerned and would call on her father tomorrow, perhaps inviting her driving in the park later this week. Other men might clamor for the young, eligible ladies' attention, but he would proceed at his own pace. Choosing a spouse was not a decision to rush.

He strolled after the Farnsworths and, when he gained the butler's attention, requested his carriage to be called as well.

"Ah, Rothwell," Farnsworth drawled. "Are you bored to death of this inane frivolity too and keen for greater excitement elsewhere?"

Farnsworth ought to watch his mouth. Their hosts were well connected and it was bad form to insult a fellow earl within his home. He glanced at the women of Farnsworth's party. Cecily stared at him with unabashed interest. Arabella looked anywhere but at him. "I have an early meeting tomorrow and must review some papers before dawn or I would be very glad to stay."

Farnsworth grunted and glanced at his watch. He had no interest in other people's affairs as far as Merrick could detect. The new earl kept to himself and played fast and loose with his fortune. Farnsworth thrust his watch away and stalked to the door, cornering the poor butler. "Where the devil is that carriage?"

Merrick was impressed the butler managed to keep his composure in the face of such violent demands.

Good manners dictated Merrick not ignore the ladies present, so he turned his attention to Arabella at last. Her color was heightened, her cheeks as fresh as a young girl's. "Did you enjoy your evening?"

Her blush increased. "I did, thank you. Lord and Lady Harrison are always gracious hosts. The music was wonderful."

He'd seen her foot tapping as the dancers had twirled upon the floor. She appeared so enamored of music that he couldn't fathom why she did not dance more often. "Did you venture into his library by chance? I mention this as I am aware of your interest in orchids through our mutual friend Grayling and remember now that Harrison has acquired a new specimen since his last event. The orchid is quite an unusual color. I've never seen its like before."

Her face fell as Lord Farnsworth snapped his fingers to gain her attention. "I hadn't heard, but it seems there is no time to look now. Perhaps I will see it on another night and with luck Lady Harrison's collection too. Good night, Rothwell."

A chill raced through him. He should have told Arabella the truth about the riding crops when he had a chance, but there was no time now. Farnsworth snapped his fingers again and grabbed Arabella's arm to steer her to the door. Merrick ground his teeth to prevent interfering. A gentleman never rushed a lady when she was in the midst of a conversation and his temper flared dangerously. "Lady Farnsworth. Miss Cecily. A pleasure to see you again."

When they were through the door, he followed to observe them together. Farnsworth appeared somewhat of a tyrant about punctuality and getting his way. He wasn't close enough to speak to them but was close enough for one last glance. Arabella appeared unconcerned as Farnsworth's tirade grew louder. She climbed into the carriage and turned her face toward the window and him immediately.

Again, Merrick was beset by a yearning for what he couldn't have. It should be enough that he had touched her tonight, kissed her till she was breathless, an opportunity he'd seized without thought. He should regret the mistake he'd made, yet he found he wasn't that cross with himself. In fact, he was rather pleased. He hoped she felt the same.

He raised his hand in farewell as the Farnsworth carriage moved off, then he entered his own as it stopped before him and gave directions to a soiree at Lady Ettington's home a short distance away. He was two blocks from the Ettington town house when he changed his mind about his evening plans. He tapped on the roof and directed the coachman toward his own home instead. There was plenty of time to search for a wife. With luck, he would find someone who liked him just the way he was some other night.

Chapter Five

Anson Holland, Merrick's assistant of several years, cleared his throat noisily, interrupting Merrick's perusal of the paper spread before him. He'd been up early to deal with his business affairs, but his heart hadn't truly been prepared. He couldn't keep his mind away from thoughts of Arabella, so as a last resort to leaving the house entirely and strolling past her home on the off chance of seeing her at a window, he'd seized on the daily scandal sheets littering the dining room to see if her name was mentioned, even anonymously.

Merrick didn't bother to look up when he spoke. "What is it now?"

"You returned home early last night," Holland observed. "I trust the evening was uneventful."

Despite his best efforts, his eyes were drawn to where Holland waited, standing at attention beside the dining table. He sighed. There were days when the man was far too nosy. Yet Merrick could never ignore him completely. Holland, though few knew it, was one of his father's extramarital mistakes. Instead of answering immediately, he continued to peruse the paper until he was satisfied. So far, no mention of his cousin, Lady Cecily, or Arabella had made the scandal sheet and that brought relief.

Yet on further reflection, he had not behaved very well last night and should be ashamed. He should have apologized for mistakenly kissing Arabella rather than thanking her. "It was pleasant."

Holland shuffled his feet. "Was that understatement for my benefit? Didn't Lady Penelope Ford attend as well?" Holland touched the tabletop with his fingertips and then peered at them as if looking for nonexistent dust. "What did happen last night? You accepted three invitations, yet you were home by half past ten o'clock."

Bloody hell. The man was keeping watch on his movements. If he weren't so loyal, Merrick would actually be concerned. "Nothing."

Holland poured a coffee from the sideboard and placed it on the paper beneath Merrick's nose, forcing him to look up. "Your face indicates otherwise."

Merrick stared at the man he depended on most. Holland's calm, organized temperament was well suited to managing Merrick's affairs. His hair was just showing signs of age in the form of patches of gray at his temples, giving him a dignified bearing, though a formerly scruffy barkeep lurked beneath. Merrick heaved a heavy sigh and sat back, stretching his legs out beneath the table, and took up the cup. "I see you've not the temperament for minding your own business."

His half brother met his gaze, familiar features creased with concern. "I cannot help it. You gave up much to offer me a position, and the others too. We are here to watch over you, and your happiness affects the whole household."

Holland was family and family, in Merrick's opinion, was never easily dismissed, so Merrick folded the paper and set it aside. "You worry too much."

Holland nodded. "Yes, you've made that very plain in the past, so tell me before I imagine the worst."

He shook his head. "Last night I prevented one Ford scandal and merely stirred the old sow. Not a bad night."

Holland's eyes grew wide. "Promise me you did not call Lady Penelope that out loud."

Merrick laughed at Holland's shocked expression. "Why do you care? The woman can hardly bear to look at you. You are far too considerate of her feelings."

"And what would a good woman such as Lady Penelope

Ford want to look at me for? You should follow your own rules and think better of her. She is family, after all."

"Not yours." Merrick drained the last of his coffee and stood. "I've told you she isn't even human. I won't pretend to like her."

Holland swallowed. "She could help smooth the way in your search for a wife. You know how important this decision is. I want you to marry well and be happy."

Merrick shot to his feet. "If she learns from you or anyone under my roof that I am surveying the field, then there will be a ruthless cleansing of the household, after which I will never allow another relation, illegitimate or not, beneath my roof. Is that understood?"

"Yes, my lord," Holland whispered, his face turning white. "You've made that very plain to all of us who depend on you."

Merrick immediately regretted his abrupt threat. Having his half siblings under his roof these past years had proved no great hardship. He slept much better at night knowing where they all were, in fact.

He filled another cup and handed it to Holland as a peace offering. "Was there something else? Your face indicates there is," he said, mimicking Holland's earlier words.

Holland took the offered cup and took his time drinking the bitter brew, a sure sign Merrick wouldn't like the news he was going to impart. "It's not urgent."

"Come on, man, spit it out." He eased back into his chair to wait. Leaving out Holland, the only sensible one in the pack, his other half brothers were not temperate creatures. There was always some to-do between their brothers. A firm warning tended to calm things down. "Who is it and what have they done now?"

"Jimmy and James." Holland quickly swallowed a mouthful of coffee before setting the cup aside. "They've been fighting."

"Not a shock there. Between themselves, as usual?"

"Yes, my lord."

Jimmy and James were the most problematic. They were arrogant little sods and proud to be employed in an earl's house where they were well treated, fed, and clothed. He even gave them leave to visit their families three times a year. "Over what this time?"

"That I cannot get out of them." Holland did not look happy about that fact. There was a pecking order in the house. Everyone Merrick employed knew their welfare depended on keeping Holland's good opinion, and Holland had mentioned more than once that their comfort depended on Merrick's continuing good graces. Most lords would not have concerned themselves with their illegitimate brothers and sisters. Merrick, the only legitimate child sired, did what he could to correct his father's wickedness.

"Bring them in and I'll deal with it."

"Yes, my lord." Holland quickly departed, returning a short time later with his two younger half siblings in tow. Both looked embarrassed to be brought before him again. If memory served, it was the third time in as many weeks. He studied them closely. Jimmy would have a black eye by dinnertime, and James' lower lip wept blood from a cut. "Explain yourselves."

When they looked down instead of answering, Merrick rose slowly and circled till he stood behind them. He reached out and caught them both about the neck and smacked their heads together.

"Ouch."

"Hey, steady on."

Sometimes being unpredictable proved very satisfying. "Idiots. You're upsetting Holland with your nonsense. Very soon he's going to request you be sent back home to Needham Hollow and two others brought up to replace you. You know how he hates disruptions in the midst of the season."

"We're sorry, milord," they mumbled in unison.

"I do not want an apology. You owe that to Holland." He sat again and folded his hands over his lap. "What I want is an explanation."

Jimmy, the smallest of the pair, fidgeted. They glanced at each other guiltily then at Holland. "James claimed a greater resemblance, sir. I don't believe it."

Merrick exchanged a glance with Holland, but the other man covered his eyes. "Resemblance to what? What the devil!"

Holland lifted his head and stared at their half brothers with annoyance twisting his lips. "Are you still debating which of you looks more like Lord Rothwell? I thought that was settled long ago."

Merrick stood quickly. "You must be joking?"

"Forgive me. I thought this matter had been settled and would not recur." Holland winced. "It seems there is a certain cache for owning a greater resemblance to yourself among those you've taken in. For some it is a point of pride and has led to some unfortunate behavior. This fight being a prime example of it all. I am sorry to have troubled you."

Merrick stared at the men before him. They *wanted* to look like him? To be known as the bastard son of their scoundrel father? His mind couldn't fathom why. He threw his hands up in the air. "This is ridiculous. Jimmy, your forehead is too wide; James, your nose is too squat. You look very little like me except for your brown eyes. I will acknowledge that at least."

Both men perked up at his words. Jimmy nodded. "If you don't mind having the final say, my lord, would you cast your vote on who out of all of us most resembles you?"

Merrick rolled his eyes. "Impertinent wretch. There is but one among you cursed with such a close likeness that it is obvious to any who observe. Holland, do send them back to their duties. I don't want to hear of this matter ever again."

Holland hustled the two men toward the door. "Yes, my lord. Forgive the interruption."

"But he didn't say," Jimmy squawked, peering behind to where Merrick sat.

When they paused at the threshold, Merrick sighed. "Holland bears the closest resemblance. Any idiot, even you pair of clods, should be able to see that."

Yes, Holland, though older by a few years, was the closest in appearance, and that was why Merrick would never return to Newberry Park and had no time for his Ford relations. They felt Holland should be sent away and forgotten for the sake of their reputation as upstanding members of society. However, Holland had proved himself a valuable man in Merrick's service many times over including that awkward first discovery, which had given Merrick the pleasure of thwarting his grandfather and Aunt Pen by turning his back on them instead.

Chapter Six

"I swear, Lady Farnsworth, you must be the worst chaperone in history," Lord Farnsworth said. "Can you not keep track of a single girl for the length of time of one ball? Perhaps you've spent too much time on your own to know what's acceptable behavior and what isn't?"

Arabella flinched at the unfair accusation. If her brother-in-law hadn't sired a devil in disguise, then they wouldn't be in this predicament. After last night's discovery, she'd reconsidered everything she knew about her niece and concluded she'd been duped. The girl was bound for trouble and by her own design, no less.

She held her tongue rather than speak out of spite. Farnsworth's temper was never far away, and she depended on his good opinion to maintain her limited independence. Although she had done everything he'd demanded with regard to Cecily's season, he continued to cast doubts on her return to Winslette House in Wiltshire in order to get his way.

She steeled herself to be agreeable but didn't like her chances of Farnsworth retrieving his good humor any time soon. The morning had not gone well. Farnsworth had received several notes from important personages that raised questions about his daughter's behavior at the festivities last night. Questions of where she may have disappeared to often led to answers he didn't like. So far, there were no reports of Cecily being seen in

Lieutenant Ford's arms, but Arabella was counting down the minutes.

Farnsworth stood and paced behind his desk, hands clasped behind his back. "Given that Cecily and tragedy are determined to be constant companions, I've taken steps to ensure the future is secure."

"What kind of steps?" But Arabella had a sinking feeling in her stomach that she already knew what his answer would be. He'd been very clear that Cecily had to marry this season and he would fund no further expeditions to London in future years.

His gaze sharpened until Arabella was near to squirming from his scrutiny. "All in good time, my dear. See that she behaves herself today and tomorrow, and if all goes to plan, we will have everything settled. By the end of the week, life could go on as it should."

Arabella's heart sank. She prayed Farnsworth hadn't already signed marriage contracts behind their backs. Farnsworth was the most stubborn of men and hated any attempt to change his mind. He had hopefully not gone so far in his plans for Cecily's future that he wouldn't see reason if he'd made a bad choice for the girl. Arabella had little influence over Farnsworth, and Cecily's tears would bring nothing but his bad temper. She just hoped if he'd made a match for the girl that the gentleman possessed a steady temperament. "Can you not offer a hint so that I may know in which direction to steer her attention? I would hate to work against your plans."

Farnsworth pursed his lips. "You may be correct. We should be of one mind on this to ensure our mutual felicity. I never could say no to you, as my brother likely could not. It should not surprise you that Lord Parker has expressed an interest in an alliance with our family, and I consider the match an advantageous one."

"Parker?" Arabella sank into the nearest chair as dismay smothered her. She had thought Parker more interested in *her*, not Cecily. How could she have been so wrong? Parker surely wouldn't want Cecily. "But he's so much older."

Farnsworth turned, his face creased into a puzzled frown. "The gap in ages is less than it was between my late brother and yourself. A very sensible match."

His response in no way comforted her. A twenty-year gap was not conducive to a happy marriage unless there were strong ties of affection. Cecily had met Parker several times that Arabella could recall, and she had detected no partiality on either side. Her niece had preferred to bestow her attention on prettier, younger gentlemen.

Farnsworth resettled behind his desk, leaning back as if his problems were already behind him. "Parker needs a wife of excellent breeding, well versed in the duties of a hostess, and one with energy and beauty to hang on his arm. He has impressed me with his enthusiasm for marriage."

Cecily would have almost the same marriage as Arabella had lived. She wouldn't wish it on her worst enemy. Women always had little choice in whom they married but still, her heart begged her to persuade him to reconsider the match. In time, the coldness and lack of affection would eat into Cecily's soul until she was left a barren husk. Arabella had only found a measure of contentment after she'd been widowed. She'd been able to establish her own friendships and in some respects could be considered happy with her life. Even dealing with Cecily's wild antics was better than her married life had been. "Are you sure about this? Shouldn't we…"

Farnsworth waved his hands to halt her questions. "It's decided. Reconcile yourself to this marriage so you may make plans for your change of location without distraction."

She stared at her brother-in-law. The offhand remark about her leaving thrilled her. "Am I to return to Wiltshire?"

"I doubt it. You've endured the season quite well, but clearly your mind has not been fully on the task at hand. Why, even Lady Penelope Ford remarked that you were ill suited as a chaperone just last evening. She suggested a sojourn in new surroundings was exactly what you needed, and I quite agree with her thinking."

Her palms grew damp. She prayed he'd not presumed her invited to stay as a guest of Lady Penelope Ford's and had said so out loud. He would have made a fool of them both. "What do you mean?"

"Depending on Lord Parker's plans, you will come to Hinkley Park after Cecily is off my hands." Farnsworth resumed his pacing, hands clasped behind his back. "Of course, I would expect you to act as my hostess on occasion and run the house again as you once did for my brother. You have not been back of your own accord since my wife died, have you?"

"No." Ants crawled over her skin at the thought of going back to Hinkley. "There never seemed to be a need since Cecily returned to school so soon after."

When Cecily married, there would be no one else at Hinkley Park but herself and her brother-in-law. There was no dower house to claim and even if there was, she doubted Farnsworth would endure the expense of the additional servants required to maintain it. She would be as trapped as she had been during her marriage. Arabella had no wish for such a retiring life. She had to prevent this. "I cannot imagine why Lady Penelope would take such an interest in me. I am perfectly happy in Wiltshire."

"The Wiltshire property is superfluous to my needs, and I intend to sell it."

"No, please." Panic assailed her. "I will buy Winslette House. I don't want to live anywhere else. Please do not make any hasty decisions."

Farnsworth laughed immediately. "My dear, you could never afford to buy or manage such a property. Lord Parker has no interest in the Wiltshire estate, so I have already spoken to several gentlemen about the matter. I am sure it will be snapped up in no time. Think no more of Wiltshire. You are done with that locale."

He dismissed her desire for Wiltshire as if she hadn't spoken, another indication that her future was fast slipping from her control. She pressed her fingertips to her temple. Why was Farnsworth so set on what Lord Parker wanted? There were many more equally acceptable gentlemen in London. Surely Cecily wasn't disagreeable to all.

Farnsworth tapped his finger to the tabletop, recalling her attention to him. "I'll be at my club tonight, but tomorrow I am sure we can expect Lord Parker to call. I'll speak to him tonight, in fact, to ensure he does. Please stress to Cecily the importance of pleasing her future husband. There will be no Lieutenant Ford in her future."

Arabella's mind raced. Had the lieutenant done what

Rothwell had demanded of him and come to call? Had he proposed marriage rather than meet in secret again? If that were so, he had come too late to do any good, but Arabella's opinion of Lieutenant Ford rose considerably. His intentions could be honorable after all.

Farnsworth snapped open a newssheet, signaling their interview was at an end. Although she'd like nothing better than to argue for Cecily's freedom, Arabella stood and walked out slowly, mind racing. Being packed off to Surrey was disagreeable in the extreme. She had vowed never to return to that miserable place. She would miss visiting her friends in Wiltshire whenever she pleased and their calls to her in return. Farnsworth valued his peace, and she would never be free to invite Grayling and his wife and daughters to visit. She would be cut off from everything she knew and loved, and that was unacceptable.

Heart pounding, she closed the library door and leaned against it, drawing unsteady breaths as frustration gripped her. Her plans to find a lover this season were no longer a priority. What she needed was a way out of her dependency on Farnsworth.

A sniff drew her attention and she raised her eyes to the stairs. Cecily stood at the halfway point of the first flight, eyes filled with tears, the butler at her side holding out a handkerchief. Given their sorrowful expressions, they must have overheard her father's plans for Cecily to marry immediately. Was a tantrum imminent? That really would seal the girl's fate.

The butler backed away with a regretful smile, leaving Arabella to the task of comforting the girl on her own. She hurried to Cecily's side, clasped her trembling hands, and led her back upstairs to her bedchamber before she did something rash like confront her father. She had a feeling that disobedience would not be tolerated. When the door closed behind them, Cecily gave in to her emotions with a loud sob. "I won't let him do this to us."

"Come now, Cecily. Surely you knew your father would have the final say in whom you married? In time, it is my hope that Lieutenant Ford will put this behind him and be happy. So will you, I'm sure." Feeling uncharacteristically close to the girl, she pressed a kiss to Cecily's hair. "We should prepare for Lord

Parker's visit."

Cecily broke away. The girl could never bear to be coddled when she was upset. "I thought Father had some foolishness on his mind these past days, but it's more important to decide how you are going to survive his plans for your life. You hate Surrey."

Arabella gaped at the girl's words. She'd always assumed Cecily cared for naught but her own happiness and had never paid attention to what she had to say. Yet Cecily had bigger problems than Arabella's exile to Surrey to worry about. "Mine? Cecily, dear. Do you understand the sort of life you will likely have as Lady Parker?"

Cecily eyed her critically even through her tears. "We need to find you a new situation and much quicker than I originally planned."

"I beg your pardon?"

Cecily sighed somewhat dramatically. "A husband you like this time."

"A husband? What plan? Now wait a moment." Arabella held up one hand. "There is no plan that concerns me more than your future happiness. I have spent the last two months in search of a good man for you. In all my thinking, it was never to someone twenty years older than yourself. Besides, I doubt we'd be able to find a husband for me. Marriage is not in my future."

Now that she'd had time to consider Farnsworth's attitude to his daughter, her ire rose. Women were not to be traded to the highest bidder. Power. Wealth. The Farnsworth men treated women no better than cattle.

Cecily said, "Oh, please. A woman as beautiful as you has many men watching her. Forget Lord Parker. Laurence's older brother, Lord Maitland, is nice—although he is a full year your junior." Cecily grinned, warming to the discussion. "Even the debauched Lord Rothwell has paid more than a passing interest in you, and the whole world knows he avoids proper women."

The mention of Rothwell and the memory of his interest and devastating kiss caused her body to quiver. He would not have plans to marry her. Seduce her, yes, but nothing so permanent as a future together beyond a handful of nights. He'd suit her plans perfectly if she still required a lover. She had considered him briefly for an affair, but her courage had utterly failed until last night, and now she had other concerns to struggle through. "I've no wish for a husband. Marriage did not agree with me the last time I tried it."

"Given my uncle's greater age and sour disposition, I'm not in the least surprised. You need someone fresher." Cecily spun about in a tight circle, her grin widening. "Forget my father. We can have any man we want for our husband. It will take cunning and bravery for sure, but you just need to choose one and offer them the right encouragement before my father carries out his plan to banish you to Surrey."

Arabella caught her niece's hands to still her. She assessed the gown Cecily wore and considered what might do for tomorrow. There was no time to dawdle. "What we need to do is talk about your future more than mine. Parker is expected to call tomorrow. You will need to be in your best looks."

Cecily's expression grew sly. "Does my father join us for dinner this evening?"

"No." Arabella studied her niece, alarmed when her smile returned so quickly. "He'll be at his club."

"Good. There is much to do. The first of which is to send a note to Laurie letting him know my worst fears have come to pass and to arrange a meeting. And the second, helping you, must be undertaken at the same time. So, who among the gentlemen I mentioned takes your fancy? Lord Wade? Although his ears are too large to take seriously. We cannot allow you to be banished to Hinkley's dull confines. You've barely left my side all season, despite my attempts to disappear long enough so a gentleman might be inappropriate with your person." Her niece giggled. "We need to discover where those you favor will be on any given night before it is too late."

Arabella shook her head furiously. "Enough of this. You cannot tell anyone of your father's plans. There has been no announcement yet."

Cecily's face grew serious at last. "I am sorry about losing your home in Wiltshire. I fear Papa used my coming out to bring you back under his roof. He can certainly bear the expense of Winslette's upkeep. He just doesn't want you so far away from his control. What about Rothwell? I really think he shouldn't be dismissed as too much a rogue. By all accounts he's a dab hand when it comes to the bedroom, and that must be a consideration at your time of life. I've just never heard of him being interested in marrying anyone, so convincing him to offer for you might require some careful planning."

Arabella quickly covered her niece's mouth with her hand, furious that the girl just wasn't listening. "Do not say such things out loud."

Cecily broke free and merely laughed at Arabella's embarrassment. "My dear aunt, you are too precious. You were married for seven years and still sound as prim as those silly girls who came out with me. I cannot wait to be a wife with all it entails. Why do you blush when a man pays you attention? I swear, if I didn't think it impossible, I would believe you a virgin."

Cecily left her then and in doing so missed the fiery blush that washed over Arabella's face. She *was* a virgin—although she'd been married for enough years to make that fact ridiculous. When she'd taken her vows, she'd meant every word. She'd hoped Farnsworth might have grown kinder, at least somewhat fond of her, but he'd passed away and she was the same as the day she married. There was nothing she could do to change that fact now. Farnsworth would pack her off to the country as soon as Cecily was wed, and her hopes for the season were impossible. Whatever plans Cecily was making would be in vain. She had no one to turn to but friends and they were all in the country.

Cecily retrieved a sealed square of paper from the depths of a drawer and then rang for a servant while Arabella looked on grimly. As the girl handed the note over to the maid they shared, she pressed a shilling into her hand. "It's time, Hill."

The maid bobbed a curtsey, bounced on the balls of her feet somewhat excitedly, and then left as if the devil was chasing her. Arabella rubbed her brow. Was there any use in trying to rein the girl in and get her to think of making the best of her future? But she was just as stubborn as her father. Standing between the two was such a strain.

When Cecily pulled a worn portmanteau from beneath the bed, alarm bells rang in Arabella's mind. "What are you doing?"

Cecily sized her up and Arabella broke out in a cold sweat.

Her niece smiled sweetly. "The only thing I can. I'm eloping with Laurie."

Chapter Seven

Family was the curse of Merrick's existence. He studied the two men seated opposite him and did his best to control his irritation at finding them in his home. The arrival of his Ford cousins always heralded trouble. Holland might have managed to send this pair away if he had not been already off on an errand.

And the pair had interrupted his pleasant fantasy of making love to Arabella in a greenhouse filled with orchids and tall palms. He couldn't ever have her in such an intimate setting, but he'd indulged himself and imagined it anyway.

"I say, Rothwell, are you even listening to us?" Quinn Ford, Captain Maitland, grumbled.

Such interruptions were not to be borne with any form of good grace and certainly not for a wedding invitation to Newberry Park, home to generations of meddling Fords and the last place on earth Merrick wished to go. He reluctantly focused on his cousins. "I have no interest in attending."

"He says you have to come or the wedding cannot proceed," Fredrick Ford whined.

Merrick raised a brow in disbelief. "For God's sake, man, it's your own wedding. Tell His Grace you'll surrender to the enemy or something equally horrifying and he'll forget about my absence simply to avoid the scandal. You'll get her dowry one way or the other."

Their mutual grandfather, the Duke of Rutherford, was as difficult as all the rest and used his rank and influence to intimidate even his own family. Arranging marriages to suit his needs was high on his list of priorities. Fredrick was the first of their generation to succumb to the pressure of the shackle being secured about his leg.

Fredrick frowned. "Do you not wish to meet my bride?"

"I think it more important that *you* meet her. How long have you known her, anyway? A bare month at most?" Merrick shrugged away his disgust. Marriages made in haste always ended badly. "I'll see her after the event when you've returned from sea and you both come up to Town."

And if it took a considerable amount of time to arrange that meeting, he would not be discontent. The less time he spent with his cousins, the better. They had nosy, prying natures. Every last one. Only a fool or a Ford relation would disturb a man before one in the afternoon.

Quinn was heir to the ducal estate after his father's passing, lifted Merrick's most prized orchid from the corner of the desk and studied it closely. "Sally is counting on you to come. She's in a complete snit about Freddy bowing to the arrangement as it is."

Merrick retrieved the temperamental orchid as Quinn started to pitch it from side to side as if measuring how it would fare aboard his ship. "Your sister has cause to disagree with the appeal of an arranged marriage."

Deprived of his amusement, Quinn sprawled in his chair as if he would never leave. "Sally is long over her disappointment, I assure you."

Merrick closed his eyes briefly. Did Quinn really not understand the cruel damage done to Quinn's sister's heart from her own aborted match? Not for one moment did he think Sally had forgotten that on the eve of her wedding, she had discovered her intended was marrying her for the guaranteed promotion it would offer him in his career. Such a disappointment would not go away so easily.

When Merrick had come upon Sally soon after, he'd calmed her down and then had the chore of ensuring her former intended suffered just enough for breaking her heart rather than let the Ford cousins kill him. That was the last time he'd involved himself in Ford affairs. He was in no rush to return to the family fold to continue old bad habits.

When he opened his eyes again, Quinn held out a folded parchment document. "His Grace sent this for you. If it's like ours, you might want to burn it before opening. It contains a special license. He's determined to have us all married before the year is out."

His cousin placed the parchment on his desk and Merrick stared at it, cursing his grandfather's meddling but rather impressed in turn. When he did decide on which woman he wanted to marry, the whole business could be concluded at their own convenience.

He smiled serenely. Since he had a special license in his possession now, it wouldn't do him any good to leave London. "Give my best to your mother and sisters when you return to Essex."

Fredrick stood scowling, hearing the unspoken "please leave" in his words.

Quinn scowled too but shook his head stubbornly. "We'll see you soon."

To make sure they left, Merrick escorted them all the way to the front door. He raked a hand through his hair when he was alone again—the unopened parchment at the forefront of his mind. He picked it up and then unfolded the paper. It was a special license and came without a bride's name upon it. He smiled. At least his grandfather had left the choice of bride open for him to decide. Now he had all that was needed to make the match he wanted.

A scratch on the door drew his attention from the paper. "Come."

Holland eased inside the room. "Excuse the interruption, my lord, but Lieutenant Ford followed me home. Laurence, that is, and he is most insistent in speaking with you without delay now his brothers have gone."

Merrick groaned. What the devil did that foolish young man want now? Since he was already disturbed, he decided he might as well add one more annoyance to his morning. "Oh, show him in. Show everyone in. I simply do not care anymore."

Holland hurried off and returned a moment later with his young cousin hard on his heels. "I need your advice," Laurence exclaimed even before Holland had completely departed the room.

Merrick waited until the door closed and he could no longer hear footsteps in the hall beyond. "You had sufficient assistance last night. I told you what you needed to do."

Laurence raked his fingers through his untidy hair. "It didn't work. He would not hear me out. In fact, I think Lord Farnsworth mocked me."

Merrick gritted his teeth. No matter how much he detested the Fords, he would not bear the insult delivered to his cousin with any form of good grace. Laurence had an earnestness of youth that was refreshingly childlike. That was why Merrick was against any alliance with Farnsworth's daughter in truth. Laurie would not bear the connection well until perhaps he had matured enough to stand up to such a man.

Merrick settled behind his desk again, securing the special license in the top drawer, out of sight, out of mind, till needed. "Start from the beginning."

"I gave your advice considerable thought last night and I wish to have Cecily for my wife. I wanted things settled before I returned to duty, and so I called on her father and asked for her hand, but he wouldn't hear me out. Kept saying I was too late." Laurence shook his head.

Occasionally, Laurence spoke as if one knew exactly what he meant without being specific. Just to be sure he'd been clear, Merrick queried him. "So you *did* tell him you wanted to marry her?"

"Yes, I managed to say marriage several times, very clearly, before he insisted I leave."

Merrick hid a grin, imagining his cousin's earnest face as he'd professed his undying love for the wild Cecily. "Perhaps Farnsworth thought your acquaintance too slight, too brief of duration, to agree to the marriage on your first request. You are very young, coz. Given time, he could very well change his mind. There is no necessity in marrying the girl immediately is there?"

Laurence shook his head, his cheeks turning red at his

suggestion that there could be an urgent reason to marry, like a babe in Lady Cecily's belly already. "None at all, although I have been led to believe she would not be adverse to that. Cecily wrote me today and I am greatly concerned by her news."

A much-folded letter was produced and promptly handed over. Merrick opened it and read the first lines, grimacing as he did so. Sugary-sweet sentiments slid from the page. No wonder Laurence was concerned. Cecily was very eloquent about her passion for his cousin. A letter like this, in the wrong hands before a wedding, could prove highly embarrassing to all parties. "I think this is perhaps too private to be shown to others." He made to fold it and hand it back, but Laurence waved his hands and refused to take it.

"The worst news is at the end."

Merrick didn't like his chances of avoiding the cloying phrases, so he skimmed them as best he could until the letter became interesting. He sat up straighter and whistled. "That's a surprise. I imagined Farnsworth might approve of someone younger, a man he could control." He'd also thought Parker's attention had been on Arabella, not the niece.

Laurence nodded. "And Parker's cruel. Just last week he beat an urchin who'd stumbled into his path."

"There is no reason to suspect he would show his wife so little consideration." Merrick caught his cousin's gaze. "Despite that, it could be a good match for her. She's bound to outlive him and can marry whomever she pleases later."

Laurence's expression became distraught. "I cannot wait forever. You were correct last night that I had not considered her reputation, but eloping, as Cecily suggests, is bound to cause a scandal for the family. I love her and want to spend every moment making her happy. What should I do?"

"There is nothing that can be done." Merrick had discovered fathers were quite an obstacle when a man had his mind on their daughter, even when he had honorable intentions. "Her father has the right to choose her husband, even if others may find the match disagreeable."

Laurence stood and paced before the desk, long legs eating up the distance in jerky strides. It was like watching a windmill, limbs everywhere at once. He pulled his temperamental orchid out of danger again and moved it to a safer position behind him to prevent an accident.

"Can you imagine Cecily wed to that man?" Laurence exclaimed suddenly. "She's far too spirited in nature to ever be truly happy with such a match."

When Merrick had mentioned last night that it was ungentlemanly to steal kisses from an unmarried girl without there being an understanding, he had no notion that his words would be taken so far to heart and so quickly. That Laurence had attempted to propose impressed him, but he couldn't fathom why he would want to be saddled with such a wild, untamed wife. There wouldn't be a lot of easy companionship in the marriage. Laurence was not thinking sensibly. "Are you sure you want to be saddled with her? I hope your decision had less to do with the threat of Aunt Pen and that you are aware of every facet of Lady Cecily's personality."

A flush of color swept Laurie's face. Anger or embarrassment, Merrick couldn't tell. Laurence sat again and drew in a shaky breath. "She may have an impetuous nature, but we do have similar interests. As you can see from her note, it is her wish to elope and avoid marriage to Lord Parker, and I'm willing to go along with that. I do want her for my wife—with or without her dowry. I've never considered such a thing as a necessity before and hoped you might advise me of how to go on."

Merrick leaned back in his chair. Making a potentially scandalous match, without the family's approval or the anticipation of the girl's dowry to sweeten the pot, raised Merrick's estimation of Laurence's character considerably. Only a man in love or a fool would go against such pressure. "What makes you think I could help with an elopement?"

Laurence colored. "My brothers have mentioned your experience with women on occasion, and you have come to Lady Farnsworth's aid before."

Merrick frowned. "What does Lady Farnsworth have to do with you eloping?"

"An unsuccessful elopement, rather than a successful one, is sure to cause Lady Farnsworth considerable embarrassment. We would rather avoid capture if at all possible."

He stood, infuriated that he was being blackmailed by his own cousin with the threat of diminishing Lady Farnsworth's happiness. There was no way Laurence had concocted this scheme on his own. This was Cecily's influence at work. "I see Cecily doesn't care one whit for her aunt's advice. If you think I'll help you simply on the threat of tarnishing Lady Farnsworth's reputation, think again. I don't believe we have anything further to say to one another."

Laurence bounced to his feet and leaned over the desk, his voice dropping low. "On the contrary. Cecily cares for her aunt's future a great deal and bemoans the fact that, as a chaperone, Lady Farnsworth has not been free to pursue her own life. She's much too pretty to be alone." Laurence's throat worked as he swallowed. "And I've noticed Lady Farnsworth has caught your attention. Do you have a special license from grandfather, too? Are you considering proposing to her?"

Merrick cursed roundly under his breath. If this simpleton had detected his admiration for Arabella, then it was likely that others had, too. He stilled. Had his aunt come out to ensure that Arabella's reputation remained intact last night?

The idea that his mother's family was set against any association, even a harmless one, between himself and Arabella infuriated him. He had never done one reproachable thing in his dealings with the lady before except accidentally kiss her last night. Aunt Pen couldn't have known about the kiss at the time. During the season, he had denied every impulse to linger near the widow because she was clearly uncomfortable around him. Last night she'd been flustered, but she would never willingly choose him over propriety. His family's mistrust was the final straw.

If he could not have Arabella, then he would help someone else find their happiness by any means. He strode to the doorway and yanked it open. "Holland, have the new coach ready to make a long journey tonight," he bellowed and then slammed the door shut.

Laurence was on his feet in an instant, towering over him. "You cannot leave now."

"Of course I cannot leave." He stabbed his finger into Laurence's chest, momentarily surprised by the resistance he encountered. Life onboard a ship had hardened the boy. "You will have your heart's desire. Tonight. Take my new coach on the journey north and you'll have a better chance of slipping from London undetected. I'll have a word with your captain and ensure you suffer no penalty. He owes me."

Laurie gaped. "Why didn't I think of that?"

"Probably because Lady Cecily has fogged your mind with her long-winded love talk. Return here at seven to collect the coach, pack sparingly, and carry sufficient funds for accommodation, food, and change of horse. I won't fund this whole affair, but I can ensure you make it to the border." Merrick held out his hand for Laurence to shake. "Best of luck to you and your true love."

Chapter Eight

"You cannot leave like this." Arabella's throat ached from the arguments, but she had to stop her niece from throwing her life away. Night had fallen and the maid had returned with the news that Lieutenant Ford was in agreement and would arrange the elopement for that very night. They were to meet one street away, on the edge of Green Park.

Cecily snapped her portmanteau closed and sighed. "Father will not listen, and I love Laurie too much to wait another day. Do you have any idea how hard it is to see him and yet have to part each night? My soul is ripped in two by constant yearning. Were you ever so aware of another person that you simply did not care what happened to you if the feelings deep inside are so stirred again and again?"

Arabella looked down at her hands. She had never felt such a way and doubted she ever would. Given recent developments, she might have no idea what love even looked like. She'd been so sure that Parker was interested. Yet it was Rothwell she'd kissed and wanted to again. "'Tis only lust stirring your body, Cecily," she whispered.

Cecily cupped her face with one hand, lifting her gaze. Steady, determined eyes met hers. The girl was reconciled to her decision. "Then I shall take lust and passion and forsake a cold alliance with a man older than my father. Wouldn't you?"

Arabella wanted to nod her agreement, but she'd hidden the true state of her life and her heart from everyone for so long that she feared their pitying glances. One kiss with Rothwell was all the excitement life had sent her way. She'd never experienced further passion or more than a passing flutter of attraction with another man. The sensations Cecily extolled as essential to life were just a dream to Arabella.

She sank onto the side of the bed, letting her niece's touch slip away. Who was she to deny Cecily a chance at happiness? If a border wedding was the only way to achieve the marriage Cecily wished for and there was love on both sides at the beginning, then surely she should offer what little support she could and hope for the best. It was more than she'd ever had. Lieutenant Ford might be young, but he was from a very good family. Perhaps their influence could control the girl where Arabella had only failed. "If you are sure this is what you want."

"Oh, I am. I cannot wait to see him again."

Since Arabella had nowhere else to go save Surrey, then the least she could do was help Cecily make it to the coach and her purported true love. She wrestled the portmanteau from her niece and opened it. "The sky is filled with clouds tonight. Do you have another shawl and a thicker pair of stockings in case the weather worsens?"

Cecily crushed Arabella in a violent embrace. "You are the truest companion a girl could want. Thank you. I will do as you suggest and add to what I have already packed."

Arabella, moved to tears by the sudden display of affection, was unsure how far to push the girl and settled for merely patting her back. "My last act as chaperone will be to come with you to meet the coach. I cannot allow you to walk the streets alone, and your luggage is somewhat awkward. What if he is delayed? I couldn't bear for you to stand alone on the street like a common strumpet."

Cecily wiped at her eyes. "It is kind of you to say delayed and not that Laurie may not come at all. I am sure you are thinking that."

Arabella squeezed her hand. "As if he would dare desert you. I'll be right back."

She returned to her room and collected her dark blue carriage cloak and fine kid gloves. As she donned them, she admired her niece's bravery. Cecily had never balked at any obstacle life had thrown after the fall that had taken her mother's life several years ago. She flew through society at her own pace, unmindful of the opinions of others or their dark looks at her daring. In Arabella's experience, such strength of character was rare in women. She could never be so headstrong, but she wished her niece well.

A tap on her door drew her attention and Cecily's pretty face peeked through the gap. She stood, portmanteau in hand, dancing on the balls of her feet in the hallway—a woman ready for the greatest adventure of her young life. Arabella checked the time. It was now or never—time to meet Lieutenant Ford and see if his heart was true.

She hurried to her niece and led her down the servants' staircase, past the servants who peered at them curiously, and out into the dark rear square. The night was overcast with clouds that promised rain but hadn't delivered, making the hour feel much later than it was. Cecily's grip tightened on hers, but her steps did not hesitate as they hurried through to the mews and out onto London's busy streets.

Mayfair teemed with fine carriages on their way to one engagement or another. Although the light was poor due to the clouds, Arabella felt exposed. "Pull your cloak closer about your face, my dear, and keep your head down. We don't want *him* to hear of this yet." By *him,* Arabella meant Cecily's father. Farnsworth would chase his daughter down and drag her back by her hair to ensure she kept the bargain he'd made with Lord Parker. Arabella shuddered at the storm that would likely land on her head because of this when Cecily was discovered missing tomorrow morning. It would not be an easy time.

Arabella stopped as she spied a gleaming black carriage standing at the appointed place. The coach bore no crest or markings that she could discern but looked very new and fine. She held Cecily in place. "That could not be him."

"I'm sure it is." Cecily hurried forward, hood falling to her shoulders in her haste, unconcerned that she could be spotted by someone who knew them.

Heart sinking to her toes, Arabella had no choice but to

follow.

"Wait," she called, but Cecily was already beside the carriage. Lieutenant Ford owned only a phaeton that she knew of. She imagined he'd hire a coach for the journey, but how he could afford such a fine conveyance in just a day escaped her.

She hurried her pace then let out a relieved breath when she spied Lieutenant Ford beside the dark carriage, one hand on the door, one held out to Cecily. He had forgone his navy uniform for this excursion but still looked every inch a sailor. As if in a daze, Cecily moved to him without a second thought for Arabella.

Lieutenant Ford raised Cecily's hand to his lips and kissed her knuckles. "My love."

Cecily's return smile was blinding.

Lieutenant Ford dragged his gaze away from his future wife and grinned at Arabella over Cecily's shoulder. "Thank you for delivering her into my keeping, my lady. I promise you we will see you again very soon."

"How could you afford...," she asked before she thought better of her question. She winced at how uncouth her blunt question would sound. It was one thing to discreetly enquire after a suitor's financial affairs, but quite another to demand answers on a public street.

"I have my cousin, Lord Rothwell's, generosity to thank for that." His eyes flickered to the impressive conveyance and the restless horses attached to it. "He is as true a believer in love as ever there was."

Rothwell was involved? That truly surprised her. She'd had the distinct impression that he didn't care to help anyone, especially not members of his family and that he considered the pair rash in their affections.

Cecily turned and hugged her tightly. "I wish I could stay to see you made happy too. I cannot bear to think of you in Surrey. When I return a married woman, you must come live with us."

Arabella could never do as Cecily wished. She could not live off their charity since the pair would have so little to live on with a lieutenant's pay. So she made no immediate answer in order to avoid the likely argument now. Time was of the essence. When she stepped back, Lieutenant Ford assisted Cecily inside. He joined her a moment later, and a groom jumped down from the rear of the vehicle.

As the carriage rolled away, the groom came closer. The man was tall and narrow, well dressed and with a mischievous glint in his eye. "Now they're on their way, I'm commissioned by Lord Rothwell to ensure you return home in safety, my lady. He had a feeling you'd follow the chit to this meeting and wanted to be sure you remained unharmed."

Arabella frowned and glanced around her. "If he thought it so dangerous, then why did he not come himself?"

"Wouldn't do, my lady. Wouldn't do your reputation any good to be seen alone with him. If you'd be so good as to return the way you came, I'm to follow at a discreet distance and ensure you're sweetly tucked up at home again before the hour has passed."

He stepped back, hands lax at his side. Why would Rothwell care for her safety and the continuation of her good reputation? He was the one to kiss her senseless and not even apologize for mistaking her for someone else. Perhaps he routinely kissed the wrong women. She shrugged aside her irritation at the idea and squared her shoulders. She was thinking irrationally to worry about that now. She had thought Rothwell uncaring of propriety in the beginning, but that wasn't true so far. He had sent his own servant to make sure she returned home safely. That had to count for something.

Confused, Arabella hurried up the street, ducking through the dark mews. Now she was alone, she was a little unnerved by the shadows, but she drew comfort from the servant who followed. When she gained the rear square of her London home, a whistle sounded behind her. She turned but detected no sign of Rothwell's servant lingering in her shadow anymore. "Thank him, please," she called out but received no reply.

The first servants she passed were silent and watchful as she entered the house alone. When the butler stepped into her path, her pulse raced.

"May I ask if the young lady is on her way?"

Arabella glanced around, swallowing her worry that they would send word to Farnsworth immediately. She nodded slowly and was pleased when the butler and every other servant grinned, though they quickly stifled the expression. They were on her niece's side about Parker, it seemed. Their reaction gave her hope that she had done the right thing in helping the girl flee the arranged marriage and that they might help delay the discovery of her disappearance by Farnsworth for as long as possible tomorrow morning.

She returned to her bedchamber and removed her cloak and gloves, satisfied that at least her niece might have a chance for happiness, if there was such a thing. She rubbed her arms. Come morning, Farnsworth would be furious. She'd be blamed and very rightly, too. She'd been a very poor chaperone. Arabella added that to her secret list of failures—wife, mother, lover, chaperone.

A miserable tally if ever there was one.

With nothing to do for Cecily anymore, she snuggled into the chair placed before the fire and tried to picture a life in Surrey again. Mind you, if Farnsworth didn't wash his hands of her entirely over Cecily's elopement, she might never see even that place in the future. What would she do then? Her portion from her marriage was pitifully small. She had no relatives that might shelter her if Farnsworth kicked her out. She'd be destitute, forced to rely on the charity of others to keep a roof over her head. Arabella pressed her head to her knees and hugged her legs as she tried to think of a solution that didn't involve a hermetic lifestyle in Surrey. The only one that came to mind was remarriage. But who would want her, and at such short notice? Could she even bear to be a wife again?

Chapter Nine

Merrick paused just inside the doorway of the coffee house and surveyed his surroundings. At this hour the business was booming, and there were very few chairs left unoccupied in the establishment. An arm rose at the back of the room, blue wool sleeve, gold lace stripe, and buttons at the cuff. That was sure to be Captain Hastings, his cousin's commanding officer, waiting to meet him as arranged.

Merrick eased through the crowd, stopping when he reached the table. "Hastings. Thank you for coming."

Pale blue eyes met his, the kind that reminded him of a windswept sky and hours of solitude. Hastings and Merrick had met in a Southport tavern some ten years ago when Hastings had been a lieutenant on leave from his uncle's command and Merrick at loose ends. They had been friends ever since, with one short period of estrangement that they both preferred not to talk about.

"How could I resist such a cryptic and urgent message?" Hastings shifted his bicorne to the side of the table. "I'll have you know I left behind a very comfortable bed that does not rock with the tide, so I hope our business does not delay my return to it for very long. It's quite a novel experience."

Hastings had become something of a lone wolf in the service, and if one believed the rumors, he was utterly ruthless in war.

No quarter given, no prize beyond reach. Some might call it ill luck that he was not on good terms with Merrick's Ford relations, but that had not stopped his rise through the ranks to captain of one of the fastest frigates in the service. That made Hastings an indispensable ally. He did not back down from a fight and had superb sense save for one notable occasion.

Merrick slid into a chair opposite him and signaled for a coffee. "How much do you like my cousin?"

"Which one?" Hastings' gaze sharpened and then his shoulders slumped. "I suppose you could only mean my lieutenant. As well as any man under my command, I suppose."

Merrick smiled and sipped his coffee, rolling the flavor in his mouth before he continued. "I was hoping perhaps you liked him more."

Hastings nudged his coffee cup to the edge of the table to be refilled. "What has he done?"

Merrick waited till the cup had been replenished and the servant had departed before answering.

"Run for Scotland to be married," Merrick told him honestly, lowering his voice so his words would carry no farther than his friend. "The family does not know that yet and don't need to be informed until the lad comes back."

Hastings rubbed one hand through his dark hair and then shook his head. "You helped him? Damn it, Rothwell. When are you going to cut all ties with them? You know how they are when they believe you at fault. They always make you do something rash you'll regret later. He could have waited out the bans, surely."

Merrick shook his head. "By then he would have been back at sea, and her father had said no."

Hastings at least took a moment to consider before responding. "I thought him a brave lad from the start. Yet I still do not understand the rush."

"If the woman you loved was about to marry a much older and undeserving man, wouldn't you try everything in your power to keep her for yourself if you could, even turning to the black sheep of the family for help?"

As Merrick had hoped, Hastings' sympathy shifted in Laurie's favor immediately. "I see why you meddled and why you came to me. This situation has a ring of familiarity about it. I, too, have stood at the crossroads before with only your support at my side. You are a good man. What do you want me to do?"

Merrick reached across the table slapped Hastings' shoulder. His friend had never forgiven himself for losing the woman he loved, and Merrick admired him for that. "I've given orders for a swift return, but there is always a chance of mishap on the road. I want to ask you not to declare him absent if such a situation delays him. He has no intention of deserting his position, I promise you."

"The correct term is run. How can you not know that given every one of your male cousins is an officer of the navy?"

"I stopped listening to them quite some time ago."

"I wish we all had that luxury." Hastings smiled ruefully. "You know, I have often wished we'd been family. I could do with a man like you in my corner. All I have is *rusticating* Rupert, and he is no help at all. Ready to believe the worst of a man and ally himself with your enemies."

"I saw him a few weeks ago. He's rounder, by the way." Merrick laughed. "Besides, you would not want me for a relation. I do more for my friends than for family anyway."

Hastings paused with his cup in midair. "Does that not go against the family motto: family first?"

"The full Ford family motto is a bit longer than that. *Never admit fault, always repay in kind, family first.* Luckily, I'm not truly a Ford. Only a half-serve was dealt me. A flaw in the makeup of my character I embrace wholeheartedly. I chose to help only where needed."

"The lad *is* your cousin."

"Yes."

A grin tugged the corners of Hastings' mouth. "So *family first* would seem to apply."

"Not in this case." Merrick was doing this to protect Arabella. Mostly. "Perhaps there was a little revenge in my decision, but my reasons are my own and I'll not share them."

"You have more secrets than a Catholic priest at confession." Hastings sat back, scowling. "Well, let us hope he's not made a rash decision. I've some leeway in my orders, but not more than a day or two."

"Thank you." Merrick eyed his friend's pale complexion. "How have you been?"

"Much the same. A skirmish or two, but no prize to add to my distinction." His eyes grew unfocused. "And you?"

"The same for the most part." He leaned forward. "Since you are not here for long, I should mention I'm going to take a wife this season."

Hastings blinked. "Dear God, why?"

"For many reasons. The succession is one."

"Love?"

A vision of Arabella flittered through his mind and he swallowed. "If I am in luck."

"Luck has nothing to do with love, but I will wish you well in finding the right woman." Hastings chewed his lower lip and fiddled with his cup. "How is she?"

Hastings could only mean one woman. Merrick's cousin, Lady Sally Ford. The woman whose heart Hastings had broken. "I imagine as irritated as ever. Freddy is to be married. Rutherford arranged it." He shrugged. "I have not spoken with Sally this season. She's still in the country, no doubt making sure this event takes place without a hitch."

Hastings wiped his brow with the back of his hand. "When you see her, be sure to pass along my compliments."

"I'll consider it, though there is every chance she will shoot the messenger."

Hastings glanced at the tables around them. "She won't shoot you. You were her champion—the one who beat me bloody for hurting her—remember?"

"Better my fists than her brother's plans." Merrick grimaced at the memory. "They would have keelhauled you if they'd gotten to you first."

"True." Hastings agreed with a heavy sigh.

He leaned closer to Hastings, noting the sweat on his brow and the tiredness of his eyes. "I say, are you sure you're at all well?"

"It's nothing. Just a chill." Hastings wiped his brow with a handkerchief, one that might once have been pristine but now resembled a rag. "Now, if the matter that brought me here is concluded, I'll be on my way. That bed I found is calling me back to it."

"Is there a woman in that bed?"

"You know me, I never carry tales."

Although Merrick grinned at the reminder of Hastings' secretive ways, he was a little worried about his friend. Hastings was rarely unwell. Perhaps a bed was exactly what he needed. "Enjoy your rest and take care of yourself, Captain. Perhaps I will see you again if you have the time during your leave."

"I'd like that, but the Admiralty will need my ship at the ready soon." Hastings collected his bicorne and then sauntered out, leaving Merrick to finish his coffee alone. Poor bloody Hastings. He'd had happiness snatched from his grasp and suffered the consequences even now for a decision he hadn't made.

As Merrick sat there thinking about love and the ramifications of foolish choices and mistakes, he decided an ability to forgive might be desired in a spouse. He'd had a lot of lovers in the past, most of whom he was still on good terms with. He should not like any misunderstandings to take place simply because some woman had touched him intimately once and his new wife learned of it and didn't like that fact.

He threw some money on the table for the proprietor and wandered out. At this time of the day, he was often at loose ends. Most of his unattached friends were still abed and did not like to be disturbed. The married ones were with their wives, and he didn't like to intrude upon them. A pity Hastings had run off so soon. But that waiting bed might be just the thing for the man.

Merrick waved for his coachman to bring up the barouche and join him before the coffee house. "I'm bored. Take me somewhere interesting, Jimmy."

The wiry man at the reins scratched his head, sparing a glance for the overcast sky. "It won't rain yet, but it might soon. Green Park, milord?"

"Yes, that will do as well as any place, I suppose." No excitement possible so close to home, but at least there was something of nature to be seen. "I might even stretch my legs for a bit and inspect the progress made on the temple."

The Temple of Concord was to be the centerpiece of the

Prince Regent's celebrations in a few months' time. Merrick had developed the habit of noting the progress, or lack thereof, since he'd come up to Town.

"Very good, milord."

As the reins cracked over the horses, Merrick settled against the squabs and considered how the family might be taking the news of Laurence's disappearance so far. He hoped they were running around in circles trying to find him. With luck, and good speed, his cousin and his love would be well underway on their adventure. The thought gave him a great sense of satisfaction. It wasn't every day he got a little revenge on the family for their adherence to an antiquated code of ethics.

Fords did not always come first. Sometimes it was better to put the needs of others ahead of self-interest.

When they reached the park, his driver skillfully pulled up under the shade of an overhanging branch and tied off the horses. "Should I wait for you here?"

He smiled. "No. Return to the house and let Holland know where I am. I'll walk back directly."

He headed toward the construction site, pondering how far they'd progressed since his last stroll past. As he approached a black poplar, a scrap of light green muslin against the gnarled bark caught his eye. When he was level with the spot, he found the scrap actually belonged to the walking dress Arabella was wearing. "Lady Farnsworth?"

She sagged against the tree and then peeked at him from beneath a large-brimmed bonnet trimmed with ribbon, her smile hesitant. "Oh, thank heavens it's you. I thought for a moment that Farnsworth had found me."

"You thought I was Farnsworth?" Merrick glanced down at his olive-green waistcoat and coat in disappointment. "I really must speak to my tailor."

"No, no." She waved her gloved hand about and laughed. "I saw the carriage and a tall man step out and hid immediately just in case. There is nothing lacking in your attire, sir. As always, you appear very distinguished."

"Thank you. And as always, you look very lovely yourself." Merrick glanced about the park but saw no sign of Lord Farnsworth anywhere, or a servant that might belong to her. "If

I may ask, why are you hiding from your brother-in-law and alone? Most women don't find the construction of the Temple of Concord particularly fascinating. Is Farnsworth angry with you over his daughter's elopement?"

"Well, not yet. As far as I can tell, he doesn't suspect she's gone, but I'd like to delay the inevitable discussion for as long as possible." She grimaced, fidgeting with the piping adorning the sleeve of her spencer. "You see, I'm a terrible liar. If he asks me directly what I know about her disappearance, I am afraid I will blurt everything out at once."

Merrick studied her. Despite how pretty she appeared on the surface, her eyes held a wealth of weariness he hadn't encountered before. "Did you worry for the whole of last night?"

She nodded slowly. "It is not every day you fail so abysmally as a chaperone."

"You did not fail." He rushed to assure her. "Far from it. Everyone has a choice in how they behave. The girl chose not to follow your excellent example and is the poorer for it in my opinion. With or without help that girl would have twisted my cousin around her finger and run off."

Her eyes widened. "After my behavior the other night, I do not feel I am necessarily an excellent example."

It was just a kiss. More or less harmless to a widow's reputation if it never recurred. Arabella made it sound as if she'd made love in a public place. "You did nothing wrong. Any blame should fall on my head."

Arabella met his gaze and her eyes softened. "Thank you."

He shifted his weight from foot to foot. He couldn't help but hope she was warming to him. Determined to find out, he took a pace toward her to see how she would react to his proximity. "If it is any comfort, there is little chance of anyone catching them. I gave orders for the team to be driven hard and fast for the border, and they are not going to the usual place where many an imprudent match is made."

"Oh," she said as she straightened, drawing closer herself. "Where will they be married?"

Merrick was mesmerized by the change in her behavior. She was no longer so timid. She met his eyes, her body turning toward him as they talked. So many unwise thoughts crossed his mind. "If you cannot lie, I'd best not mention the name, but there was a little town not far from the border where I've stayed once or twice. The first time I went there, my driver had gotten us thoroughly lost. The second time, I went by choice and stayed a good long while. The place is little frequented by travelers, so they should not be discovered until the deed is done."

"That does relieve my mind. Thank you."

Still, she did not smile with her usual good spirits and that puzzled him. "There is something else, isn't there? Are you angry about the kiss? I will apologize if necessary."

"No. It's not that. Quite the contrary."

He moved closer, intrigued by her response. "What then? I know we are not the closest of acquaintances, but if I can ease your mind, I would gladly do anything you ask."

She bit her lower lip a moment before turning her head, denying him a view of her face because the bonnet brim was so large. "Aside from Cecily's elopement, I do have something preying on my mind. Not that my problem is her fault, of course, the two events are simply inexplicably tied together, if you take my meaning."

He wanted to reach out and turn her lovely face his way again. Instead, he curled his hands into fists at his side. "No, you have lost me, in truth. What problem do you face? I may not be Grayling, but I will help if I can."

"I fear there is nothing you could do. Farnsworth wishes for me to return to the family estate in Surrey, Hinkley Park, after Cecily marries. With Cecily's elopement, and his expected anger with her, I believe that may change."

"So you want to return to Hinkley?"

"In truth, no. I never liked living there."

He still did not understand her concern. "Then remain in Wiltshire."

"Winslette is not part of the entailment and Farnsworth has informed me that he intends to sell it despite my wish to remain living there. So you see, I may find myself without a home anywhere at all if he believes me responsible for Cecily's actions."

Merrick rubbed his hand over his mouth to hold back the

curses he couldn't utter before this elegant lady. Farnsworth was an utter bastard to sell her home out from under her very feet and force her back to an estate she didn't like. Plus, if she went there, he didn't like his chances of seeing her again for a very long time. She would be cut off from her friends too, and he could see why she appeared so troubled. He glanced around the park quickly. "It is not your fault. The girl is willful and headstrong."

"True, yet Farnsworth will hold me accountable. He would never admit himself a failure in raising the girl. I dread returning to that town house today." Her eyes grew fearful and Merrick longed to comfort her. Perhaps to hold her against his chest and promise everything would work out for the best in due course. But he could not touch her nor make promises he could not deliver. The frustration that realization brought soured his mood. He had no business getting involved, but he wanted to help very much. It was then he noticed a group of official-looking sorts pointing in their direction. "I should leave you to continue your stroll."

Her smile returned but it was forced. "I suppose I should go visit the ducks as I usually do. Thank you for helping Cecily, my lord. I hope she will return a married woman and not be caught beforehand."

"I wish for that too. Farewell." He nodded and retraced his steps to Piccadilly Street, his mind filled with Arabella's fears. At the border of the park, he met with another half brother coming down Half Moon Street.

Archie, one of the youngest in his employ, smiled eagerly. "Mr. Holland sent me to see if you needed any assistance."

"What possible need could I have so close to home?" He shook his head. "No, don't answer that. He's sent you out on a fool's errand."

"Didn't mind in the least, milord." Archie grinned and craned his neck to look around. "There's always something exciting to see in the park."

Archie hadn't been in London long enough to set aside his awe of his surroundings. Merrick glanced behind him. Leaving Lady Farnsworth alone in the park, with her mind so full of her worries, did not sit well with him. He crooked his finger at

Archie. "I need you to do something for me, lad."

The boy's head whipped around so fast it was a wonder it didn't fall off his neck. "Anything."

"There is a fine lady in the park, possibly down by the water's edge now, dressed all in green and wearing a large bonnet. When I saw her she was hiding behind a black poplar, in fact, so you may overlook her. I want you to keep a discreet eye on her until she returns to number eight Half Moon Street. I saw no sign of a servant attending her, and her mind is too full of her own cares for me to have any peace. If she senses your presence, introduce yourself as my servant, but it is important that no one else know you are watching over her on my behalf. She is a very proper lady, if you take my meaning, and I would not like any harm to come to her reputation. Is that clear?"

"Of course."

Merrick slapped Archie's shoulder to send him on his way. He cast one last lingering glance behind him before he turned his thoughts to the other matter Lady Farnsworth had mentioned and headed for home. Winslette was for sale. A rare opportunity that intrigued him. The property had significant esteem, so the price would be steep to match. Farnsworth wasn't one to bargain about anything. If Grayling were here and not buried in the country with his new wife and daughters, his friend would certainly consider purchasing the property that adjoined his to expand his holdings.

In his absence, Merrick could at least inquire. If a deal could be made, then there was no need for Lady Farnsworth to ever remove to Surrey at all. Grayling would never send her packing, and if Merrick kept the place himself because Gray didn't want it, he would not either and would gain a decent excuse to visit and spend time with Arabella.

By the time he let himself in his front door, he had decided purchasing a property in Wiltshire was a sound investment and addition to his estates. He had no qualms about serving his own interests first before consulting his friend's wishes.

He handed his hat and gloves over as Holland approached. "I've decided to buy another country estate. See what you can find in Wiltshire, my good man. There must be something close to Grayling's estate that will be tolerable."

Holland passed him the day's mail. "Wiltshire? Very good, my lord. I'll make enquiries on your behalf and have an answer by week's end."

"Today, Holland. I must have an answer quickly and the deal done without delay." He flicked through the invitations, saw the promised one for Lady Berry's dinner, and discarded the rest. It was not for a few days. Perhaps tonight he would stay in and read a book, recharging his enthusiasm before resuming his search.

Holland cleared his throat. "Why the urgency for a Wiltshire property?"

Merrick clapped his hand to his half brother's shoulder and squeezed. He could have a little fun at Holland's expense by knowing something before the other man did. "All in good time, Holland. Just wait and see what you find for sale."

Chapter Ten

As Arabella had foreseen, Farnsworth was enraged by the elopement of his only daughter for the embarrassment it inflicted on him and the stain to the family reputation. What she couldn't fathom was why he had not set off in pursuit of the lovers to Scotland to prevent the match from taking place straight away.

"I wash my hands of them and rue the day I ever came to London," he said sourly as he poured another drink, his fifth since Arabella had been summoned to dinner this evening. "He'll not get a penny of her dowry."

She winced. A lieutenant made little enough from his commission to support a family without denying them the dowry. She hoped her niece had considered that. After returning from her walk, Arabella had been on tenterhooks because Cecily's elopement was still unknown. An hour later, Farnsworth discovered the situation. His bellow of outrage, heard clearly through the floor of her bedchamber from below, alerted her to be ready for his anger and made her tremble. She had been questioned harshly until he had received a note he wouldn't share the contents of.

At first, she had assumed it was about Cecily, yet Farnsworth was still in their Half Moon Street residence, complaining at every opportunity. The butler appeared and delivered yet another note to Farnsworth. When he picked it up and read it, his eyes darted in her direction. He smiled, yet kept the details to himself again.

Arabella began to feel distinctly uncomfortable.

"What will you do?" She posed her question carefully, uncertain of whether she wanted his answer or not. Rothwell had eased her mind of Cecily being abandoned when the idea of elopement lost its appeal to Lieutenant Ford. As far as Rothwell was concerned, Cecily would marry without a shadow of a doubt and she had to believe it would be so.

Farnsworth sighed. "There is little to be done. She left very early last night. She has a whole night of travel between us, and according to my reports, this Ford fellow has disappeared without a trace. He'll not stop long on the way to the border. Only a fool would attempt a recovery, and I am not dancing to that tune. It will take time for the stain to be forgotten by society, but Parker will overlook the impropriety and that is all that matters."

Farnsworth was so wrong she wanted to laugh at him. They were in Town and everyone they met with would soon know exactly what had befallen the house of Farnsworth. The man had been obsessed with keeping up appearances prior to Cecily's elopement. He was always throwing out little remarks about how a lady should conduct herself in public. No matter how much money changed hands or what apologies were made to Parker, the scandal would not subside for some time and would remain a black spot on the family's reputation.

A tap on the front door reverberated through the house. Although Arabella strained her ears, she could not discern who it might be. When the butler interrupted their dinner yet again a few moments later, he went directly to Farnsworth, holding his little silver tray before him. A single note rested on the silver surface and he read it quickly. Farnsworth met her gaze. "You must excuse me. A matter of business has arisen that must be dealt with."

"Do the notes concern Cecily?"

"No." Farnsworth slipped the note into his pocket, his expression thoughtful. "You would do well to focus on the future. I'll need a few minutes to conclude my business, and then

I will join you in the drawing room."

He retreated and rudely left Arabella seated at the dining table amid a feast better suited to a celebration. Tomorrow Arabella would speak to cook about extravagance. It was not necessary to dine so lavishly when it was just herself and Farnsworth sitting down to dinner. She reached for her wineglass, startled to see her hand shaking. Just contemplating bringing order and good sense to Farnsworth's homes unsettled her.

Without Cecily to talk to, Arabella was not certain what she would do with herself tonight in the drawing room. Since she'd come up to Town, she had concentrated on what Cecily needed. Practice at the pianoforte, dissecting the peerage to determine familial connections of those they met. During the day, they went out—shopping for new gloves, visiting the modiste, accepting invitations to parties and fetes that would show the girl off to advantage. Farnsworth had insisted they decline tonight's round of amusements given Cecily's embarrassing elopement, and she had to agree with his decision. If they went out without Cecily in their ranks, someone would ask of her whereabouts.

Without a pressing task before her, Arabella retreated to the drawing room as Farnsworth had demanded and stopped before a window facing the street. Outside, a steady rain had fallen since midafternoon, cocooning her with her thoughts and worries. Rain would slow Cecily and Lieutenant Ford's flight to the border, though it might just prevent any pursuit being made by the Fords. She hoped Rothwell had factored bad weather into his calculations. She smiled ruefully. She had completely underestimated that gentleman. He was not the pleasure-obsessed rogue society made him out to be. He believed in love and helping those in need. Not at all what she'd imagined he might feel.

She leaned toward the window and tried to see the façade of his town house far down Half Moon Street, toward the park. If she pressed her nose to the glass, she could just see enough to determine its location. Were the windows lit more brightly than normal tonight? Possibly. Perhaps she was not the only one to eschew the pleasures of Town on a rainy night, or it was more likely Rothwell had his own private entertainment indoors. All she had was Farnsworth and his odd looks.

Dispirited by that thought, Arabella turned from the window and then shrieked. Farnsworth was standing immediately behind her, smiling down at her in that odd way he'd adopted today, another refilled glass in hand. She pressed her fingers to her chest, attempting to recover her calm and control her racing pulse. "Gracious, I did not hear you come in, Farnsworth."

He did not move back. "Did you not plan to be so artfully displayed when I returned? You must do exactly that tomorrow when Parker calls."

"Artfully?" She scowled at him for frightening her and babbling nonsense. "Really, Farnsworth, you must moderate your consumption of spirits. They make you imagine any number of ridiculous things."

"Not so ridiculous." Farnsworth placed the glass on the nearest table. "We are alike, you and I. We each hesitate to say what is on our minds."

Arabella had had enough of his moods today. Farnsworth held nothing of his opinions in reserve. She'd learned so much while living beneath his roof to determine she had to do everything she could to avoid continuing the conversation. "I believe I should like to retire early tonight. Excuse me."

Farnsworth's hand rose and cupped her face. "I was thinking the same thing. You should be refreshed for when Parker extends his offer of marriage tomorrow."

It took a moment to make sense of Farnsworth's words, but when she did, she staggered back against the window. "You must be mistaken."

"Not at all." He held up a scrap of paper for her to see. "It is all arranged. Since Cecily has eloped, your days as a chaperone are done. You shall marry Parker by special license tomorrow and any embarrassment to the family will largely be erased by the connection."

"I am not marrying Parker," she insisted. Arabella had only wanted a lover, not a man to tell her what to do with her days. "Whatever possessed you to think you could arrange such a thing without consulting me?"

He grabbed her arm and jerked her hard against him, well

beyond the bounds of proper behavior for any gentleman. "You will do what I say or you will get out. Have I not been patient while you mourned? Have I not allowed you certain freedoms while keeping a roof over your head and providing you with endless luxury? If you had any family, I'd have sent you back to them, but I thought you could be useful. Well, you will be now. With your help, Cecily managed to repel every proper gentleman save that Ford runt and ruined us in the process. It's up to you to smooth the way forward."

"What do you mean ruin us? What haven't you told me?" Arabella struggled and his grip tightened. Such a situation she had never imagined she would find herself in. What woman did? She would not marry Parker. She would not marry anyone. Unfortunately, the more she fought against his hold, the tighter Farnsworth gripped her. "Farnsworth, release me at once or I will scream."

The next moment, his open palm slammed against her cheek, sending her spinning across the room and into a side table. Small ornaments shattered as they hit the floor. Only a single, unlit silver candelabra remained on the surface and even it tipped on its side.

"You will do as I say, woman," he growled, stalking toward her. "Don't tell me you're not in the mood for a man after all your come-hither looks you've sent the fellows about London this season. You ruined my daughter, planted wild notions in her head about love and personal freedom. I won't suffer the expense of you under my roof a moment longer without the promise of a dividend in return. Luckily, Parker isn't repelled by a more experienced woman and has settled my debts in full in order to have you. Be grateful it's marriage he offers and not an affair. You'll marry him or live on the street with the other tarts for all I care."

She stared at him, shocked by the way he saw her actions. She'd created no scandal herself. She'd done not one thing to feel embarrassed about. "I don't know what you're talking about. I have done nothing to deserve being treated in this manner. I am not a horse to sell at Tattersall's."

"Oh, come now. I'm not a fool or blind." His hand shot out and wrapped about her throat, hauling her upright to meet his eyes. His bloodshot gaze skimmed over her body once, a sneer forming on his mouth. He was far more intoxicated than she'd first suspected. His grip tightened as he pressed her against the table. "New dresses designed to arouse, the absence of my brother's wedding ring upon your finger. You had but one plan in mind when you came up to Town. Seduction. Well, you got your wish. There is one gentleman among the many prepared to seize what's on offer."

Arabella clutched at the table behind her for support. "I came because you gave me no choice," she croaked.

Farnsworth's face came closer. "You always had a choice. Pretend all you like, but you'll get your wish for a man between your legs. You'll be married before the sun sets tomorrow and business with Parker will be complete."

Arabella groped behind her. Her fingers closed on the lone candlestick. The cold, heavy silver reassured her somewhat. "You're mad. I am not marrying him or anyone."

He drew back, but his free hand rose as if to strike her again. "Then get out of my house."

As his hand fell toward her face again, Arabella swung the candlestick, clubbing Farnsworth on the side of his head with all her might. It wasn't enough to drop him to the floor, but he staggered back, clutching at his head and bellowing his rage. She took one instant to decide she shouldn't stay another moment to try to reason with him. She flung the candlestick from her fingers and ran for the door. She passed the butler, ignoring his expression of horror, gained the entrance hall, and wrenched open the front door and stared out into the night.

"Arabella! You have no choice," Farnsworth bellowed.

But she *did* have a choice. Despite the rain, and having no possessions save the gown she wore, she plunged out into the safety of darkness. She chose freedom.

Once on the street, she glanced left and right through the rain and knew she had little time to decide her direction. She hadn't wounded Farnsworth greatly, and he seemed convinced she'd fall in with his plans. It was possible he might follow and force her to return. She chose left and the open space of the park ahead, moving off at a normal walking pace to avoid scrutiny. By the fourth house, the trickle of rain had grown to a downpour, slick cold water sliding beneath the neckline of her flimsy dinner gown and between her breasts.

A carriage clattered past her on the narrow street, flicking dirty water across her lower skirts. She swiped at it ineffectually and then gave up. She couldn't keep going like this without a specific destination in mind, so she stopped in the servants' stairwell of a house she knew to be vacant this season to think for a minute or two.

The park ahead would be dangerous at this time of night for a woman alone. Farnsworth might come upon her there and do even worse.

She looked around her quickly and shivered as rain slicked her skin. She had few friends in London that would accept her arrival and ask no questions about her disheveled, rain-soaked state. Anyone with a sense of honor would demand answers that she didn't want to give.

Footsteps pounded past where she hid and she huddled against the stair wall, desperately trying to control her fear and not give herself away. When all was silent again, she risked a peek. There was no one in sight or carriages drawing close, but across the street stood Lord Rothwell's house. The fanlight and lower street-front windows were brightly lit, casting the only welcoming glow to the evening that she could see. Rothwell might shelter her if he were at home, at least for a few hours until she could make up her mind where to go.

He had proved himself a gentleman of sorts. She had never feared him, only found his intense stare strangely unsettling. She didn't believe he would take advantage of a woman in her position. Tonight, of all nights, he was her best bet for safety.

With a quick check of the street, she bit her lip and stepped toward that light, trusting that her good friend's best friend would be the right option. At least if he were to ravish her, she might actually enjoy it.

A ripple of fear raced over her skin as she knocked on the blue door and huddled against it, making herself as small as possible. She glanced up and down the street swiftly but detected no movement coming after her. Through the rain, she thought the doorway of her own home was dark, which led her to believe Farnsworth might expect her to creep back.

She knocked rapidly again on Rothwell's door and it opened suddenly. "Help me," she said to Rothwell's servant and stumbled over the doorstep, quickly shoving the door closed behind her.

She ran her hands over the comfortingly solid door and turned the locks herself, dragging in several ragged breaths in relief. Farnsworth might never consider she would come here and it would take him a while to get through that door when it possessed so many stout locks. She might even have enough time to escape through the rear exit if no one stood in her path.

After a time, she grew aware of the repeated clearing of a throat behind her. Knowing she couldn't avoid it, she slowly pivoted to face the room. At first glance, she thought she stood before Rothwell himself, but this man was somewhat older and had none of his intensity.

"May I be of assistance?" The stranger's eyes widened suddenly. "Lady Farnsworth?"

Arabella smiled awkwardly. She had hoped not to be recognized at all, but anonymity was impossible given the help she needed. "I need a moment."

"You may have as many as you wish for, of course." His eyes dipped lower and then narrowed at her sodden gown. "Perhaps you would be more comfortable beside a fire. Given the weather outside, I believe it very likely you may be soaked through to the bone."

Arabella cautiously glanced down at herself. Her gown was plastered to her breasts and legs as if she were wearing rags. Smears of something dark ruined the hem of the once lovely light blue muslin she'd worn for dinner. There was also a puddle forming at her feet and more droplets of water adding to it from her elbows. She swallowed the tide of nausea that tightened her throat. She wanted to hide, but this man had already seen too much. "I fear I am. A fire would be very much appreciated."

"Come this way. Please."

Her elbow was grasped lightly and the man steered her toward a closed door to the right. She appreciated his help. Once she'd begun to move, her legs were not very steady. Inside was a warmly lit chamber, a drawing room perhaps, but one designed for comfort rather than appearances. A pair of booted feet overhung the end of the longest settee.

The feet moved and Rothwell sat up. He shook his head suddenly. "What the devil? Dear God, what the hell has happened? Holland, send for Farnsworth at once."

"Don't," Arabella shouted and then clutched her hands over her mouth in shock at her panicked yell. "Oh, please don't."

Arabella shivered at the flare of puzzlement forming in Rothwell's eyes. She'd been around enough men to understand their moods. He would want to take her back where he thought she belonged as quickly as possible. She couldn't allow that.

The man holding her arm, Holland, she recalled, eased her back a little, glancing distrustfully at Rothwell. "This wasn't your doing, was it, Merrick?"

Rothwell scrambled to his feet. "Of course not."

Surprised by Rothwell's hasty move, Arabella shifted closer to the older man.

"Just as well." Holland patted her hand, brought her to the fire, and released her near a well-padded chair. "I'll fetch a blanket to wrap her in before she takes a chill."

When he was gone, Rothwell moved to stand before her. His hand rose and she flinched away unconsciously.

"I'm sorry," she said quickly, taking rapid breaths as panic seized her. After the events of tonight, she wasn't sure she wanted anyone to touch any part of her ever again.

His brow furrowed but he did not withdraw. Instead, he moved his hand toward her again, much slower this time. Arabella was better prepared for the second attempt and did not flinch as his fingers slid over her jaw gently. He tilted her face toward the light so he could view her neck. His touch was light and impersonal. Very soon his eyes darkened, his jaw clenched, and then his gaze sharpened on hers. "Who did this to you?"

"Don't ask me that." Arabella wrenched her face from his grip and hugged her arms around her body. She struggled to keep calm. She had come to Rothwell for shelter, not questioning. She didn't blame him for wanting answers, but she had none to give. She didn't understand Farnsworth's behavior. She knew he had a temper, but this was far beyond her experience.

She peeked at Rothwell and saw he'd not moved away. She

shouldn't have jumped from him like that and she wanted to apologize, but the words were stuck in her throat. She raised her hand to caress her cheek, feeling tenderness and discomfort there. Slowly, Arabella lifted her chin, but Rothwell wasn't watching her. His eyes were fixed on the distant windows where the rain still drummed, deep frown lines etched on his brow.

"Best keep your questions for later," Holland said to Rothwell as he rushed back into the room. When the man held out an opened blanket, Arabella allowed him to wrap her up in it and gently press her into a chair again.

When Holland was done wrapping her snugly in the blanket, he moved to Rothwell's side. "She's had a terrible fright and will need time to calm her mind."

"Of course." Rothwell caught her watching them and his lips lifted in a smile Arabella found infinitely reassuring. "You're safe here, Lady Farnsworth. I promise you that."

"There's tea coming," Holland added helpfully.

Arabella nodded, sinking farther into the soft wool blanket and hoping the night was all a very bad dream. "Tea. Yes, tea will fix everything, I expect."

Chapter Eleven

Merrick wasn't a violent man, but given the last startling hour, he could be persuaded to kill easily enough. He'd stood aside when Holland had fussed over Arabella, keeping her close to the fire and forcing hot tea down her bruised throat. Holland was a natural at mothering. He'd continued to reassure Arabella that Farnsworth would never learn her location whenever a door closed with too loud a bang. Given her extreme anxiety about Farnsworth being summoned, Merrick could only assume that Farnsworth was somehow responsible for her appearance. The bruises forming across Lady Farnsworth's skin enraged him still, but he'd held back his questions as Holland had advised.

Had his own actions today concerning the purchase of her home incited Farnsworth to anger? Their bargaining had been brisk during the day and he was afraid their negotiations, on top of his daughter's elopement, had pushed Farnsworth into a temper.

He approached the huddled woman and perched on the footstool placed close to her knees. "Do you feel calm enough now to tell me what happened?"

Her head lifted a touch but she did not meet his eyes directly. "I shouldn't imagine I will ever be, but you've been so considerate. You deserve to know what brought me here."

He held out one hand, palm facing upward, hoping to reassure both her and himself that she had suffered no lasting harm. Seeing her flinch every time aid was offered was tearing his heart in two. "I don't need to know the particulars if you do not feel strong enough to speak of it. I merely wish to assist you in whatever way I can."

Her hand slipped from the blanket and she laid it over his. Her flesh was still chilled and she trembled. He closed his hands about hers and chafed her skin, hoping to warm her. Her face fell so low he could not see her expression.

"Farnsworth insisted I marry again."

"What?" Merrick drew back in shock. "The devil he did."

Arabella disappeared into the blanket as she hugged herself. "You don't believe me?"

"I believe you," he whispered urgently. "But the mind does not want to imagine you placed in such a situation. You have a choice about who you marry. He should not force you."

Her hand rose to her neck and she hunched a little more into herself. "That is what I said. He was determined to give me little choice in the matter. He's far stronger than I am and insisted that I accept Lord Parker's proposal when he calls tomorrow."

"Parker?"

"So he claimed."

The last was said barely at a whisper. Merrick dropped to his knees, yet hesitated to come any closer. No man should have the right to abuse a woman just because she disagreed with him. It went against everything he believed in.

Her breath grew rushed. "He hit me when I refused to do as he demanded, then wrapped his hand about my throat and would have killed me for going against his wishes. I've never seen someone so enraged. He was deep in his cups, but I didn't see the danger until too late. I either had to accept or he threatened to throw me out. When I gained enough freedom to escape, I left the house. I don't want to marry anyone. I couldn't think where to go and I was alone on the street with only the dark and the rain to hide me and the park ahead. I am so sorry to involve you in my problems. I'll rest here a bit longer and then be on my way."

Dear God. What might have happened if he'd not changed his plans and remained at home tonight? "There's no need to rush back out. There is no need to go anywhere just yet. I would never turn you out into the night to fend for yourself. I would not do that to anyone."

Against his better judgment, he placed a hand on her shoulder. She started instantly but soon stopped trembling when he merely held her shoulder through the blanket. As he continued to hold her thus, Arabella slowly toppled toward him until her damp head rested against his chest, a broken sob tearing from her throat.

Gingerly, Rothwell embraced her. He stroked her back, noting that while she shook in the grips of her misery, she did not resist or pull away from the scant comfort he could offer. At least he was able to do some good. When her sobbing began in earnest, he didn't think she noticed much of anything he did, and he simply held her tightly against his chest until she stiffened and moved away again.

Merrick sat back on his heels and gave her space enough to pull herself together without feeling rushed to do so. She glanced at him timidly, fingers clenching and unclenching on the edge of the wool blanket wrapped around her. Merrick moved farther away, regaining a place on the footstool and simply watched her.

"I don't know what to do," she told him softly, wiping at tears that continued to slip down her cheeks. "I wish I had never come to London."

When she sobbed again, Merrick moved toward her. He had never been particularly comfortable around crying women, but he could not watch her suffer like this at a distance. Arabella came to his arms easily, clinging to him in a way he had once dreamed of but discarded as merely an impossible fantasy.

She turned her face into his cravat, her breath warming him through the thin material. "I cannot think of what to do. Where should I go tonight?"

Merrick glanced out the window at the rain that continued to fall. There were few choices at this time of night. Taking her to his aunt might be a possibility. He wasn't certain whose side she would take, Arabella's or Farnsworth's, but he didn't want to risk a scene that might upset Arabella even more. If he delivered her to Aunt Pen and convinced her to hold her tongue, he would owe her, of course. The Fords would expect something from him in return for their aid.

Other acquaintances of good standing would be even more problematic to beg help from. Yet there was another possibility that required no effort at all. Arabella could stay with him. Farnsworth would never look for her here, and she could make her decisions in the morning when she was calmer. Blundering about in the night in her distressed state would only upset her more. She would sleep far more peacefully under Merrick's roof. There would also be no awkward questions to answer about the bruise forming on her cheek or neck in the morning. There would be no discussion either of why her personal belongings were not with her.

But if she were found out, her reputation would be in tatters.

If he opened his mouth and made the suggestion, would she be shocked even more? Was he asking too much of her to let him watch over her for one night? He was getting used to being viewed as a friend rather than a seducer. Asking her to stay risked her reputation and was likely to destroy the small tendrils of friendship that had led her to seek safety with him.

Yet in the end, Holland returned and saved him from any decision. "I took the liberty of preparing a bedchamber for Lady Farnsworth," Holland said softly. "If you'll but come with me, madam, I am sure you may rest your head in more comfortable surroundings."

Arabella jumped, her head snapping upward, her eyes widening in fright as she stared across the room. The blemish to her pale cheek would be unmistakable by morning. Anyone who saw her would question her appearance. Her face turned a fiery pink. She bit her lip but eventually faced Merrick, her eyes full of hope and misery. "I should not like to impose."

She wanted to stay. Though his heart leapt at keeping her here, he patted her hand again in what he hoped was a brotherly way. "It is no imposition. Holland has already made arrangements for you it seems, and I would certainly feel easier knowing you were beyond Farnsworth's reach. Go with him, and tomorrow we can discuss how to go on."

Her relieved smile was fleeting, turning into a grimace of pain. She lifted her hand to her tender face and held it there, letting the blanket fall at long last. The state of her gown, ruined by the elements outside, reminded Merrick of what had brought her here.

Any thoughts he'd entertained about pursuing her for himself crumbled to ashes. Arabella had fled from one arranged marriage. She might not be at all interested in becoming a wife even to save her reputation. All he could be to her was a friend, and she needed him to be only that tonight. He would be the best friend he could be and never let her know he'd considered more than that.

She glanced at him, a shy, hesitant smile lingering on her lips. "You, sir, are not at all as your reputation marks you."

His pulse pounded at her compliment, but he merely stood by and gave her room to stand unaided, anxious that too much proximity might make her fearful again. "Goodnight, Lady Farnsworth."

She reclaimed the wool blanket and clutched it around her and her sodden dress. Her hesitant shuffle across the room broke his heart. There was little left of the confident woman he had admired two nights ago.

At the doorway, she turned back. "Goodnight, Rothwell, and thank you."

After about an hour, Holland joined Merrick in the study, where he sat staring into an empty brandy glass. Holland closed the door behind him and leaned against it. "She is resting now, I believe. Everything has grown quiet."

Merrick rolled the glass between his hands. "Where did you put her?"

Holland crossed the room, took the open decanter of brandy, and replaced the stopper. "Your mother's old room has recently been cleaned in preparation for your marriage, so I took the liberty of putting her there. It is the most comfortable bedchamber in the town house save yours."

"Did she say anything else?"

Holland took the empty glass from his hands and set it aside. "Not a word beyond thank you. I left her with a nightshirt of yours and a glass of port to sip. I thought she might sleep better for having it."

"I own a nightshirt?" Merrick bowed his head, marveling at how calm and practical Holland could be at a time like this. "Holland, I need your advice."

"Of course."

Anger flared to life again. "Lady Cecily eloped. Farnsworth compromised on the price for Winslette and then insisted Arabella marry someone she didn't want. Am I to blame for her injuries? Is this my fault?"

Holland came closer and perched on the edge of the desk. His hand settled on Merrick's shoulder a moment before he drew back. "Farnsworth's temper has always been quick, or so the servants I've come across have remarked in the past."

"A refused match has often resulted in quarrels, but this is beyond anything I could have anticipated. She's his sister-in-law for Gods sake." Merrick rubbed his hands over his face. He couldn't rest until he was sure he hadn't caused this. "Just yesterday he sold her home to me for what I believed was a fair price. Though the bargaining was brisk, I detected no desperation in the negotiations."

"There was none. I believe you. The deal was fair, generous even, and he was indeed very happy with the bargain he struck with you."

"Ugh." Anger propelled him to his feet. He had never felt so utterly useless. He wanted to return the damage done to Arabella tenfold. "I cannot help feeling that my actions set her up so Farnsworth could control her and give her no choice. What did he hope to gain?"

"I am not sure." Holland poured a drink and held it out to Merrick. "I confess I had concluded Farnsworth liked everything his way. From what I could glean, there were three other parties interested in that property. You were simply faster and fairer in naming a price. If not you, then someone else would have taken Winslette off his hands. Lady Farnsworth would likely have been in the same situation if you had not made the purchase."

Merrick took the glass but slid it back to the table untouched. He didn't need to start down that drunken path tonight. He needed to keep a clear head and decide what to do. "I don't think she knows yet that he sold Winslette."

Holland drained the discarded glass in two swallows and set it aside. "Then you will have to tell her yourself that she has no home and see how she takes the news."

"She has a home still." Merrick raked his fingers through his hair. He'd never explained the matter fully to Holland and now seemed an opportune time to get the matter out into the open. "It was never my intention to evict her."

Holland's eyes narrowed. "I had assumed you intended to make Winslette your country residence for a while, given the proximity to Lord Grayling and his family and the distance from Newberry Park. I had considered you might set your wife up close to your friends so they might become better acquainted in a shorter space of time."

"I never intended to live there. My first thought was to buy it so Grayling might not miss out on the opportunity. Winslette does share a boundary with his estate. But then I reconsidered and decided to keep it."

"I see." Holland's frown cleared. "Well, then, you should be up-front with Lady Farnsworth as soon as possible to set her mind at ease. She is probably worried for her future, and that of her staff. I am told she is very kind to them and may be concerned for their security."

"Arabella is kind to all who cross her path."

He sensed Holland's scrutiny before the man spoke.

"And is that why you like her so well?"

Merrick could not get much past Holland. His half brother would have made a fine Ford, always prying into matters that were better left alone. He faced his brother and shrugged. "One of them, at any rate."

"Ah, I did not realize the wind blew in that direction." He chuckled briefly and then his head tilted. "You do realize that Lady Farnsworth would make you a fine wife."

"I hardly think a marriage would be on her mind after this." He sighed. "The most I can hope for is to make her feel she is safe again."

"Ah," Holland said, and a grimace crossed face. "No wonder you seem so out of sorts. You cannot blame yourself about tonight's events. It was not you who struck her and she will need your help on the morrow to make the right choices."

"Assuming there are any," he muttered as Holland drew closer. "Her gown appeared ruined. She will need a new one and other personal items for tomorrow—items not readily found lying about this house."

Merrick kept no female servants.

"Everything can be bought if you have money enough."

Merrick knew that, but there could be complications. He did not ordinarily buy women's clothing for his household. He had no sisters, not even half sisters, nearby to spoil with pretty dresses or even ribbons for their hair. "Everything can be gossiped about too."

Holland paused while straightening up the room. "Are you still on good terms with the courtesan Lottie Townsend?"

"Yes." Relief filled him. He had not considered approaching that particular woman for aid, but Lottie would be just the ticket. If he explained enough details of what had transpired, the woman would surely make the purchases on his behalf and see they were delivered discreetly. "I'll write a note containing what I need for Arabella's comfort. If you would take it to her tonight, I would be grateful. Lottie will keep quiet."

"Are you sure?"

"Lottie would never betray a wronged woman, and I'll send a gift along with you as thanks." He quickly scrawled a note, giving only the barest of particulars and requesting her silence and, after describing Arabella's dimensions as best he could, requested at least a suitable day gown for tomorrow.

"You're a good man, Merrick," Holland said suddenly. "You never fail to surprise me in your quest to do the right thing. I am sure it's not always easy."

"Nothing ever is." He glanced at his brother, gratitude filling him. He might not have won wider society's approval in everything he did, but his brother knew him best of all. "Just don't tell anyone. They likely wouldn't believe you."

Holland took the note and slid it into his coat pocket. "Then they are fools."

When Holland was on his way, Merrick climbed the stairs toward the room where Arabella slept. He cast an anxious glance in that direction before turning for his empty bedchamber. At the entrance, he left his door ajar. It might be foolish to hope, but if Arabella needed anything during the night, he wanted to be the first to know so he could be there for her.

Chapter Twelve

Horse hooves clopping past her window woke Arabella from a deep, dreamless sleep. She blinked at the shadowed, unfamiliar room around her, taking a long, terrified moment to remember where she was. Once she had, her panic subsided quickly. She'd fled to Lord Rothwell's home last night. She'd sought safety with one of London's most notorious rogues and had slept the whole night alone as if she were in her own bed. If she had not lived the experience, she might not have believed it possible.

She stared at the soft blue linen canopy above her as a tear fell from the corner of her eye and slid over her cheek. She wiped it away furiously, determined not to cry again. Farnsworth wasn't worth shedding another tear over. She still could not believe what he'd attempted and she considered herself fortunate to have gotten away when she had. Even if she were ruined in society's eyes by being in Lord Rothwell's home, it was much better to think of herself as his lover than Farnsworth's property, to be discarded because he blamed her for Cecily's behavior and wouldn't bear the small expense of her upkeep.

Arabella took a deep breath and slowly sat up. Her jaw ached when she yawned and she tested the skin there, finding tenderness and perhaps some swelling. She climbed from the bed and hurried to the mirror, peering at herself in the poor light. A battered stranger in a man's borrowed nightshirt stared back, lifting her hand to her mouth to bury a cry that burned her throat.

Arabella closed her eyes to block out what Farnsworth had done. She couldn't let anyone see her like this. They would ask questions about last night. She didn't want anyone to know she'd been so utterly powerless. Determined to hide, she climbed back into bed and pulled the covers over her head. She would stay here all day, for several days in fact, until she was presentable again. At least then she might have an idea of where to go. As it was, her mind would not settle on any one person to trust. The only thing she felt certain of right now was that her present location was the safest place she knew.

A scratch at the door had her pulling the sheets tighter about her.

"Lady Farnsworth, would you care to break your fast?"

The voice of the kind man from last night, Holland, soothed her a little, but she still did not want to be seen. She remained silent, hoping he would go away. He knocked again and then the sounds ceased.

After a time, when she'd grown uncomfortably warm beneath the blankets, Arabella threw them off her face. She was being childish and fearful, two traits she rarely admired. It was not the man's fault she wasn't fit to be seen. She should have answered him and suggested he come back later. Much later, in fact. A whole week would do.

The scratch came again. "Arabella? We know you're awake."

Rothwell. She bolted upright and grimaced at the idea of him seeing her. She glanced at her ruined dress where she'd hung it across the chair to dry and shuddered. It needed much work to be presentable by anyone's standards. She'd been too shocked to consider how she might have appeared last night, but hoped he had not paid too much attention to her ragged appearance. Since Rothwell always gravitated to the finest looking women at a ball or party, she dreaded the revulsion she would see on his face this morning. The knock came again.

She could not ignore the earl. "Yes, I'm awake."

"Good." The door handle rattled but thankfully did not open immediately. "Holland would like to deliver a few necessities for your comfort. May my staff come in?"

Arabella slid down the bed again, hands on the edges of the sheet, ready to cover her face when the door opened. "Oh, very well."

She tossed the covers over her head and lay still as china rattled beyond her safe cocoon beneath the blankets. Other footsteps came and went. Water poured as if from buckets into a tub. The comforter covering her twitched as if someone had touched the bed. She stiffened, wondering what was going on, but dared not look for fear of letting someone see her so battered. When nothing else happened, she calmed herself. Rothwell had promised she was safe.

After a time, the footsteps filed out, and the door handle rattled again. "They will not come again until you ring for someone to attend you," Rothwell informed her in a kind tone that brought warmth to her cheeks that had nothing to do with embarrassment. "I have to go out for a while. I thought it best to keep up appearances as if nothing untoward had occurred, but call if you need anything. Holland will deliver whatever you need."

The door closed with a soft click, and Arabella lowered the sheet carefully, checking that she was indeed alone again. Alone again, but not forgotten. A feast covered the dressing table, a bath of steaming water sat before the fireplace. On her bed lay a peach-colored day gown she had never seen before and a few wrapped packages. She darted a glance at the chair and saw her poor ruined dress had been taken away. Rothwell had provided her with the means to dress for the day. She covered her face as her true situation struck her forcefully. She had nothing. Had no one now. Had it not been for Rothwell's aid, she did not know what would have become of her last night. She pressed her hand to her eyes and held back further tears.

She had to put herself back together again. The situation wasn't completely hopeless. For now, she was dry and warm and by all appearances would be well fed. Arabella would not let her host's generosity go to waste. She hurried to the door and locked it, as she'd neglected to do last night before sleep claimed her, and then she slipped off the borrowed nightshirt, shivering a little as she stepped into the warm water. She scrubbed her skin, washing away the terror of the night before with masculine-scented soap. She raised the bar to her nose and inhaled, liking the fragrance of sandalwood more because she recognized it as Rothwell's own. When she was clean and dry and bundled in a man-sized banyan while her hair dried, she inspected her small world and found nothing wanting.

The hot chocolate was warm enough to still be delicious; the bread rolls were cold but appetizing. She ate slowly because her jaw tingled with pain whenever she bit down with any enthusiasm. Arabella experimentally tapped at her teeth and discovered one to be the source of her discomfort. She was lucky not to have lost it completely when Farnsworth had struck her so hard that her head had spun. The one thing she'd feared most of all until yesterday was to have a tooth pulled.

Other food had been delivered, too—exotic fruits and small cakes in covered dishes. She had enough to last her most of the day without ever needing to show her face outside this room and would save them for later. Relief trickled through her that Rothwell had planned everything so she did not have to make any immediate decisions about her life. Another sign that she did not know very much about him at all but what she discovered now proved him extremely generous.

Arabella moved to the bed where clothing had been laid out in readiness for dressing. The parcels were a mystery but clearly meant for her. She opened each one, blushing with each new discovery. A chemise, corset, and fine silk stockings were terribly personal but essential if one cared to be properly dressed. How had Rothwell acquired ladies' clothing so quickly by this hour? Given her gown of last night had disappeared when the servants had come, and she had nothing else to wear, she couldn't refuse to put them on.

Feeling extremely self-conscious, Arabella slid the stockings up her legs and secured them beneath her knees. Next she slipped from the robe and drew the chemise over her head. The fit was good and she lifted the corset. Luckily, it was a style she could manage alone without a maid, and it fit snugly around her body.

The last was the dress, a simply styled affair that didn't look too fussy. She stepped into the peach muslin, securing the material around her and at last feeling ready to face, well, anything better than last night.

However, dressing did bring to mind her future destination. She wasn't wanted by Farnsworth except to marry off. He would sell her home and leave her with nothing but her pride to warm her. She had only friends, and none of them in London. Every decision required an effort and more hours of travel than she cared to contemplate.

She moved to the window and carefully peeked through the gap in the curtains at the street below. The view was one she'd never had before and she took a moment to reacquaint herself with Rothwell's nearest neighbors. None of them were friends to Farnsworth, though they were little known to her too. The relief of that eased her mind. She leaned against the wall, hiding behind the safety of the drapes, and watched the comings and goings of those below. She was relieved to be here and not out there where who knows what else could have assaulted her.

She touched her face again and then moved to the mirror. The bruise was not as bad as she had imagined this morning, but it definitely did not make her pretty in any way. She lifted her chin and moved her damp hair back over her shoulder to inspect the bruises made by Farnsworth's hand about her throat. A shudder raked her. She'd never been subjected to violence before. Her father had been the gentlest of men, and her late husband had left her alone. At no time in the past had she ever imagined Farnsworth capable of such cruelty, although his temper was easily provoked.

Arabella pulled her hair forward so it covered her neck and the bruised side of her face. She would keep it down today to hide the damage even from her own eyes. She poured another cup of lukewarm chocolate from the pot and settled in a chair to think. Perhaps if she was as undemanding as possible, Rothwell might allow her to remain hidden in his house for today and maybe, if she was extremely lucky, until she was fully restored to her usual appearance. She couldn't face the world like this, but to make plans for her future she would have to speak to others. At the moment, she might only have the courage to let Rothwell see her face. He'd been so kind, but she didn't want to shock him. There was nothing else she could do now but wait for her appearance to heal itself or for Rothwell to grow bored with the situation and suggest an alternative that involved leaving.

Sometimes to get to the heart of an issue, a man has to skirt very close to the border without actually asking a direct question. Merrick judged himself most fortunate for crossing paths with Mr. Milne outside the coffee house he frequented and garnering an invitation to step inside the man's home for a drink after their short walk. He wouldn't quibble at so sudden an invitation, and with any luck, he would get the answers he needed to make a decision about Miss Milne.

He studied the numerous small curios that littered Mr. Milne's desk and every other available surface in the room. "You have a lovely home. I imagine your wife, and to some degree your daughter, like everything just so."

"That they do," said Mr. Milne, nodding enthusiastically. "Sensible management leads to a well-run home. My own wife began with pin money of six hundred a year, but she's a kind soul with an exceedingly generous heart to those less fortunate. My daughter takes after her in that respect. Always ready to spend a shilling for another's comfort. They do love to patronize the craftsmen of our great city."

"I honor them for their generosity." Merrick smiled at Mr. Milne, judging the last few moments had considerably advanced his knowledge. Despite a timid nature at balls, Miss Milne appeared rather free with purchasing unnecessary things.

As many fathers in the merchant class were, Milne was eager to have his daughter marry into a titled family. He didn't appear unduly concerned about his reputation today and had been rather happy to relate particulars of his daughter's nature. He proudly boasted of her accomplishments and even mentioned some early setbacks best forgotten.

Such candidness pleased Merrick. He did not mind if his future wife had the odd incident in her past, nor a tendency to shop, so long as he was made aware of it before he proposed. He had enough scandals in his own family to make him a less-than-stellar candidate for marriage and had no illusions that his wife might have habits in her life best forgotten or at least overlooked.

Eager to be on his way home to his unexpected houseguest, he stood to leave a short time later. "I should be going and let you get on with your business. Thank you for seeing me, sir."

Milne surged to his feet. "I say, Rothwell, is anything the matter? I would have thought you'd wish my daughter to be called down to speak with you."

Merrick smiled. He was not ready to propose. He wanted to observe Miss Milne when she was not aware of his presence and also talk to her once or twice before he declared his interest. And he was later than he hoped to be in returning to Arabella. She had barely been out of his mind all day and had proved quite the distraction, but running into Milne had been an opportunity he hadn't wanted to pass up. "Another time perhaps."

Mr. Milne sat back, his hands resting on his overstretched belly. "Yes, indeed. I'll likely see you next in Essex for the wedding. Looking forward to sampling the duke's hospitality. They say Ford affairs are very fine."

Merrick peered at Mr. Milne. "I had not known invitations had already been sent for my cousin's wedding."

"I had a note from Rutherford just this morning, inviting myself, my wife and my darling daughter to join him." He touched the side of his nose with one finger and grinned. "Your grandfather assuredly plays a long game, but he will be proved right in the end."

What the devil was this? "Will he?"

"It takes a brave man to stand in the Admiral's way when he wants something done. I've no objection to his laying out the timetable at all for a match. Either way, we'll each get what we want." Milne saluted him with the remains of his drink. "Until the wedding."

Merrick strode out, puzzling over what he'd learned. His grandfather was no friend to Mr. Milne. At least not to his knowledge. He'd never known they were acquainted, which had added to Miss Milne's appeal. Until now. Was a scheme at play? Merrick had a sinking feeling he'd already been cast in the central role with Miss Milne as his leading lady. That his grandfather was likely meddling placed a pall over getting to know her. He had hoped to avoid family interference, but it might just be impossible.

As he reached the entrance hall, his remaining good humor vanished. Farnsworth stood before him, a condescending smile spreading over his face. "I say, Rothwell. Well met."

Merrick itched to wipe that expression off his face. "Farnsworth."

The stupid man came closer, giving Merrick a glimpse of the left side of his face. A cut oozed red at his hairline. Arabella hadn't mentioned that she'd fought back, but he was pleased. A little harder and Arabella might have killed the man. A pity she had not.

Farnsworth's expression grew serious. "Now, this is fortuitous. Do you have a moment?"

Whatever Farnsworth had to say would not be worth listening to. "Actually no. I have somewhere to be and cannot delay. Good day to you."

"Wait. I wanted to warn you to be cautious. I was attacked in my home last night. A terribly brazen affair, indeed." He pointed to the wound on his head. "I discovered the villains in my home quite by chance and routed them, or so I thought at the time."

Farnsworth had to be joking. "Really? How terrible for you."

"It was, but that is not the worst. You see, while they were taking my candlesticks and silverware out through the back window, my sister-in-law, Arabella, fled the house in a wild panic and hasn't been seen since. I truly fear for her sanity. She must have been quite overset with fear for us all."

Merrick stared at the man. This was how he would explain Arabella's disappearance to any who questioned her whereabouts? The fool. Anyone who knew Arabella would know she wasn't one to suffer panic without cause.

Farnsworth pointed to his wound again. "This is what they did to me. I truly fear for Arabella's safety if the brigands followed her into the night. I dread to think what has happened to her. I am sure she fled far into Green Park. I followed as long as I could, of course, but lost sight of her in the heavy rain. Keep your eyes open would you, and do be discreet. My dear Arabella means the world to me and to my daughter. We would hate to lose her though will gladly take her back no matter what evil has befallen her."

Merrick held on to his temper by the skin of his teeth. Arabella's happiness meant much more to him than to this bastard. However, the time wasn't right to reveal he knew her location, so he kept his mouth shut. He wanted to see how far Farnsworth would go in his lies first. "What have the Runners to say?"

Farnsworth's expression grew evasive. "I'm on my way to them now."

No, he wasn't. It was three in the afternoon and the man was paying house calls. Milne had no ties to the runners or the law. Merrick had a suspicion that Farnsworth wouldn't hire even one man to find her. It had been hours since Arabella had fled Farnsworth's home, and he'd likely done nothing more than design a story to explain his injury and garner sympathy should Arabella reveal what he intended for her. If pressed, would Farnsworth weep over a vacant grave bearing her name? He probably hoped she would return to him properly chastened and cowed into submission so she would marry Lord Parker without fuss.

Milne's butler gestured to the doorway Merrick had just walked through. "Mr. Milne will see you now, Lord Farnsworth."

The sorrowful expression instantly slipped from Farnsworth's face at the news. "Excellent."

Merrick again forced himself not to pound the man to a bloody pulp. He had no right to do so. Not yet. But once Arabella was healed and settled in an alternate safe haven, Merrick would pay a call to Farnsworth and avenge her. There were any number of ways to make the man suffer that would be undetectable.

Chapter Thirteen

Merrick let himself into his home and immediately looked around for Arabella. When he heard and saw nothing but the usual household sounds and sights, he sighed. It was foolish to hope her nerves had relaxed sufficiently to make her feel safe enough to come out of hiding.

"Has she come down yet?" he asked Holland as soon as he appeared.

"No, my lord." Holland frowned, his glance rising to the ceiling. "She is up and moving around but will not allow anyone to see her. I fear the bruising must be quite bad."

Merrick shared that fear. He'd worried for her welfare all day while he'd continued about his business as usual, as if he did not have an unexpected houseguest resting in his future wife's bedchamber. There had better not be any lasting harm done to her appearance. Farnsworth had done enough to shake her confidence already and with the lies he was spreading about her flight into the night, he feared any disfiguration would break her confidence completely.

Merrick slapped Holland's shoulder and then slid his hat and gloves onto the hall table. "I'm sure she will come down in due time. However, I'll look in on her directly to see if she needs anything."

"She should not stay here much longer," Holland said

quietly, for his ears alone. "We should have let her catch her breath and then taken her to your aunt this morning."

Merrick did not need Holland to voice the doubts that had already invaded his mind. He'd spent the morning roundly chastising himself for selfishness on his part for wanting Arabella to remain where he could keep an eye on her. The cost to her reputation could be severe, but he felt better knowing she was truly beyond Farnsworth's reach. "My aunt would have questioned her. You saw her last night and her behavior this morning. She wasn't ready to face any of that."

"And now?"

"And now I do not know, but I will ask what she wishes to do. If she wishes to remain or will not see me, then she may stay exactly where she is. If she wishes to leave, then I will see that it's accomplished in a way to avoid discovery and spare her reputation any stain. Is her presence any great hardship for the household?"

Holland shook his head quickly. "No, my lord. It's just that I'd thought of her reputation, too. The gossip could be quite vicious if she is found out. There has never been a hint of impropriety attached to Lady Farnsworth before and we have no female servants to attend her or female family in residence."

That was a problem. He scratched his whiskered jaw, wondering if he should shave off the new growth before he saw her. He was eager to see her now and did not want to wait another moment. "It cannot be helped. We've run the house without for so long that if I employ a female servant now to attend her, it could draw unwanted attention. I trust everyone to hold their tongues, but a new face in their ranks could reveal Arabella's location before she is ready to face anyone."

"She will have to come out eventually, or let us in," Holland said. "The water from her morning bath is still within her bedchamber. It is unhealthy to let it remain there for much longer. If you could persuade her to retire to another room, perhaps we could attend it and anything else she needs."

Merrick glanced up the stairs. Holland had come up with the flimsiest of excuses to get through the door, but he would take it gladly just to know how badly Arabella was suffering. "Very well. I will go see her now before I change to go out for dinner."

"Do you think it's wise to carry on as usual, given you have a woman sheltering under your roof?"

He'd questioned his actions all day, yet whatever happened with Arabella, he still wanted a wife. Quitting the field now might mean he'd have to start over again. "Going out as usual offers an advantage in drawing attention away from the house. Arabella may have come to me in her time of need, but to assume anything more would be presumptuous."

Holland frowned. "I suppose it would be."

When Holland hurried off into the depths of the house, Merrick headed upstairs. He straightened his waistcoat and coat and smoothed his hair before he tapped lightly on Arabella's door and waited.

"Who is it?" Her voice was a soft whisper through the door. The shy, cautious question tore his heart.

"It's Rothwell. May I come in? I'd like to talk to you."

"Ah, I don't think so," she said quickly. The door handle rattled as if to prevent the door from being opened without her permission. "I'd rather not let anyone see me like this."

"It's just me. No one else has to come in." He eased closer to the door and laid his head upon the wood. He would never force her to do anything she didn't want. "Arabella," he said softly. "Please."

There was a long pause and then the door he leaned his head against fell open. Arabella stood opposite him against the wall, her eyes wide. He stepped inside and she gave ground. Her injury was nowhere near as bad as he thought it would be. The swelling to her cheek had lessened quite a bit. In a few days, there would be no trace. He smiled in relief and lifted a hand to brush her loose, pale hair back from her neck. The finger marks were distinct but would fade in time too.

"I was worried."

Her brow creased and she hurried to cover her abused skin again with her hair. "I look terrible."

"You look better than my imagination supplied. Thank you for letting me see you." He glanced around the room while he nudged the door shut with his foot so no one passing could peek in. "Do you have everything you need?"

The simple gown and accessories he'd begged the loan of from Lottie Townsend clung to her curves in all the right places.

The only thing he hadn't accomplished was acquiring right-sized footwear to replace her evening slippers. As she fidgeted in place, her stocking-covered toes peeked out from beneath her gown.

"Yes. I can never repay you for your kindness."

"It's an honor to be of assistance. Think nothing of it." He glanced around the room one more time, noticing the differences from the morning. During the day, Arabella had kept busy by rearranging a few items. A chair had been moved closer to the window. The writing desk was angled differently to catch the light. He didn't mind the changes. If such activity kept her occupied and distracted from her troubles, she could rearrange his entire house to her heart's content. "Holland would like the servants to clear the room of the bathwater and perform other tasks. He wanted me to ask if you minded stepping into another room for a short time."

Her gaze dropped to the floor. "I'm an inconvenience."

"Not at all." He lifted her chin gently and smiled to reassure her. "Holland likes to fuss. Leaving anything unfinished is beyond him, but I think he'd rather not upset you by coming to your door again."

"I am sorry for my earlier churlish behavior." Her smile was hesitant and brief. "Very well. As long as no one sees me. Lead the way, my lord."

Merrick stepped back into the hall, checked that no servants lingered nearby to startle her, and then gestured for Arabella to come with him. He lived alone and most rooms in the house were closed up, so he opened the doorway to the only acceptable quarters and allowed her to pass. "I'll return for you when they are done and gone away again."

She stopped three paces into the room and looked about curiously. "Whose room is this?"

"Ah, this would be mine. You should be comfortable here for a little while." Merrick turned away before she could protest that being in his bedchamber was highly inappropriate. However, the other rooms would be dusty and provide little comfort. Leaving her there was the sensible thing to do.

As he closed the door, he heard her mutter, "Oh, the injustice of this."

Although puzzled by her words, he called for Holland and waited in the hall. The servants trooped back and forth, Holland hurrying everyone along as quickly as he could. Holland nodded when he was done and disappeared downstairs again. When the house was quiet once more, he returned his bedchamber and knocked on the door.

As before, Arabella faced him through the opening. "You grow orchids?"

He smiled quickly. "I dabble."

"So do I."

He nodded. "I know. Grayling mentioned that you and his late wife would spend hours in the conservatory he had built at his estate."

She opened the door fully and with a quick, furtive glance at the empty hallway beyond stepped toward him. "Why did you not tell me? We could have spoken about propagation and such."

"When? We've only ever spoken briefly before now."

"That is true. I cannot imagine why." When she strolled out into the hall, there was a book in her hands. She lifted it, a small guilty smile crossing her face. "I've not read this one. May I borrow it to read this evening?"

He nodded and gestured for her to walk beside him. The urge to curl his arm around her back and draw her close against his side grew to an impossible ache. He clenched his hands behind his back instead of reaching for her. "Yes, of course. I finished it last night, actually, so you may have it for as long as you like. There are many more in my study downstairs, too. You're welcome to borrow what you like while I am out tonight."

Her frown returned. "You're going out again?"

Was that disappointment or disapproval? He nodded. "I have an invitation I cannot decline at this late an hour, and I thought crying off might draw unwanted attention. Holland will be home all night should you need anything."

She sighed, then cast an impish smile in his direction. "You are very fortunate in your choice of butler. It's a wonder someone hasn't tried to steal him for themselves."

He smiled at her mistake. "Holland acts in my stead in many things, but Jenkins is actually the butler, though he's away at present. I don't believe there's a high enough offer that would convince either one to leave my employ, but that's a conversation for another day."

She reached her doorway and paused. "When I am better, we have much to discuss. You have been keeping secrets from me. I dislike secrets between friends."

He studied her face, noting that the light in her eyes had returned, and leaned against the wall as close to her as he dared. "Are we friends now?"

The corner of her mouth lifted in a gentle smile that had his body reacting before he could prevent it. "We surely must be."

Then she was gone, disappearing inside her bedchamber without another word or an invitation to follow. Merrick paused a long moment and then turned for his bedchamber, aware that while he was disappointed to part company with Arabella so soon, he was grinning like an idiot. Arabella liked him enough to call him a friend. That made any inconvenience her presence caused worthwhile, at least on his part. He could get to like being gently admonished by her, but he would still keep his secrets.

Now that Arabella had been dealt with, he had a dinner to prepare for. While he dressed, he practiced the things he might say to Lady Mary Crawford at dinner. He could ask her about her season. He could ask her if she liked the country. He could ask her if she knew about his past and his father too, and if so consider overlooking it. He shook his head. Didn't women claim that reformed rakes made the best husbands? To do that required they rise to the challenge and give a man a chance. He could certainly make the attempt to prove his sincerity if the lady was open-minded.

Holland nodded his approval as he stepped through the front door and into his carriage. The journey to Lord Crawford's residence was not far, and he had little time to catch his breath. He pushed Arabella's situation from his mind for a little while. Holland would take care of her and refuse Farnsworth admittance should he knock on the door.

That left him free to pursue his own agenda. Lord and Lady Crawford would be gracious hosts, their daughter full of energy and chatter. He put on his best face and stepped out of the carriage, determined to make the right impression.

Chapter Fourteen

Arabella closed the book as she reached the last page and laid it aside. She'd been Rothwell's guest for three days, and the marks on her face and neck were finally reduced to faint smudges. In the course of her recovery, Arabella had discovered herself as vain as the next woman. She'd feared permanent harm and men's reactions to her loss of beauty. Rothwell's reassurances had gone a long way to helping her adjust. If not for his gentle kindness, she'd still be hiding in her bed.

The clock downstairs struck four o'clock and chimed out the close of another day. She stood and brushed off the skirts of another day dress that had appeared without explanation as to its origins. One day she would make Rothwell answer her questions and she would find some way to repay him for everything.

Now in need of a new book to while away the afternoon, she ventured out into the hallway with a plan to surreptitiously explore the rest of Rothwell's home. The floor she'd spent the last few days on contained only bedchambers, dressing rooms, and a few closets containing bedding. Most were neglected, which fit with what Arabella knew of Rothwell. He didn't have family save the Fords, and his tendency to avoid them made his home little visited. The lower floors were mostly a mystery.

When she reached the top of the stairs and started down, she was surprised at seeing Rothwell rushing up them toward her. He barely saw her before they would have collided. She jumped aside, only to run into him when he swerved too.

"My apologies," he said quickly, his breathing rushed, his riding coat half off, and his cravat dangling from his fingers.

Arabella dragged her eyes from the patch of chest exposed by his undressing. "None needed," she reassured him, fighting the blush threatening to give away her feelings. "I am sorry to be in your way."

"I was on my way to see you, actually." He grinned and lifted his arm to his nose. "I fear I smell of the stables. I'm just back from Tattersall's with one of my men and a new horse. I was on my way to change first though."

She swept her gaze over him and liked what she saw. Even though he appeared slightly rough around the edges, the air of vitality brought about by exercise and likely excitement over the purchase suited him well. "I see that."

A throat cleared nearby and when Arabella peeked around Rothwell's broad shoulders, she found Holland waiting on a lower stair.

Rothwell grinned again. "Where will you be in twenty minutes?"

"Downstairs, if that is all right with you." She waved the book in her hand. "I need a new diversion."

"Perfect. By all means, help yourself to anything you like. I'll join you shortly if you'd enjoy company."

She nodded quickly. It had been a long, slow day with only her own company for amusement. Rothwell's eyes glowed with pleasure and he leaned just a little closer—just enough that the scent of horses did reach her. She couldn't help but wrinkle her nose.

He eased back quickly. "Do excuse me."

He passed her by without another word, leaving Arabella standing with only Holland for company. The older man nodded to her, his gaze speculative, and then followed Rothwell at a more sedate pace to his bedchamber.

When the door shut with a solid thud, Arabella hurried down the remaining stairs. The more time she spent with Rothwell, the more she wilted beneath those smoldering eyes, which caused her no end of blushes.

As she'd noticed before, the household was a quiet one, but

there were masculine voices coming from parts of the house sure to be servant's quarters. She paused to listen. In the days she'd been here, there had been few whispered conversations to be overheard. Rothwell's servants were quick and efficient and, to her surprise, rather happy in his service. As she thought about that, she discovered a surprising fact. She'd only ever heard male voices in the town house. There might be no other women beneath this roof aside from herself.

As she remembered from her arrival, a door to the right led to a drawing room where she'd warmed herself by the fire. That room had not contained any books that she remembered seeing, so she turned beneath the staircase and made her way to the rear of the house. There was a closed door at the end of the short hall and she leaned her ear to the door. After listening a long while and hearing nothing, Arabella released the latch and let herself in.

She smiled at what she found—an empty room but for the books behind glass doors and dozens of rare orchids littering every other space. Rothwell had said he dabbled, but this was so much more than dabbling. He truly had a green thumb.

She inspected each plant gently, smiling at the variations he'd chosen to cultivate. So very pretty and not at all the type of plant she'd expected a man like Rothwell to have. She shook her head. The man was a walking contradiction. Wicked in public, proper in private. At no time had she thought he might fall on her in a passion.

She turned next for the nearest bookcase and tugged at the door. Locked. She glanced around uncertainly. No sign of a key anywhere. Rothwell had said she might read anything she liked in his collection. He'd never mentioned needing a key to get to them though.

She eyed the desk as doubt filled her. Should she disturb him or attempt to find the key herself? It was not on the desktop or around on any other surface. That left inside his desk to investigate, although she was not sure he'd meant her to do so. Arabella bit her lip as she slid open a shallow upper drawer. A folded note lay on top of a stack of papers, but she could just make out the edge of a metal key hiding beneath. Arabella lifted the note and claimed the key quickly, casting a nervous glance at the door.

Snooping through Rothwell's papers hadn't been part of her plan. She was just about to close the drawer when curiosity got the better of her. She flicked the large note open and then stared in shock. Rothwell had a special license to marry, though the bride's name had not been filled out.

The paper tumbled from her numb fingers. Good grief, when would she learn to mind her own business and ask permission first? The discovery answered her questions and raised yet more still. Rothwell was always going in and out in a rush, but given her recent isolation, she had no idea who he was courting. She'd never suspected he had formed an attachment to anyone in London. Which meant her presence in his home was indeed an imposition.

"Ah, good. You found the key?"

Arabella looked up, sure that guilt was writ large on her face. Instead of a scowl, Rothwell stood at the doorway with his arms folded across his chest, smiling in a way that immediately set her heart racing. Instead of angry, he looked quite delicious. Maybe he hadn't seen her reading his private papers. She hoped not. It would make her seem an ungrateful wretch. She quickly nudged the drawer closed and moved away from the desk. "Yes, just this moment."

She glanced at him and then paused as she took stock of his appearance: neatly pressed, boots gleaming, gloves and top hat in hand. He was devastatingly handsome in a finely tailored navy-blue coat and embroidered waistcoat. Her awareness of his appeal multiplied. "Are you going out?"

His finger dug beneath his cravat to loosen the starched material as if he wished to be rid of it entirely. "To the park in an hour to meet with an acquaintance."

Was he courting a woman she knew? "You look very fine."

"Thank you." He leaned against the bookcase, a grin twisting his lips. His gaze roved over her body and caused a tremble in her legs. "You too look quite lovely, in fact."

"Thank you." A blush warmed her cheeks and she turned to the bookcase to unlock the door, willing her hands to cease their fumbling. She stared at the volumes before her, not really seeing them. Her mind raced at the notion that Rothwell was hunting a bride. The idea of him marrying had never occurred to her, although at his age he would have considered the necessity of taking a wife to acquire an heir long before this.

At that moment, Holland joined them, apologized for interrupting, and then crossed the room to check if the spirit decanters on a far table needed refilling.

"I'm glad to see you making yourself at home." He pointed to the man across the room and smiled. "Holland's been fretting again about your lack of company. Anyone would think he's your father the way he's been carrying on, and I've been meaning to ask you about that. Do you have any family left? I've never heard mention of anyone from you or from Grayling in the past years."

Arabella winced. "My parents died a year after I married. My mother first, and then my father very soon after, as if he couldn't go on without her. The loss of them broke my heart because they were my whole world too. They were older when they had me, you see, but had married quite young and were never far apart. Any cousins or aunts I might have had are unknown to me. All we had was each other and our neighbors, but that was enough for them."

"I'm so sorry." Rothwell's gaze softened and he reached out to squeeze her hand.

Rather than feel uncomfortable relating the impact of the loss that felt as fresh today as all those years ago, Arabella felt better. She hadn't spoken of them in a very long time.

Rothwell turned away suddenly. "If only that were the case for me. I find it nearly impossible to escape my family."

Holland's head snapped around to stare at them. His cheeks grew red as he checked the time on his pocket watch. "Time's passing, my lord."

"Yes. Yes." Rothwell shooed him out. "I'll be there soon. Jimmy can just wait a few minutes longer."

Holland bowed to Arabella and hurried out.

Rothwell merely smiled. "Since you are downstairs at last, may I ask if you have made any plans for the evening ahead?"

Arabella bit her lip. What would any lady Rothwell was courting think if she discovered Arabella had lived beneath Rothwell's roof these past days? If it were Arabella being courted, she'd be utterly humiliated by the discovery.

Sure she'd overstayed her welcome and was about to be asked to leave, she shook her head. "I hadn't made any as yet."

He smiled and set his hands behind his back. "Well, I have an invitation to offer you. Join me for dinner. You've eaten in your bedchamber every night since you've come, and you must be utterly bored with your surroundings."

She should say no and make immediate plans to be on her way, except she'd managed to push her decision from her mind time and again. She'd placed Rothwell in an awkward situation. "I don't mind my own company."

"As you wish." He relaxed and eased away a step. "I thought you might have enjoyed furthering our acquaintance, but I will leave you to your own devices instead."

As she realized she'd snubbed his company quite thoroughly and offended him in turn, she panicked and grabbed his arm. "Oh, no, I'm sorry. That didn't come out the way I planned. I just mean that I don't mind being alone. I wasn't in the best of moods these past days to be good company for anyone."

Beneath her hand, a muscled arm, warm and solid, twisted. "Then you'll dine with me?"

Arabella released him and nodded. One last night alone in his home and she'd find another situation for herself tomorrow. "I would enjoy that."

"Excellent." Rothwell passed behind her and moved to his desk.

Arabella sighed softly. She would be sad to leave. However, the next moment her breath seized as Rothwell bent to pick up a paper lying on the floor. *The special license.* As his lips pursed, Arabella spun about, attempting to focus on the books before her rather than the man with the plan to marry. She hoped he didn't ask her about disturbing his desk. Dropping it had been purely an accident, but not the fact that she'd read it and knew what it was. She pulled the first book her hand touched from the shelf and opened it, pretending to be considering the volume.

The drawer scraped open slowly and shut again with a soft click. "I'll see you for dinner at eight, yes?"

Arabella swallowed nervously. "Yes, eight o'clock would suit me very well."

She glanced at him over her shoulder and saw him smile in return. He moved closer, fitting his hat to his head, pulling his gloves into place. His dark eyes searched hers. "Until then, my lady."

His hand brushed her back softly, just across her shoulder blades, and her pulse raced beyond her power to control it. She bit her lip, saw his eyes follow the nervous gesture, and quickly released it to clear her throat. "Until you return."

His mouth quirked into a sensual smile just before he headed to the door. When he was gone from the house, when all was silent again, Arabella snatched up two volumes at random and practically ran the whole way back to her bedchamber so she could blush to her heart's content in private. She didn't know the first thing about seduction, but from that one scorching kiss days ago and the brief touch just now, she was sure she wanted Rothwell to be her first lover.

Chapter Fifteen

Merrick tooled his phaeton through Hyde Park in a glum mood and considered his behavior of late. At his side, Lady Mary Crawford chattered nonstop, smelled of lilac, and mentioned at least a dozen times how much she admired his aunt, as if that were any incentive to call on her again.

Mention of Aunt Pen had the opposite effect, in fact. He didn't need his aunt to loom large in his intended's life. He wanted to marry a woman who didn't need to please everyone she met, and most especially didn't mind *not* having closer ties to his mother's family.

But the truth was that the existence of that damned special license had soured his mood for courtship. He was certain Arabella had seen it. In truth, he'd felt somewhat embarrassed at having one. Would she be sitting in his home wondering about it? Speculating on whom he was with in the park today? Who he'd been calling on at other times? So far he'd deflected her inquiries on his return from similar outings, but if he intended to marry by special license, there was a time limit to her stay. She would have to go before he could propose to anyone.

And he was quickly coming to the conclusion that he did not want her to go at all.

He nodded to acquaintances gracing the park for the fashionable hour, but his mind was firmly on deciding the fastest way to return Lady Mary to her parents. Looking down to talk to a woman, even while sitting, made him feel he was conversing with a child. The truth was, he'd grown used to speaking with Arabella. Sitting or standing, her height placed her almost eye to eye with him in every situation. Today he'd seen a glimmer of the woman he'd known before Farnsworth had abused her. Her confidence was returning, along with her blushes. And yet he still could not decide whether they were silent invitations or not.

At his side, Lady Mary fluffed out her gown like a bird feathering its nest. "Do you spend much time in the country, my lord?"

"Not really. London mostly or Needham Hollow and Wiltshire, visiting with friends."

Her face creased with confusion. "Not Essex? Surely you are at Newberry Park with your cousins most often."

He glanced at the young woman at his side and shuddered. "Good Lord, no. I'd rather spend a night in Marshalsea Debtors Prison than voluntarily visit my grandfather's estates. I spend as little of my time as possible with them."

"Oh," Lady Mary said at last, a frown growing on her face. "I had not known that. What about your cousin's wedding? It will be the talk of the season."

"I'm sure the event will be a success without me. I make no apologies for the estrangement." He smiled at her. "They like to meddle and I do not appreciate it."

Lady Mary faced forward, her brow furrowing. "I spend much time with my family, so I always thought you'd be at the wedding."

"I enjoy the peace without that sort of thing."

"I see."

At last the chit fell silent, her attention fixed on her gloves. Was she thinking as he did now? They would not suit. Not at all. She would want and miss her family, inflicting them on him when he craved peace and quiet. He would have to reconsider his choice of bride. He might have to reconsider quite a lot.

It was a sad fact that he compared each woman he met to Arabella. Their height, their manners, their interest in the natural world. Each time he'd discovered a similarity that gave him hope, he'd also found fault. Was there not one woman in London to come close to Lady Farnsworth in accomplishments?

He was starting to believe he'd set himself an impossible goal. If there was no one like Arabella, then perhaps he should ask her to marry him instead.

However, she'd made it quite plain that she wasn't keen to marry and nothing in the past few days of conversation had hinted at a change of heart. But perhaps her distaste for it was largely due to the arranged match with Lord Parker and the way she'd been given little choice. She might react very differently should he propose, but he might be wise to wait until he was confident his proposal wouldn't send her running for the street.

Could she overlook his debauched past, accept the secrets he could not turn aside from, and consider another marriage? From what he had learned of her first, she had not liked being a wife. There was the possibility he would fail and be disappointed, but there was also an equal chance that he might succeed.

He deposited Lady Mary at her door and cheerily waved good-bye, fully intending to never see her again as a would-be bride. He would return home and dine with Arabella and see if she might be interested in more than simple friendship.

The instant he stepped inside the door, he knew something was terribly wrong. Holland wore the expression he adopted when faced with being the bearer of bad news. Merrick braced himself. "What?"

"Lady Penelope Ford is waiting to see you."

Merrick glanced left and right and then finally up to the ceiling. "Blast."

"She hasn't said anything," Holland whispered. "I placed her in the parlor while she waited your return."

"Thank you, Holland." Merrick handed off his hat and gloves and strode into the room. He decided not to mince words today. Aunt Pen rarely made surprise visits to his home, and this was the worst possible time for one. "What do you want?"

His aunt paused with her teacup to her lips. "You're in a mood, so I will come straight to the point. I've come to question you about Lady Farnsworth and her niece, Lady Cecily."

As he'd suspected, his aunt's arrival signaled trouble. "What about them?"

Aunt Pen leaned forward, her brow furrowing with deep lines of concern. "Lady Farnsworth and Lady Cecily have not been seen for some time. Lord Farnsworth tells quite a tale, that she ran away in terror of a horde of brigands."

Merrick frowned at the growth of Farnsworth's lie. Fairly soon it would be apparent to even a fool that nothing of the sort had happened. He had to tread carefully. It seemed possible that Aunt Pen knew nothing of Cecily's elopement with Laurence, but the woman was a master at intrigue and could lie better than anyone he knew to serve her own purpose. "Something about midnight abductions and thievery." He shrugged. "I saw Farnsworth at Mr. Milne's just yesterday. It has the ring of nonsense."

"Milne, you say." Her lips lifted in approval. "His daughter is lovely."

Blast. Aunt Pen approved of Miss Milne. That had not been part of his plans but her support didn't matter as his interest was with Arabella now. He shrugged and didn't comment.

Aunt Pen smiled again, but Merrick still did not trust her one bit. She studied him carefully, then said, "So, you think they have not been abducted and likely ravished in some den of inequity?"

"I am sure Lady Farnsworth is snugly settled with friends somewhere." He pretended to think about where she might be for a moment and moved into the room. He stopped behind a chair, a little barrier between them for his peace of mind. "What has Grayling to say? I'm sure if she's anywhere, she would be there."

His aunt peered at him. "Because you purchased her home from beneath her feet and she cannot possibly return to it?"

He smiled tightly, hating that his every word and deed eventually fell into his aunt's lap. "Word travels fast. Actually, when I see Lady Farnsworth, I thought to enquire if she wished to continue on there under lease. Grayling has suggested before that she is inordinately fond of Winslette and manages it well."

Aunt Pen set her cup aside and folded her hands in her lap, a sure sign she was just now warming to her inquisition. "When I heard of the new purchase, I assumed you might want to live there with your new wife."

Since there was no chance of avoiding the subject, he chose to tackle it head on. "I've not married yet, and Grandfather sending me a special license will not spur me to propose." He shook his head. "I own many properties, both in England and abroad, though I have not seen many in some time. An inspection is overdue at many. I really must attend to that soon."

It was a risk mentioning any future plans to travel. He hoped offering up a bit of his life would distract her from asking further questions of Arabella and Cecily and any likely bride.

Her eyes narrowed. "Very well. Since you claim to know nothing of her disappearance, I will leave you in peace. When you do see Lady Farnsworth, be sure to give her my regards. Lovely girl, but so terribly tall."

Aunt Pen stood and made her way to the door. Merrick watched her the whole way just to be sure she'd gone.

When the door closed, he strode to Holland. "She knows."

His half brother stared at the closed door his aunt had passed through moments before. "About your pursuit of a bride? That was always in the cards the minute you took Lady Mary driving in the park."

"No, she knows Lady Farnsworth is here."

Holland shook his head. "Surely not or she would have said something. She would have demanded to see her."

Merrick checked the time on his pocket watch. An hour until dinner with Arabella. Would he get to dine with her without his aunt coming back with Farnsworth in tow? "She uttered not one word about Laurence being missing from Town, and mention of having called on Mr. Milne yesterday barely stirred a ripple of interest. She left the house too quickly. She came for confirmation and somehow she got it." He stared hard at Holland, wondering what had been said in his absence.

The other man shook his head, but his expression grew worried. "I swear I did nothing to give Lady Farnsworth away. How could she possibly know?"

He tucked his watch away and straightened his waistcoat. "I've no idea, but unless we want a scene that will be talked of for a decade should Farnsworth come pounding on my door, Arabella must leave my house."

Even now, well before his aunt could reach her home, he could imagine the flurry of letters she would write. If not tonight, then by morning they would be besieged. Farnsworth would come and upset Arabella. His own family might just come too, all very ready to remind him that the surest way to avoid scandal for the family was to marry Arabella immediately. He had the special license. It could be done tomorrow.

Being married in such circumstances was not part of his plan. He had wanted to avoid his family's interference in his choice of bride. He growled his annoyance and stalked past Holland, taking the stairs two at a time on his way upstairs. When he reached Arabella's door, he knocked, immediately hoping the loud sound would not startle her unduly.

As soon as the door opened, he stepped inside. "My aunt knows you are here. You have to leave before she can either come back with other Fords or return with Farnsworth. The man has been looking for you everywhere."

Arabella's face leeched of color. "You never mentioned that before."

"I didn't want to upset you." He moved closer to her. "What do you want to do? By morning my aunt will have told those she deems worthy of the news that you are in my power. We could tell the truth about Farnsworth striking you and attempting to force you into a match you didn't want, but one is as bad as the other. Your reputation will never survive."

She shivered and hugged her arms about her. "From my point of view the two are widely different. I'd choose being in your power over Farnsworth's any day. But where can I go?"

"There is always Wiltshire."

She nodded slowly. "Grayling would take me in surely. I had not wanted to impose on him and Rosemary. They are only just married. I suppose I could be of help with the children."

He frowned at that. There was no way he could imagine she'd be content looking after someone else's children. "Winslette is there for you to return to if you wish."

"If Farnsworth hasn't sold it already."

Merrick hadn't found the words or the opportunity to mention her estate. In truth, he had never wanted to add to her disappointments by mentioning the transition of ownership. Given the circumstances, Merrick hoped she would not take his purchase of the property badly. "You can return. This may have been presumptuous on my part, but I purchased the property from Farnsworth the day you came to me. I didn't know how you'd take the news and kept silent. Forgive me."

She closed her eyes. "Then I truly am dependent only on him."

"Not if you don't want to be." He caught her hands in his and brought them to his chest. "Farnsworth seemed very keen to be rid of it and now it seems clear as to why."

"He wanted me in his power. He wanted to make sure I had nowhere to go but where he told me." She freed her hand from his grip and pressed her hands to her face, hiding behind them momentarily. When she emerged, her expression was bitter. She rubbed her throat, caressing the place that Farnsworth had held her and caused such injury. "Cecily tried to warn me, but I dismissed it. I never imagined the scenario reaching this conclusion."

"I doubt few would have foreseen this occurring." He caressed the back of her clutching fingers. "Farnsworth cannot come to Winslette now that I own it. He has no right."

"Why did you buy my home?"

Merrick moved Arabella to the setting by the window as he tried to put his decision into some form of order that would make sense to her. "The property is a beauty and is well situated. At first I considered whether it might do for Grayling, an expansion of his property, but with no time to get word to him, I purchased it first. I own nothing in Wiltshire but am often there as Grayling's guest. It is a good investment. If later he's keen to add the acres to his own, it's a matter that will always be open for discussion. But you must believe I never had any intention of throwing you from the estate."

"But you intend to live there?"

"No. When you told me it was on the market, I couldn't imagine you not living there. Having Grayling as a confidant means I knew much more about the property than most interested buyers would. By all accounts, you managed it well without assistance. I have no qualms at all for you to remain as long as you wish."

"You would let a woman manage one of your properties?" Her eyes widened and then she shook her head. "Farnsworth would come every few months and make me feel my decisions were foolish. I guess now I must concede he only left me in peace and limited freedom because I mourned his brother. Coming to London changed that."

The color in her cheeks drained away. Merrick quickly touched her arm in an attempt to send her insecurities into the far distance. "Enough of Farnsworth for tonight. He is no longer important."

"No. No, he certainly is not."

"That's my girl." Merrick swallowed against a suddenly dry mouth. "I should mention from the outset that I should only need visit once or twice a year to assure myself that all is well with you. I doubt I would ever reverse any decision you made. Grayling has indicated you take a very sensible and farseeing approach to land management."

She nodded slowly. "I had ample time to read about many things most married women do not. My husband had his own life and was rarely underfoot."

Curiosity got the better of him. "Did you like being married?"

Her face changed to one of bitterness. "Not really. But after my husband died, I came to enjoy the freedom to come and go at will without explaining my every movement or expense. Then Farnsworth summoned me to be his daughter's chaperone and I was once more forced to account for my every action and shilling spent. I miss Wiltshire and my friends. Farnsworth insisted I do things his way in London, far too often."

"I see." Merrick bit his lip. Arabella hadn't been treated very fairly. While he could understand her frustration, he wouldn't ever treat his wife that way. He hoped they would share a life. Given her wish for freedom, he decided then and there that he wouldn't impose on her by staying at Winslette. He'd ride across from Grayling's estate and keep his visits as short as possible. "Arabella, are you ready to go home? I fear if you remain much longer under my roof my aunt will do her worst to ruin you or force the alternative."

She looked up at him, confusion clear in her expression. "What alternative could there be?"

He eased back from her disappointed that a marriage between them had to be discussed under such circumstances.

"My aunt would do everything in her power to avoid family scandal. She would insist I marry you."

Arabella drew back a little. "But I don't want to be married. Certainly not to avoid a scandal. I was naïve in marrying the first time, and I like what little freedom I have gained since. I abandoned my life to avoid a marriage I didn't want. I doubt even your aunt could persuade me to anything right now."

"I assumed as much." He smiled, though his disappointment was acute. He did not blame her. Marriage required sacrifice. "Can you be ready to leave early tomorrow? If so, I'll take you home."

She stared at him a long moment, her teeth worrying her lower lip. "Are you not busy with the season's amusements? You go out so often that I would not mind if you'd rather remain here. I can easily make the journey alone."

His heart clattered against his ribs frantically at the speculation on her face. Was she curious about whether he'd found a bride? "I wouldn't dream of it. I assure you there is nothing of importance to keep me in London at present."

"Oh." Her eyes held his for a long moment, her expression clearing as she smiled shyly. "I will not mind going home with you."

Chapter Sixteen

In a world where every word had to be guarded and every decision weighed carefully, Arabella's choice to place her trust in Rothwell was extraordinary, even to her. At the end of each day of their journey home to Winslette, they'd had a quiet dinner together and then she'd spend the long hours of the night tossing and turning, finally to be awoken by Rothwell's quiet tap on the door each morning so they could enjoy a very early departure, as was his preference.

They had been traveling since before the sun rose each morning, leaving London sleeping in their wake. They'd taken rooms at pleasant inns along the way, but had resumed their journey each morning without incident. She had barely spent a moment alone and was not sorry for it.

Rothwell remained alert on his side of the carriage, Arabella facing toward home. It was not lost on her the sense of peace that came with leaving London. What she wasn't so sure of was why Rothwell expected nothing in return for his assistance.

His head turned from the window and their eyes met across the carriage. He neither smiled nor frowned, simply held her gaze a long moment before returning his attention to the view. It was almost as if he felt nothing about helping her. That was comforting but also a touch insulting. After giving it some thought, she realized she would miss his quiet company and the way he instantly made her feel safe.

Her gaze traveled to the man seated at his side. She had been rather startled to find Mr. Holland seated inside the carriage before she entered it that first morning. Rothwell gave no explanation for Holland's presence, but the man made as unlikely a chaperone as there had ever been. He smiled as he turned the page.

And there it was again. A resemblance she couldn't dismiss after so many hours of close confinement. Holland's lips quirked often, a reaction perhaps to a passage in the book he was reading, and he turned the page, looking very much like Rothwell.

Arabella leaned her head against the squabs, allowing her deductions to form, unimpeded by emotion. Rothwell and Holland were related of a certainty. There was similarity in much of their faces, though only Rothwell could truly be considered handsome. Holland was shorter and seemed a few years older. She had few doubts they shared the same blood—they appeared as similar as brothers.

"It won't be long now, I should think," Rothwell murmured.

She smiled as she noticed that Rothwell spoke both for her own benefit as well as for that of Mr. Holland. Despite being lord and servant—or were they even that?—Rothwell appeared to consider the comfort of the other man quite often.

She said, "No, not long at all. Just along the way is a little bridge where the local children like to fish. After that is a row of very large oak trees beside a long stone wall. A short distance from there we turn right, and another mile after is Winslette."

"You know the way home very well indeed." A frown marred his handsome face. "You were from Essex, Maidstone, were you not? Do you visit there often?"

She was surprised he knew where she'd grown up. "Not very often now, but I do long to travel to see old friends. I suppose that will be difficult in the future. I did not consider this before, but given how things stand now, I know not how I will support myself."

Rothwell smiled to acknowledge her situation. "Old friends are often the very best. They forgive lapses of communication more easily than newer acquaintances, in my opinion."

She appreciated that he made no mention of how to solve

every difficulty in her life. Having him, a friend of a friend, purchase her home was a remarkable boon and certainly removed one burden from her mind. Her servants would not be dismissed out of hand, but there was only so much she could ask of him for herself. Their friendship was far too insubstantial to risk. One demand too many and his aid might disappear completely. "I had a best friend when I was growing up there, but she married and moved to the north. We still write each year. I had wished to see her again one day."

"Where did she move to? Do you know?"

"Somerset, a house east of Taunton."

Rothwell smiled suddenly and glanced out the window. "I have an estate near there, don't I, Holland?"

"Yes, my lord." Holland closed his book. "A small house on a hill in the middle of several hundred acres, I believe."

Rothwell frowned. "The roadway floods during the spring rains."

"I believe that was why you bought the place." Holland grinned. "You said the flooded road would lessen any interruptions from unwanted visitors."

"Sounds like a very good reason to buy any place the Fords cannot reach." Rothwell smiled cheekily in Arabella's direction. "I like to avoid them at all costs."

Arabella laughed. "So if I confess that your aunt quite terrifies me, you will not think too badly of me? I always wonder why she smiles at me so much when we have little to do with one another."

Rothwell appeared startled by that revelation and glanced at Holland. They exchanged a long look, quite like one seeing a reflection in a mirror, before Rothwell returned his attention to her. "She would be hard-pressed to find fault with you, but you are wise to regard her with caution," he said in all seriousness. "My aunt cannot help but meddle. Ah, we're here at last."

Arabella stared out the window. *Home.* As had happened so often during the journey, she'd lost track of time while speaking with Rothwell. She was just getting the man to open up and now the journey was over. She was very sorry it was. She'd love to know why he avoided his family, aside from wishing for no interference in his life. There was something he would not say.

A disagreement that had never been settled, perhaps. Now there was unfortunately no time to discover it.

When the carriage rolled to a stop before the front steps, Rothwell climbed out and then extended his hand to her.

Her butler, Mr. Piper, appeared almost instantly, hastily rushing to greet them in the drive. "My lady?"

Arabella set her hand in Rothwell's and joined him. There was nothing like returning to the place you feel most comfortable. Despite how she must appear in the company of a strange man, she grinned at her butler to assure him she was exactly where she wanted to be. "Did I catch you unawares?"

He peered hard at her, color draining from his usually ruddy cheeks. "Indeed you did, but I am very glad to see you looking so well. The house is closed up as you requested on your departure, but I'd expected a message a few days ahead of your return so all that could be attended to."

He turned questioning eyes toward her companions.

She did not want him to misunderstand the reason for her current company. Rothwell had done more for her than she'd dreamed he would want to. She turned to the man still holding her hand, her cheeks warming because his presence always had an impact on her. She owed Rothwell a debt that could never be repaid. "Under normal circumstances I would have sent one, but I wanted to come home. Mr. Piper, you have the pleasure of meeting Lord Rothwell. Farnsworth has sold Winslette to him."

All the blood drained from Piper's face. "Sold, you say?"

Rothwell released her hand, his expression growing serious as he appraised the butler with a haughty disdain so unlike his recent countenance. "Nothing changes for your mistress. You will go on in the manner she wishes."

"It is not that." Piper rubbed his hand over his face. "Lord Farnsworth is here. He's looking for Lady Farnsworth. He told us she was missing."

Arabella glanced at Rothwell nervously. Farnsworth was in *her* home. A place she'd been assured of sanctuary. "Why would he look for me here. The sale was completed, wasn't it?"

Rothwell rubbed her arms and then shrugged out of his coat and wrapped her in it. "Yes it was, he hasn't the right to be anywhere on the estate. Holland, remain with Arabella and do not let her come inside till I say so. Jimmy, you're with me."

Arabella caught Rothwell's arm and kept him with her as the coachman bounded toward the door, rolling up his shirtsleeves. "What do you mean to do?"

He brushed the thumb of his free hand across her cheek gently, the same cheek Farnsworth had struck when she'd refused to do his bidding and marry Parker without complaint. This time the sensation was pleasant. One she would remember fondly forever.

"I intend to teach him the manners he clearly lacks." A smile grew on his face. "I'm so pleased he decided to trespass. His comeuppance is days overdue. Wait for me and all will be well."

She let him go and watched his departure anxiously, the coachman and Piper flanking him seeming far too little support. She edged closer to Holland. "He'll be all right, won't he?"

Holland might have smiled, but his eyes were filled with concern. "He may claim to dislike the reference, but he is a Ford. He can handle himself in a fight when necessary."

From within the house came a shout, the crash of wood splintering, and then a long silence. Arabella craned her neck but could see nothing through the open doorway.

When Rothwell finally strode out, his cravat was askew, his breathing hurried, but the look on his face proved he was pleased with events. He reached for his coat without a word and shoved his arms into the sleeves. "The vermin is being removed by a side door as we speak and will be escorted some distance from the house to ensure the fool leaves. I'm sorry about the table. I'll replace it with whatever your heart desires."

Arabella bit her lip as he smoothed his waistcoat and straightened his cravat. The fool grinned. She could not believe he could smile at a time like this. If not for Rothwell's escort, she would have faced Farnsworth again and alone. She buried her face in her hands, overwhelmed with relief to have gone to Rothwell for aid in the first place.

After a long moment, Rothwell's arms slowly encircled her and tightened about her. "He will not bother you ever again, I swear. You will never need to see him."

When released, she glanced around swiftly, aware that there were servants around them and they had viewed her behavior.

To her surprise, not one faced her. They had all turned away. "Thank you."

Recalled to their audience too, Rothwell's posture stiffened. "Holland, see to the carriage and have everything ready for our return to London."

A rush of panic seized Arabella. For the whole of the trip she had not thought of what would happen next. She wasn't prepared to let Rothwell go just yet. In the distant carriage house, servants could be seen rushing to hitch the horses to ensure Farnsworth's immediate departure. But what if Farnsworth returned tonight while she was sleeping? The idea of it brought on fresh panic.

She grabbed Rothwell's hand and held it tightly. "Surely you wish to inspect the property you purchased," she blurted out, purely as a means to delay his departure.

Rothwell glanced around, eyeing his new possession and then the distant carriage house. He nodded slowly. "I suppose I should."

Holland edged closer. "Are you forgetting those matters in London that required all your attention, and the other one to be attended to on our way back?"

"There is plenty of time to accomplish everything."

Were they speaking of the special license or something else entirely? She had a nagging feeling something was to be done when she wasn't around. The sense of exclusion grated. Given the aggravated expression on Rothwell's face, he didn't want to discuss it before her either. But to make use of the special license, Rothwell would have to marry before the march of time made it worthless. He had a month, or so she believed, but she did not know when the license had been issued.

To her surprise, Rothwell took her arm and threaded it through his. He led her toward the front door. "I would be very happy to have a tour if you can spare me an hour."

"It will take quite a bit longer than an hour to view the property properly," she confessed. Arabella quickly tallied a list guaranteed to keep Rothwell occupied and with her for as long as possible. He should have an intimate knowledge of the estate before he left. He would probably be hungry too. Besides, any good hostess would see his appetites were fully catered to.

Chapter Seventeen

It might be wishful thinking on his part, but Merrick was almost certain Arabella sought to delay his departure and keep him at Winslette until approaching nightfall made traveling impossible. He poked his head inside a milking shed, noting the care and attention made to keep the stalls clean, and faced Arabella again. She gestured to the next structure and moved in that direction.

Their progress was steadily leading him far away from the main house and his waiting carriage. Not that he minded spending even more hours in her company. Speaking with an intelligent woman who never once tossed out lures or flirtations was something of a rarity. And she'd been through a lot in the last days. If she felt safe in his company for the time being, he would be a fool to rush away from her if he was doing some good.

Back at the house, Holland would be fretting by now. They'd sent word to their married half sister to expect them tonight at her inn, and Holland simply hated letting anyone down. However, Merrick found the position he was in quite amusing. When he'd decided to return Arabella home, Holland had insisted on coming to act as a chaperone of sorts and to make good on a promise to their sister. Since Arabella had never once made allusions to intimacies between them, a chaperone hadn't been necessary.

She was nervous though, and he suspected he knew the reason.

Farnsworth's behavior still preyed on her mind.

Unfortunately, it preyed on his too. That Farnsworth had come to Wiltshire from London in search of Arabella was no small matter. He might have used the excuse of trespass to trounce the man, but there was always the possibility that he might return once he was gone. When she was easy again he'd return to London and make sure Farnsworth understood that he was not to contact Arabella except to discuss her pension, and then only through her solicitor. She was to be free of him or Merrick would finish their fight.

As the last building inspection was concluded, Arabella scanned the horizon. Ahead, he thought he detected what looked to be a small stream, and across from there a ruin of some sort. He could see nowhere to cross without getting wet, so he concluded his inspection might be over for the day.

Arabella noticed the direction of his gaze. "The ruins were once an old manor house, fallen into disuse long ago. There is a road, barely more than a deer track now, I suppose, leading to another roadway to the south. My late husband told me the house was quite unsafe and forbid anyone to venture there."

"Well, if it's forbidden, we will stay away." He grinned. "Are there fish to be caught on the property?"

Arabella smiled too. "Why, yes. I believe there are. Do you enjoy the sport?"

"Not since I was a boy." He smiled to himself. It was nice his company was wanted so badly that a woman seized on any topic of conversation to keep his interest. "Will you show me?"

Her blush returned. "Of course."

Merrick could get used to seeing blushes every hour. Arabella wore them so charmingly. The grass was thick and clumped in this part of the property and he caught Arabella's elbow to steady her as they walked to the stream. In closer proximity, he couldn't help but notice that the exertion of the inspection was taking a toll on her stamina. The light sheen of perspiration on her forehead reminded him that a pause in their meanderings might be warranted. When the stream came into view, he directed her to the shade of a large tree near the water's edge and settled her there.

He took a place himself a short distance away. "What is it you want, my dear, and do not say I must be acquainted with every blade of grass I have purchased."

Instead of answering immediately, she hugged her knees to her chest. The posture reminded him that just a few nights ago she'd been frightened out of her wits by a man she trusted as a brother. She had placed her security in his lap and he would do well not to rush her to the confession he'd already guessed.

She was still afraid. Perhaps mortally. She might always have this fear. It might be that only when she was distracted did she not imagine Farnsworth's assault.

Merrick plucked a blade of grass and ran it though his fingertips. "He has no right to come back. I made that very plain to him."

"I believe you, but what if he guesses I was with you the entire time? He might make trouble for you. Tarnish your reputation. It would be very easy to have one of your servants confirm that you lied to him about my location these past days."

She was worried about his reputation? Merrick had not thought it possible to admire her more, but he did. She was remarkable. "None of my servants would dare."

"How can you be so sure?"

Holland would dismiss them immediately if they said one word that implicated him in scandal. His half brother had adopted the Ford motto of family first for his own. He'd rather not explain the real reasons for Holland's loyalty or the others as yet. She'd be rather shocked that she'd been in the company of several bastard brothers these past days. "Because I can."

"And if Farnsworth deduced on his own and makes trouble for us both?"

He shifted on the ground to face her. "Grayling should have the truth told to him so he is not surprised and can support you. Grayling will understand and ensure your reputation remains unblemished. The worst Farnsworth can say against me is nothing I haven't heard before. I'll survive it."

She laid her head on her knees and stared into space. "I want to be here, but I fear what Farnsworth might do if he comes again."

Merrick did not want to leave her in such a state, but it was the right thing to do. Every moment he spent alone in her company, regardless of their distance, put her reputation as a respectable lady in jeopardy. Arabella appeared largely unconcerned about that, he noticed. Yet Merrick couldn't be. He had always held Arabella in the highest esteem, the model for all other women's behavior. To imagine her brought low by false accusations pained him. Perhaps she was too caught up in her own concerns to notice the implied impropriety of them being together.

He'd have to watch out for both of them. "Speaking of Grayling, have you considered moving to Stanton Harold Hall as a guest until the matter is behind you? You may feel more secure there. His daughters and wife could be a welcome distraction to you and he could ensure Farnsworth stays away. I promise you the house will remain yours for as long as you wish, despite any absence."

"I don't wish to impose."

Merrick pursed his lips. "You say that quite often. Why? I would not offer if I had any hesitations about such a suggestion."

"Habit, I suppose." She sighed softly and stretched out her legs before her. "When I was a little girl, my parents impressed on me the need to be compliant, and my husband was of the same mind. I never argued with any of their decisions and that made them happier."

Merrick frowned at her words. Such a repression of her desires was unnatural. One of the Ford rules came to mind: always repay in kind. From Grayling, he knew she had brought the man's wife into his orbit and sought to make a match of them. Surely they should not begrudge her aid now? "Friends expect to be imposed upon or they are not really friends, are they? It is a balance. Something given, something gained."

A curious expression crossed her face and she peered at him. "You do not follow your own rules it seems."

"How so?"

"I cannot imagine what you gain by your assistance to me. You have gone above and beyond the bounds of friendship to aid me. We were not very well acquainted in the beginning, were we?"

"I suppose I imagine I know you better than I actually do. Grayling speaks of you a great deal. I always thought you two would make a match, but you went and paired him with someone else. That surprised me." He grinned. "As for what I gained, my legs have gained the exercise of a walking hither and yon today, and I had the pleasure of throwing Farnsworth out on his backside. Both very pleasant activities, I assure you."

"That is not at all the same, and you know it. You brought me into your home, concealed my whereabouts from everyone, including your family and mine, and returned me to the property you'd purchased just because you cannot imagine me not living here. You give too much."

Damn. She would not let the matter drop. He drew in a deep breath and exhaled slowly. Now was not the time for a glib answer to appease her conscience. He could tell her some of what influenced him and see how she might view his ideals. "Women are largely at a disadvantage in our society. It is a circumstance that has disappointed me many times in the past. They are expected to be silent when mistreated and have no grounds to complain or receive compensation for cruel use. It is wrong, Arabella."

"I don't understand." She inched closer to him. "What wrongs have you witnessed?"

"Far too many and too close to home." He scrubbed a hand through his hair. He wanted to tell her the truth. To explain why her suffering affected him so strongly and yet still not tell her every secret. He could tell her of his father, though. What that man had done likely still circulated as gossip about his family, so she might have heard the whispers. It would be a small thing to confirm what she possibly knew already. "My father was not one to deny himself life's pleasures. He never once counted the cost of his actions, and many lives were ruined as a result of his desires."

Her brow furrowed. Perhaps not all of his father's misdeeds were widely circulated and in this case had not reached her ears. "Go on."

He swallowed the lump that formed at the base of his throat. He'd started down this path, to explain a bit of himself, so by rights he ought to keep to his decision and hope he didn't shock her completely. "To be blunt, my father sired a number of children outside marriage, most to servants in his employ or in the great houses he visited. My mother knew and the humiliation was more than she could bear. My last memory of them together is my father backhanding my mother for speaking against him and his many disgraces."

Her skin paled and she shivered. "I'm sorry."

He shook his head. "'Tis nothing to be done about it now. They are alive in the world and made poorer by his choices."

"They?"

Merrick smiled grimly, staring out at the slow-moving water. "My half brothers and sisters. I am sorry to say there are rather a lot of them."

Her gasp struck him like a blow. "Holland?"

Merrick nodded slowly, glancing at her for the signs of shock he expected. When none appeared on her face, he pressed on. "He was the first I grew aware of when I was a young man and suffering through an education I didn't want at Newberry Park. Holland worked at a tavern I frequented and often he was the one to put me on my horse and send me home when I was too deep in my cups and growing quarrelsome. I liked him very much then. He did not bow and scrape as many men did to those of Newberry. One day I came upon him surrounded and outnumbered, bloody and beaten but still not cowed. I offered my fists and then offered him a better position as my valet. My grandfather and particularly my aunt were furious when I brought Holland home to Newberry and it was only then I discovered exactly who he was to me. My disagreements with the Fords began then."

"What of Holland's mother?"

"You know, I've never heard Holland speak her name, but she lives, I'm sure of it. I have pieced together what I think happened. She lived in a great house, probably a servant. But she couldn't keep him with her and had to give him up. It is a situation that has occurred many times over."

"It is kind of you to employ him as you do."

"Holland enjoys managing me and ensures our siblings are fed, employed usefully, and have a roof over their heads."

"How many?"

"A dozen or more. Holland keeps track of them." He sighed at the folly of revealing this side of his personal life. "Almost every servant in my London home is a relation, every man on the carriage that brought you here also. I take care of them and they take care of me. They will say not one word of this excursion to anyone for fear of Holland's wrath. My half brother will brook no disobedience from them. He knows their situation is tenuous."

He continued, knowing revealing so much would likely ruin everything but feeling lighter for the unburdening. He tossed aside the blade of grass he'd been running through his fingers while he talked. "My point is that not everyone has someone to watch out for their welfare and not every debt needs to be repaid immediately. I have had the pleasure of your company, a situation that would never have presented itself at any other time. So you see, without knowing it, you have already held up your side of our friendship."

"It is very good what you do. Most lords would not do so much." Arabella plucked a blade of grass and handed it to him to replace the one he'd mangled. "Why do they believe their situation is tenuous?"

"Because it is true. My father sired only one legitimate son, and I have not married as yet to produce the required heir. The next in line is a cousin, a pious prig who would sooner brand them all vile creatures to be cast out onto the street than spend the shillings required to feed even one."

Her eyes widened. "You would marry just for them?"

"Not just for them. I did have other hopes when I eventually wed."

A rosy blush spread over her cheeks and her neck too, yet relief filled him. She did not appear too shocked. He'd always intended to be honest with his wife about his half brothers and sisters, so gaining Arabella's understanding went a long way to proving he'd made the right decision to tell the woman he married too.

"You're fond on your siblings, despite their origins?"

Merrick supposed she was right. "Family first."

"That is not at all a bad thing." She shifted closer, tucking her knees beneath her and giving him all her attention. "Having none I care for now means I'm made more aware of my lack."

Merrick glanced across the stream to hide the sadness that filled him. It was not easy to ignore that Farnsworth's actions had revealed just how alone Arabella was in the world. Leaving would be difficult. He lifted his eyes to the horizon with a heavy heart. Storm clouds had gathered to the west of the estate. His brothers were going to get wet on their way home. Yet if he didn't go now, he feared he might never walk away from her. His hopes for his life would go unfulfilled if he stayed.

He stood and dusted off his trousers, then held his hand out to Arabella. "We'd best be on our way."

He helped her up and brought her back into the field, holding her arm as they walked over difficult terrain, releasing her when their way was free of impediment. They had not traveled very far when he spotted Holland and his coachman, Jimmy, in the distance, striding toward them in a hurry. "Ah, a family reunion. I wonder what the fuss is about now."

Arabella chuckled. "Oh, dear. Did they think your virtue in danger?"

"No. I'm very sure they are attempting to protect yours." He laughed too as his good mood returned. He had been alone with Arabella and had thought very little of getting beneath her skirts. It was not the first time Arabella had lured him to speak his mind rather than contemplate the delights of her body. Despite her troubles and the delicate topic he'd broached, he'd never had a more enjoyable day. If he told Holland that she knew all their secrets now, the man would likely fall over in a faint and never wake.

She stopped suddenly. "Will you dine with me this evening?"

"If I stay that long I'll have no chance of returning to London as expected."

"You had other plans for the journey home too, didn't you? I'm sorry. I shouldn't delay you." Her throat moved as she swallowed, proving her disappointment was acute.

"My plan had no date affixed to it." He smiled. "My half sister is an agreeable creature and will understand the delay was for a good cause."

"You have a sister?"

"Several. The one I am to meet runs the Castle Inn at Fox Hill with her husband. I often break my journey there when I come to Wiltshire. She had a babe recently and Holland wants to see the lad and another one residing close by before we return to Town. They can wait a day more."

Her gaze turned to the building storm clouds. "If you're sure it's not a bother I'd appreciate it if you would stay for the night. There is ample room for everyone and I should not like your brothers to get soaked before half a mile is passed."

Merrick threw his head back and laughed. "Now that is a first. Most women invite me to stay for anything but my ugly brother's benefit."

A brilliant blush stained her cheeks and he caught her arm and steered her toward the fast approach of Holland and Jimmy. Did she blush when men shared her bed? He frowned at that idea. Arabella had been a widow for some time, yet he'd never heard of her taking a lover. She cast no lures that he could detect. He pushed the idea from his mind firmly. It was better to be friends than lovers. Friendship lasted far longer than the sudden rush of lust.

"Jimmy, we seem to be staying the night. Have the carriage and team put away and the men dispersed where they will fit. Make sure they help out where they can. No sense being idle if there is work begging to be done."

Holland glanced between himself and Arabella, his expression curious and wary. "My lord, this is unexpected. What about your plans?"

"It is unexpected, isn't it? Ease your mind, Holland. My plans can wait. Lady Farnsworth would feel more secure if Lord Farnsworth found the place still occupied by my servants and myself should he return tonight. I would not like to disappoint her by refusing her hospitality."

Holland didn't appear happy about it but eventually nodded. "Of course. I would not be easy to have him return either."

When Holland hurried back to the house, Arabella swatted Merrick's arm. "You beast. You enjoyed tormenting him."

He studied his brother's fast retreat. "I'll be suitably lectured for it later."

"What could he have to say about the matter?"

"He's concerned for you."

"I'm in no danger with you."

"Quite the contrary." He faced her so he could judge her reaction. "Have you even thought your invitation through properly? While we were in London, I was confident I could remove you from my house undetected, but here in the country our *togetherness* will not be so easily overlooked. People will assume there is something between us if I stay. We have already been too long alone together as it is."

Her tongue darted out and licked her lips. A distinctly nervous gesture that made his pulse race. "You've never…" She waved her free hand about as she sought the right word to describe his lack of seduction.

"Oh, I've been interested, but you would surely be the poorer for it." Merrick was glad they had some distance to walk before they reached the house again and he curled her arm about his and drew her in that direction. "After your recent set of troubles, I wouldn't be surprised that you'd want nothing to do with men again. You've been very clear that you oppose marriage."

"I don't exactly oppose marriage. I just never want to have to make another because I've no choice." Her free hand clenched at her waist. "I'd always thought of Farnsworth as a brother. Not a particularly close one, though, so I was shocked that he thought to sell me like he would cattle." She tightened her grip on his arm. "Can we talk of something else?"

"Anything you like."

Yet silence fell between them. As they drew closer to the house, Arabella's steps slowed. She kept sneaking glances at him until he couldn't stand it. "What?"

She paused beneath a tall tree and faced him. "I have a favor to ask."

"Name it."

"When I close my eyes, I see Farnsworth's face right before he would have hit me. I would like not to see that image anymore."

"I don't imagine that's very pleasant. What can I do?"

"Will you kiss me again?"

Merrick held himself very, very still as his pulse bolted. "Ah, I don't think that's such a good idea."

"Please. I would like something pleasant to think about at night."

The plea in her eyes broke him. Perhaps a kiss would take her terror away quicker than time and distance would. A glance around them confirmed they were alone and could not be seen from the house. He could kiss her and no one would be any the wiser.

He didn't want to say no, so before he reasoned out the whys of not doing so, he leaned toward her and brushed his lips across hers. He drew back quickly when Arabella froze in place. "I'm sorry."

Her brow furrowed. "For what?"

"I startled you."

Her cheeks brightened with hot color. "No. It was not that at all."

"What then?"

"I don't know." Her lips pressed together briefly. "Would you kiss me again and I will try to remain still?"

"Arabella, another kiss may not change anything."

"Perhaps not, but please, Merrick. I'd rather think of you."

She gave so much more than she realized. Merrick tried again, more slowly this time. The first brush of lips was gentle and soft. A temptation to ease her mind. The second kiss was firmer. He cupped her head, eagerly ready to tangle tongues with her. However, her lips remained closed as if she were not used to being kissed.

Slowly, Merrick sought her waist with his free hand and drew her against him. She sighed as a third kiss began and finally kissed him back the way he wanted. Her hands touched his chest as he tasted her with his tongue. The sweet suction of their lips sent his pulse out of control, and his cock thickened and strained immediately against the placket of his trousers. There was more, so much more, passion to come between them, but in everything to do with Arabella, he hesitated. He wanted her so badly and did not want to make a mistake. He drew back reluctantly with one last soft kiss and waited for her reaction.

Arabella opened her eyes slowly. Her cheeks flamed to a vivid pink, so bright he had to run his fingertip across the smooth surface to test how warm they were.

"Oh my." She slapped her hands over her blushing cheeks and a throaty laugh burst from her lips. "I see now why every woman who's ever spoken of you was mad for your company."

There was his reputation, come to remind her of his debauched past. He bit back his disappointment that she listened to gossip and looked away. "I have my uses."

After a moment, her arm slid back through his and they continued their walk toward the house with her holding to him firmly. Her eyes fluttered shut as she walked, an unwise decision on uneven ground, and her lips pressed together tightly.

Although intrigued by her reaction to such a simple kiss, he waited till she opened her eyes again before asking what he most wanted to know. "Is Farnsworth gone from your memory?"

"Who?" She faced him and her smile was sweet and intimate. "After such a kiss I am capable of very little recall. It's a wonder my legs can hold me up. Do you kiss all women like that?"

He'd used no more skill with Arabella than anyone else, but it *was* different kissing her. Unique and undeniably tender. An idea formed in his mind, but he pushed it away as a foolish wish brought on by an even more foolish desire that she might never belong to anyone but him and only smiled.

Chapter Eighteen

Arabella rolled her face into the pillow as frustration grew. Kissing Rothwell had ruined everything. Now instead of the memory of Farnsworth's red, angry face filling her with terror, she saw Rothwell, and not just in that moment before he'd touched his lips to hers and ripped her contentment apart. Every kind and gentle moment between them flickered through her mind, adding fuel to her memories of kissing him.

She burrowed beneath the sheets, irritated by herself more than anything. During dinner tonight, Rothwell had acted as if that kiss never happened. He'd been charming and kind, always smiling and ready to converse. He'd had no problem upholding his side of the conversation at all. Arabella had barely managed to finish her meal. How could he not feel anything after such a kiss?

She was thankful he'd been taken away by Holland to speak of something so vitally important that Rothwell had not reappeared. Arabella rolled over and tossed the covers from her body. Her nightgown was twisted completely around and she lacked the will to straighten herself. The advice she had received months ago on how to seduce a man played through her mind again. The ring on her finger was gone, just the faintest trace of the depression remained. She had restyled her hair and worn more revealing gowns than normal.

Even close proximity to a rogue had made no discernable

increase in her attractiveness.

Perhaps she was doomed to die a virgin.

She sat up quickly. No. Absolutely not. She would not allow life to pass her by. If not for Rothwell's being home, she might have fallen prey to Farnsworth's evil intentions and been coerced into marrying Lord Parker.

How long could a man like Rothwell resist a woman if she were to climb into his bed? He had said he was interested but had assumed she was put off by men entirely. She wasn't, but if Rothwell was waiting for some sign from her to proceed to intimate relations between them, she had no idea what gesture to give.

She bit her lip. Rosemary had promised that her body would appeal to any man. She wanted to test that theory with Rothwell before he found himself a wife. Nervous but committed to her decision, she climbed from bed. She just had to allow Rothwell an opportunity while he was still here. He'd been amenable to a kiss that had scorched her senses. She would go to him tonight before she changed her mind.

Arabella drew in a deep breath to steady her nerves and stepped out into the dark hall. It took a few moments before her eyes adjusted to the gloom and without the aid of any other light she padded toward the room her butler had assigned to Rothwell on his arrival. Steady rain beat against the windows she passed and disguised the sound of her passage. Light flickered beneath his door and she raised her hand to the wood. Her knock sounded loud to her own ears, so instead of waiting outside where a servant might see her, she quickly entered.

But the room was empty. The bed was made as if Rothwell had not been in it. Crushed, she turned on the spot and retraced her steps. So much for having dishonorable intentions about a man. She would have to try again later or give up her wish as a fool's errand.

"Arabella?"

She jerked her head up and stared into the shadows lingering beside her bedchamber door. Rothwell stepped from them.

"Oh, there you are."

He came closer. He was still dressed as he'd been at dinner, but his coat was missing. He looked rather dashing in his shirtsleeves and embroidered waistcoat. "Were you looking for me?"

As during dinner, his deep voice did funny things to her nerves. A ball of uncertainty settled in her stomach. She took a deep breath and took a pace toward him. "I was. I have another request to make of you."

"Are you thinking of Farnsworth again?"

"No. I was thinking of you."

"Me." His fingers brushed the sleeve of her nightgown. "In what way?"

This was the moment. "I'd like you to kiss me again and not stop."

He studied her for a long, uncomfortable moment, eyes skimming her body as if he were touching her. Warmth pooled between her thighs and she clutched her robe tightly to stop her hands from shaking. When he blinked, his expression grew shuttered. "This is an unexpected request."

Arabella brushed her suddenly sweaty palms over her robe. There was only one thing left to do. She'd have to be honest and as bold as Cecily could be. "I wanted you to seduce me," she blurted.

Rothwell drew back a pace as if she'd struck him. For the first time ever, he seemed at a loss for words. He shook his head. "I'm sorry. My mind wandered for a moment. Could you please repeat that?"

His words bolstered her courage considerably. The tables had turned. Now he was the one flustered.

Yet Arabella hesitated. She hadn't actually thought she'd need to ask to be seduced. She'd assumed Lord Rothwell would understand what she wanted without being told and act accordingly. How else did one invite seduction if there were no right words to request it? "I want you."

She stared at him, hoping a blunt invitation would be acceptable. Time slowed. The clock ticked loudly nearby and then Rothwell finally seemed to catch on. But still he did not sweep in to ravish her. Perhaps additional conversation was a requirement in a seduction. She smiled. "Are you not pleased?"

"Don't mistake my silence as displeasure. I am honored." He swallowed and dug a finger beneath his cravat to loosen it.

"However, before I consider how to proceed I want to know why me and now."

Because there was much about Rothwell to be impressed by—tall; dark haired; broad, muscled shoulders. He commanded attention wherever he went and to be alone with such a man in her own surroundings did terrible things to her senses. She might actually swoon.

That he was so out of countenance pleased her. From the moment he had kissed her, she had hesitated to name the force that plagued her. It might be described as lust, but she'd never experienced that. Yet the heat of his gaze now seared through her body and did terrible things to her composure. She wanted to twine her body around his and never let go.

Even now, with her interest in the open and the heat in Rothwell's gaze evident, he still refused to act. Perhaps he looked at all women as potential candidates to grace his bed but he didn't necessarily follow through in bedding every one.

The thought was disheartening. She liked him best of all the gentlemen she knew. Disappointed, she pulled her robe closer about her body. "Forgive me for taking up your valuable time. I'm sure you have other, more interesting activities planned for your evening."

He caught her arm to prevent her flight. "Wait. Our discussion hasn't ended."

"But my courage has." She turned for the door and an end to her embarrassment, slipping from his soft hold easily. "Good evening, my lord."

He caught her before she made her door, his hands firm on her upper arms, his body behind her. "I'm willing. I'm just surprised. Why would you need courage for me? Has Farnsworth given you another fear to conquer? I promise you few men are cruel like that."

She drew in a shaky breath. "I hope not."

They were alone. His seduction could begin. He drew her against his body and when her spine landed against his chest, she shuddered. Warmth penetrated her robe where they touched and took her breath away. His hands slid up her arms firmly and she tried not to start from the unfamiliar sensations he stirred. Yet her whole body thrummed with anticipation at the sensation of his attention.

His soft sigh against her hair made her jump. Rothwell stilled, breath caught as he inhaled, and after a time, he released her. "Are you sure about this? I will not seek to detain you should you change your mind." Rothwell's voice was a soft murmur, full of patience and perhaps even a touch of understanding.

She faced him. "This is what I want."

Rothwell twined his fingers through hers and tugged. "Then follow me." He drew her back to his bedchamber and through the door, shutting it softly behind him.

Ahead lay his large, empty bed. She risked a peek at him. Although this moment marked a turning point for Arabella, Rothwell appeared calm, as if such an act was almost mundane. He didn't immediately ravish her. He seemed completely at ease.

Could she really hope that London's most debauched rogue would introduce her to carnal pleasures? It seemed she could.

The next moment, Rothwell stood before her, a devilish grin on his lips. He caught her fingers in his and squeezed, then dipped his head to brush his lips over her hot cheeks. "Lovely."

Arabella shook her head, puzzled by his behavior. "Thank you."

When he loosened the tie on her robe, his fingertips brushed her stomach and she sucked in a sharp breath. She swallowed past the lump forming in her throat. She could do this and not feel fear. Yet, as her robe slithered down her arms and Rothwell tossed it across the room to land on a chair, she feared her legs might give way.

His arms curled around her back and held her against him. "You can change your mind."

She met his gaze quickly. "No, I couldn't do that to you."

He frowned. "Arabella, you are trembling."

"I'm sorry. It's just…" She swallowed quickly. "I've never been in this situation before. I find you quite overwhelming."

"I don't mean to be." He grinned suddenly. "Shall we talk first?"

All they had done was talk. Arabella leaned forward to kiss him instead. Although taken by surprise, he quickly kissed her back. As before in the gardens, Rothwell's kisses turned her legs to butter. She sagged against him for support even as he drew her closer against his chest. Through the thin nightgown, the cold metal buttons of his waistcoat dug into her body, reminding her how little she was dressed by comparison. Was there a polite way to ask a man to disrobe?

Rothwell eased back a touch even while he continued to kiss her. His fingers flew over his waistcoat and discarded the garment, ending the discomfort. He broke the kiss and stared at her. "I was leaving tomorrow."

Arabella frowned. "You were."

Rothwell leaned his head against hers and sighed. "I thought it best, but now I don't know what to think."

All the gossip she'd heard of his restless habits crowded her mind. He was hardly the type of man to consider a long-term relationship that gave him so little, and she could never forget he was on the hunt for a wife. She had only tonight left with him. "You always do the right thing, Rothwell."

He met her gaze and then smiled, the same devilish smile that she had seen before but never received. "Flatterer."

She laughed too. "The truth."

Of course he couldn't stay with her forever. Even tonight, she'd practically forced him to make love to her and whatever happened between them she wouldn't regret it.

Rothwell circled behind her. His fingertips brushed her spine above her nightgown and she shivered again. "You are the most sensitive woman I have ever met."

She glanced over her shoulder. "Is that good or ill?"

He reached around her body without touching her and caught the ties on her nightgown. "You are so aware of everything I do. Every touch. Every brush of my hands about your beautiful body. It's as if you've never done this before, but that couldn't be so."

Her anxiety returned as he loosened the cord holding her nightgown in place. She should tell him. Confess her most embarrassing secret. She was eight and twenty years old and still a virgin. It was humiliating to need another man to fulfill her husband's failing.

Her nightgown fell to her feet and she stared at it, her face heating. She was naked. After a few more moments, Rothwell's fingers traced a short distance down her spine and then back up again. She dragged in a deep breath, expecting him to pounce, to touch flesh that craved attention.

When he walked away, she followed his progress. He picked up a banyan that had been draped across the end of his bed, the one she'd always worn at his London town house, and flicked the silken fabric around her. She stared at his face—his mouth was pursed as he tied the robe securely around her waist.

Why had he stopped? Had she done something wrong? Did he not like what he saw?

His hands rose to cup her skull. "May I take your hair down?"

In all she had heard about seductions, they were quick and required the minimum of undressing. Taking her hair down hadn't come into her calculations.

When she nodded, Rothwell lowered his head and brushed his lips against hers. She sighed at the warmth of his kiss, and he took advantage and swept his tongue across her parted lips. She kissed him back, glorying in sensations as he drew her flush against him. Kissing Rothwell was something she would miss when he was gone.

Chapter Nineteen

Damn it to hell. *Arabella was an innocent.* Merrick would stake his life on it. Since their kiss that afternoon, he had watched her closely for signs that she'd welcome further intimacies between them. He'd been disappointed until she'd said she wanted him, but had then wondered why she was so nervous about being with him in his room.

He ruthlessly reined in his impatience. He had been attracted to the woman since the moment they met, but he'd never imagined her to have been untouched. It explained so much about his fascination with her. She might have been married for half a dozen years, but he'd bet her spouse had never laid a finger on her.

Which meant that Merrick couldn't rush this. He had to prepare her properly. She was utterly terrified and yet utterly determined to be seduced. He couldn't risk botching the job or he'd never get another chance to have her in his arms.

He smoothed his hands down her back, feeling her curves beckoning him to strip her naked again. Removing her outer garments had been his way to level the field and give her time to adjust to intimacy, but he'd gone too far too fast. He'd covered her in his robe as a means of reassurance. At least now she'd ceased trembling.

He broke the kiss and moved his lips to her neck, nibbling a path across her flawless skin. Such soft, delicate flesh deserved every consideration. He kissed just below her ear and then concentrated on removing the ribbons from her hair. Once freed the blonde tresses cascaded down to the middle of her back.

He combed his fingers through her hair, catching the odd snarl and then smoothing it. He wanted Arabella so much he ached. Still, one could not rush a virgin into bed. He wouldn't want her to regret her faith in him. He could scarcely believe she had come to him in the first place, and he wasn't so foolish as to send her away unsatisfied.

He smiled at her, saw the same dreamy expression she'd worn the first time they'd kissed, and brushed his lips over the tip of her nose. "Come sit with me." He caught her fingers and drew her to the settee.

She settled primly beside him, appearing uncertain of herself again. Did she really expect him to have just thrown her over his bed and be done with her already? "What did you do after dinner?"

"Not very much at all." She sighed when he leaned into her and nibbled her throat. "Was Holland's news urgent?"

"Not really." Holland had lectured him about Arabella again until Merrick had confessed to his change of mind about the urgency of marriage. He wanted to see what came of a longer friendship with Arabella before he hunted for a wife again. "I swear that man should have been a woman the way he fusses."

"He is very fond of you."

"And of course I am so very lovable." He laughed as he removed his footwear and flexed his toes. He wanted Arabella comfortable with nudity, hers and his. He planned to explore every inch of her lush body, and it would certainly not be under the cover of a comforter. He would coax her lustful impulses and hope she enjoyed his.

She smoothed her hands over his banyan, straightening what didn't need straightening. Merrick removed the pin from his cravat and tossed it carelessly behind him. Holland would find it in the morning. There would be little chance of hiding what he was about to do anyway. Merrick untied his cravat. "Have you written to Grayling and his wife yet?"

"Not yet. Grayling will be sorry to have missed you."

He shrugged, finished removing his cravat, and dropped it to the floor. "I will catch Gray another time or he will catch me in London."

When Arabella smiled, a little of her tension seemed to slip away. He moved closer and set his lips to her neck again. Her spine arched and a soft moan left her lips.

Merrick cupped the other side of her face. "Enough of tomorrow. What will come will come."

He kissed her lips when she turned her face to his. He brushed his thumb over the smooth curve of her dewy, soft cheek as he deepened the kiss, using his tongue to induce further pleasure. Her response was to clutch at his shirt and pull him closer. Merrick quickly shifted her onto his lap and plundered her mouth, listening to the little whimpers she uttered. Pleasing Arabella was the one thing that mattered tonight. He would face the rest tomorrow.

He cupped her breast gently in the palm of his hand, noticing the way she stiffened against the intimate touch and treasuring her response all the more. Truly untouched. He thrilled to know he would be her first lover. He had never expected that.

Merrick slowly thumbed her nipple, brushing over the peak until it pebbled. When she pushed her chest into his hand, he squeezed and massaged her, all the while giving in to the impulse to indulge in never-ending kisses.

She had a mouth made to be kissed. Sweet, lush, and hungry like his. He slowly removed his hand from her breast and stroked down her body. She tensed again when he touched her hip and he lingered there a long while, allowing her to grow used to the pressure.

When her hands threaded through his hair, he progressed down her leg, caught the bottom of the banyan, and lifted it until he touched her bare knee. Arabella broke the kiss and squeezed her eyes shut, her breath a fast pant against his cheek.

He stroked up her calf. "You have lovely legs. It is a pity ladies' fashions hide them from proper admiration."

She drew back, stared at him, and then buried her face in his throat with a laugh. "My whole life I have wanted to be short."

Merrick smiled at her mood. Playfulness in bed was preferable to terror. "You are the perfect height. Never doubt that." He raised his hand higher, sliding it under the banyan she wore, letting her warmth brand his fingers. When he touched softer skin, he paused. Smooth, slim thighs greeted him. But they were firmly pressed together.

Determined to proceed, he sought her mouth and when she kissed him in return and relaxed again, he took the opportunity to part her thighs. She squeaked a protest, but he continued, sliding his hand up her inner thigh until he reached the apex. Damp curls brushed his fingertips and he lingered, knowing by her trembling reaction that he was the first to touch her there.

The experience was heady and he drew back to look into her face, to memorize the moment. She looked so surprised that he kissed her cheek. "Sweetheart, I cannot wait to bring you pleasure."

Her hand settled against his chest, her fingers playfully twisting into the light dusting of hair revealed by his parted shirt. "And how will you do that?"

"Wait and see."

He nudged her thighs wider and then stroked between her legs. Arabella jerked away, but he soothed her with inarticulate words and brushed against her a little more firmly. She was wet, but she likely didn't know why. Poor darling. He'd soon show her the pleasure he could give. He stroked his fingers along her sensitive skin, catching the twist of her hips when he neared her clitoris.

He focused there, softly at first but returning again and again with firmer pressure until she was sobbing, churning her sex against him. He paused to probe her entrance with the tip of his finger and then alternated the pressure so she'd grow accustomed to his invasion.

The tension in her thighs softened and allowed greater access. His fingers slipped through her moisture easily, and encouraged, he kissed her brow. "Ready for more?"

Arabella nodded quickly as he slowly pressed one finger inside her tight confines. She squirmed, clearly unnerved by his actions. As he teased her, repeating the movement, he brushed his thumb over her clitoris, bringing her deeper into her desires. Merrick increased his movements, listening to the rasp of her breathing, enjoying the scrape of her fingertips against his chest, and finally the sudden tension that clamped her body around his finger. Her breath hitched as she experience her first release of the night.

Merrick stilled the movements of his hand but laid it over her mound. "There now. Isn't that better?"

She gulped air and when she finally looked up at him, she appeared dazed. Merrick kissed her lips, drew her tightly against his chest. There was so much more to give her. So much joy and tenderness that he couldn't wait to bestow on her. He stood, taking her with him, nestled in his arms.

She clutched his shirt. "What are you doing? I'm too tall to be carried."

"Not to me, and I'm taking you where you've always belonged. Into my bed."

Arabella stared at Rothwell as he placed her in the center of his large bed. She had never dreamed such pleasures could be found simply from a man's hand. She'd be embarrassed or worse except her limbs were as heavy as lead and coherent thought was a struggle. No wonder the ladies sighed over him.

Rothwell stripped her of her remaining clothes and she allowed it without considering a word of protest. When he removed his own clothing and climbed in beside her, displaying his bare skin to her startled eyes, she glanced at the candles anxiously. "Shouldn't you..."

Rothwell smiled widely and then kissed her cheek, his breath hot enough to make her sigh contentedly. "No. Seductions are much more decadent when you can see the effect you have on your lover. And Arabella, I want to see all of you. Every moment between us must be remembered."

A little startled by his statement, she dropped her eyes to his bare chest, studying the unfamiliar sight that stirred her all over again. She peeked lower and couldn't miss his arousal. So many unasked questions flooded her mind but she hid them, determined not to give herself away.

He eased onto his side and the heat in his gaze warmed her

all over. "Have you grown shy of me again?"

Perhaps she had. There was quite a bit more to making love than she'd first expected. Rothwell's intensity was overwhelming and would take some getting used to. "I'm sorry."

His fingertips skimmed her hipbone and she jumped because it tickled. A soft chuckle left him and he laid his hand flat over the place. "Don't be. There is nothing more appealing than seeing you in any state. Shy or bold, I have always admired you."

As Arabella met Rothwell's gaze, she wondered how far his admiration went. His behavior was nothing like she'd expected, and she definitely liked getting to know his character better. His consideration and tenderness was rather sweet actually. The smile on his face showed he was not alarmed or even disappointed by her timidity. She'd made the right choice for her first lover.

Determined to press on, she set her hand to his bare chest and fluttered her fingers over his skin the way he had done to her. A low groan left his mouth as she touched him. He remained still and let her explore and learn the warmth and contours of his upper body. He was remarkably robust and appealing, and she circled his flat nipples, smiling to herself as he groaned. When she'd touched all she could reach, her face was hot with a fiery blush.

"Bella, my darling," he whispered against her lips. "Dear God, I want you more than words can say."

A burst of happiness caused her to smile and she stretched to press her lips to his. Rothwell dragged her flush against him and she didn't resist or mind his sudden impatience. He draped her upper leg over his, aligning their hips quite scandalously. But he didn't let her remember where she was for long. His kisses filled her awareness. The occasional rasp of new whiskers against her skin was pleasant, and the scent and warmth of him turned her mind in one direction only—experiencing more bliss.

She curled her arms about his neck as he rolled to bring her beneath him. His strength and muscular thighs between her own caused her breath to catch. She clung to him as sensation upon sensation swamped her. His hard length brushed her leg, burning hot and foreign to her. She broke the kiss and met his gaze.

He swallowed. "You are everything I dreamed of and so much more."

"You dreamed of me?"

He buried his face in the curve of her neck. "Every damn night." His words were a coarse growl, swiftly followed by a change of position. He slid a hand beneath her hips as his jerked forward. A sudden sharp pain caused a yelp to leave her throat before she could prepare herself for the loss of her virginity.

Arabella waited for Rothwell to denounce her. To cry foul that she'd tricked him. However, he remained still within her, motionless above her, his rough pant against her throat a comforting presence. He groaned and eased back. "I'm sorry. It'll pass soon," he whispered.

After a few thrusts, the pain faded only to be replaced by urgency. She threaded her fingers through his hair and held on, certain that he would bring her to that perfect place of passion again. His movements grew wild as he urged her legs farther apart. She wrapped them about his hips when urged to do so and hung on as her body once more tensed and shuddered with the force of her desire.

Rothwell's rumbling groan ended with his sudden stillness and then he jerked from her body, his shoulders shaking violently beneath her clutching hands. Warmth splattered across her thigh and she lifted her head to see. The next instant, he collapsed atop her, hot, slick with sweat, and more familiar and dear than Arabella dreamed anyone could ever be. He rested his weight on her briefly before rolling off again.

She was no longer a virgin, but was now Rothwell's lover. The thought made her happy. Now she knew why other women smiled so smugly when they whispered about their gentlemen friends. Rothwell was so skilled that making love again, even with that necessary first burst of pain, was highly desirable.

Rothwell wriggled closer and when he offered a place in his arms, Arabella snuggled against his side and listened to the fast beat of his heart. He held her firmly against his chest, pressed a long kiss to her hair, and sighed deeply. He didn't speak, and Arabella didn't mind the silence. His hands wandered restlessly over her skin, and she touched him in return. A candle spluttered and died, casting the chamber in deep shadow.

She held herself to Rothwell, unwilling for their time alone to be over. If she had but one night to spend with him, she would revel in every moment. "Thank you."

His fingers fluttered over her lips to shush her.

When she lifted her chin, Rothwell kissed her lips softly and dragged her atop his body before sighing deeply. The unfamiliar position alarmed her momentarily until he drew her higher and brought one nipple into his mouth. He suckled on the peak and she squirmed.

Although it barely seemed possible, warmth pooled between her thighs again. Could all men elicit such desires, or was it simply Rothwell who sparked the flame? She met his gaze and her body shook until finally she grabbed his head and held him to her breast.

It seemed there was quite a bit more about pleasure that Rothwell could teach her. She'd be a fool let one last opportunity slip away so soon. She loosened her hold on him and ran her fingers through his wavy dark hair. The firm tug on her nipple made it hard to remain still. "That was perfect."

Rothwell released her and feathered kisses all over her breast. "No, you are."

He tumbled her over onto her back and held her down with the weight of his body, his teeth flashing white in the dim light as he grinned. "We've hours of night left to play and please each other."

"Hours?"

"Certainly." He lifted up and then rolled her onto her stomach. "Take your back for instance." He shifted her hair aside and kissed the top of her spine. "A tall woman has much more skin—a man can devote hours to kissing."

She squirmed as he proved his point, giggling from the certainty that he was teasing her and thoroughly enjoying doing so.

"Then there are her delightfully long legs. You have no idea how many hours of thought I've put into imagining them wrapped about my hips." He kissed the back of her knee suddenly and she flipped over.

"Please be serious."

He rose to his knees at the foot of the bed. "Arabella. Sex

doesn't have to be a serious matter. It can be a great deal of fun and delight for both of us. A man doesn't have to be inside the woman for them both to find fulfillment."

"Really?"

He caught her ankle and ran his hand up her leg, forcing her to part them involuntarily. He slid between them on his stomach and laid his head on her inner thigh. "Nothing would please me more than to prove it."

And without another word, Rothwell showed her exactly what he liked best. Again and again through the long hours of the night.

Chapter Twenty

Merrick crept across his bedchamber and stared down at the sleeping woman strewn across his bed. To finally make love to Arabella, to have been her first lover, was a heady, exhilarating experience. One of her long legs was in plain view, not under the bedding, tempting him to return and make love to her all over again.

Yet he could not. Not until he had taken care of a few things first. He and Arabella had to talk about the consequences of last night. Merrick would never abandon her. Not when she made him feel things he'd longed for all his life.

In the early hours of the morning, when Arabella had succumbed to exhaustion, he'd imagined a pleasant fantasy of a life with her as his wife. He would be so good to her. She would never want for anything. The one difficulty that blackened their happiness was her determination to keep her freedom.

He sighed and leaned against the bedpost. He did have to leave today, but he wanted to be certain he could return. He hoped to convince her to visit with Grayling and his wife while he was away dealing with family affairs, and then they could continue what had only just begun between them.

She stirred as he sat on the edge of the bed. It was like watching his sun rise. She stretched beneath the sheet and blinked up at the curtained canopy, a contented smile playing at the corners of her mouth. His heart tumbled over, adding to his certainty that she was the one for him.

"Good morning," he said gently.

Regardless of his soft tone and their passions of last night, she scrambled for the sheets to cover her body. "Rothwell?"

He perused whatever curves remained in view and then forced the memory of her passionate responses firmly aside. He couldn't think clearly around her when he was aroused. Last night had been bad enough. She'd almost escaped him because of his befuddlement. But in the morning light, mussed from sleep and his lovemaking, Arabella was near to irresistible. A siren unveiled. He met her gaze and tried his best to keep it there. "I think, perhaps, we are beyond the use of titles. I would be pleased if you would call me Merrick."

"Merrick," she said softly, her lips curving into an inviting smile. No blush today, but her skin glowed with health and vitality. The siren had woken and he was powerless.

He leaned in and paused a moment before he brushed a light kiss across her lips. "Did you sleep well?"

When he drew back, Arabella was blushing. "I did, thank you. Could you please tell me the time?"

"Almost nine."

She sat up suddenly, glancing around the room. "Oh no."

Merrick sat back with a satisfied smile. The siren was adorable when she was uncertain. "Did you not factor the morning into your plans before you came to seduce me?"

She held the sheet tightly against her breasts, depriving Merrick of the perfect view. "I did not imagine I'd fall asleep. Usually I have trouble sleeping anywhere else but in my own bed."

He smiled. "It can happen if one is properly sated. I can happily accept that I exhausted you."

Another blush swept her cheeks and she glanced down. "You did that very well."

Merrick slipped his finger under her chin and lifted her gaze. "You were untouched before you came to my bed. You should have been honest with me."

Her eyes widened in panic and he tightened his grip so he was holding her chin firmly. He wanted nothing less than her complete honesty.

She quickly nodded. "I was, and I'd be grateful if you could keep the embarrassing discovery to yourself. I'm in your debt."

"My debt." Merrick stood, suddenly irritated by her attitude. The gift she'd granted him was beyond price. "I should be the one to be grateful."

"I don't understand. You seduce women every day."

A bitter laugh slipped past his control. "Not respectable women like you. An honorable man would offer to marry you after such a night and the discovery he'd taken something so precious, but you don't want that, do you?" He strode to the tall windows and threw the drapes wide, unnerved by how easily his own truths tumbled from his lips when in her company. If this continued, he'd be confessing the secret of his first boyhood fantasy.

The bed sheets rustled. "Last night doesn't necessarily need to change things between us."

He glanced over his shoulder and immediately wished he hadn't. Arabella sat in a puddle of bed sheets, legs crossed and her shoulders bared to his gaze. Long strands of pale hair tumbled over her limbs, tempting him to wrap his hands around her and never let go.

"How many times have I wanted you and thought you disinterested? But you were not the woman of experience I imagined you must be. You were as innocent as any new bride come to her husband's bed," he said quietly.

A rush of color swept her cheeks at his observation. "Those days are behind me. I was a virgin. But that was yesterday."

Merrick could understand her willingness to throw propriety aside to experience passion, but what did that mean for him? Did she view him as a passing fancy? He had to know. "And what will you do now that your virginity has been taken? Bat your lashes at gentleman and invite them to your bed while expecting me to ignore your trysts without a word of protest?"

"No." She fought to free herself from the bed and scrambled into his discarded banyan. "I'll go on as I always have. I thought we were friends. You're still friends with your previous lovers, are you not?"

"I am, but everything is different now. There is the slightest chance you could be carrying a child at this very moment. Did you even think of that?" He was satisfied when her hand touched her belly. She appeared startled but not unduly alarmed that she could be carrying his babe. "I do not usually make mistakes in such matters, but with you I am utterly reckless. With all the half brothers and sisters I have, I can ill afford to continue that family tradition." He set his hands to his hips. "What if I cannot forget last night? What if I cannot ignore the fact that I had you in my bed? I want you back there already."

Her brow creased in a frown. "I…I'm sorry. It was my problem I sought to remedy, and I thought this wouldn't change anything for you."

He moved close to her. He needed to be near her again. In his arms would be better. "I cannot forget last night as easily as you will forget me."

Her eyes widened. "I never said I would forget you. You've been so kind to me."

"I'm not kind, Arabella. I'm in love with you." At her silence, Merrick spun on his heel and headed for the door. "I'll see your breakfast is brought to your bedchamber so we might say good-bye in proper surroundings."

Merrick slammed the door behind him, appalled that he'd blurted out the state of his heart and received nothing in return. *Devil take it.* Pleasing Arabella last night had not been in his best interests. He couldn't let her go. The idea was impossible.

He made arrangements for a breakfast tray to be prepared and then sat down on the staircase steps to await its delivery, pondering his next actions. He still had to order his carriage and gain Arabella's agreement to visit with Grayling for the day before he could attend to family matters and then return to plead his case. In all he had at most an hour without interruption to get her agreement that marriage was the next logical step, or at least as something to consider.

Holland appeared before him, a deeply disapproving expression on his face. "Do you want the carriage brought up now?"

Merrick stared at Holland. "In an hour."

Holland's brows pinched together. "What troubles you?"

"Oh, everything. Go away, brother. I have no need of your counsel right now."

"Suit yourself." Holland's eyes turned pitying.

"Wait. Be a good fellow and hurry that breakfast tray along."

Holland rushed off and, a few minutes later, returned with the tray in his hands. "It goes without saying there are no secrets in a country house. I assume you would prefer to deliver her tray yourself?"

Merrick held out his hands and took the tray. This was what came of giving in to his yearnings for Arabella. He'd ruined a very proper lady. He plodded up the stairs, stopping when Arabella's bedchamber door was before him. He juggled the tray and knocked, half expecting to be kept waiting a very long time. She bid him enter immediately, though it was with a voice so quiet he grew afraid he'd ruined everything between them.

Merrick slipped inside, making sure to lock the door behind him. Arabella had taken refuge on a crimson settee, still wrapped snugly in his silk banyan. He set the tray on the small side table and uncovered the dishes.

She leaned over immediately and took a warm fruit scone. "These are my favorites. Thank you."

"You have your cook to thank, not me."

He took one himself and moved to the very end of the settee. He might want to sit nearer and touch her body again, but he wasn't sure of his reception after his sudden confession that he'd fallen in love with her. They ate in silence.

"No one has ever loved me before," she said softly.

She'd been untouched for certain. The blood on his previously pristine bedsheets attested to that fact. A small wave of guilt swept over him. He could have been gentler. "I promise you will feel no further discomfort from now on."

Her brow creased and she clenched her hands together. "You misunderstand. No one has ever told me they loved me. I'm not certain what you want from me or what to do."

Her eyes were twin pools of confusion and he slid along the settee until they sat side by side. He took her hand in his. "There is nothing you need do if you don't wish to. 'Tis the state of my heart, and I doubt it will deviate from its chosen path."

"Surely there's hope your feelings will pass. We've known each other for so short a time."

He winced. "I'm told you cannot choose who you fall in love

with, and I have discovered it's impossible to fight it. You were happily married when we first met, and then I thought you might make a match with Grayling. I never dreamed I'd get a chance to know you better."

"Oh?" Her hand landed on his thigh and the touch seared through his trousers.

He picked up her hand and pressed his lips to her knuckles. "I am so glad you came to my door."

She leaned her head against his shoulder. "I was never happily married, you know."

Merrick drew her into his arms and held her. Such a sad statement and one he'd certainly heard from other women in society. But Arabella had hidden her misery better than most. If he'd had the smallest inkling, he'd probably have acted long before this. He rocked her in his arms, so grateful for the chance to be alone with her.

But he did not want her to dwell on the past. He wanted to make her happy now. He kissed her lips gently, and then deeper when she held on to him. "I have to go soon."

"Back to London?"

"No. There is nothing I want in London now. I have to visit my half sister and decide what to do about another of my father's illegitimate sons."

"What's happened?"

"His mother died and he's been living with another half sibling, but she's overwhelmed. We promised to take the boy away this trip and lighten her burdens."

"Oh." She sat up and grabbed his hand. "May I help in any way?"

He shook his head. He couldn't take her to meet other members of his family and have her become more involved in his life. There was no need if she didn't love him in return. "I'd like to take you to visit Grayling for the day before I go, and when I come back I was wondering if we might talk again."

Her thumb caressed the back of his hand. "I should like that. I can be ready to go in an hour."

He raised her hand to her lips one last time and kissed it. "Thank you, Arabella. I hate to go, but I have obligations that I cannot avoid no matter how much I wish to stay."

She smiled suddenly. “That is actually one of your best qualities, Merrick. You never turn your back on your family or your friends.”

Chapter Twenty-One

Visiting Lord Grayling's neighboring estate and sipping tea on the lawn was a beautiful respite for a troubled mind. Arabella smiled as Grayling's children cavorted on the lawn with hoops and brightly colored leather balls in the company of their new mother and doting father. The happy scene made her heart lighter, but she was aware she was feeling out of place. Matching Grayling with his lover, while scandalous and not without risk, had been the right thing to do. They were all so happy together.

Yet part of Arabella's mind was as restless as a stormy night. She'd had a hard time conversing with her friends while she grappled with the concept of Merrick in love. And with her, no less. She'd never imagined him besotted with anyone, and she didn't know what to say to him when he returned from his errand.

Grayling sank into the chair beside her. "You're quiet today."

"It's been a troubling week or so."

"So Rothwell mentioned." Grayling took her half-full cup from her fingers and set it on the bench beside him. "He was a trifle vague about the details though. I trust he's been on his best behavior?"

"Yes. He's been a great friend to me."

"Well, then. I am glad to know he's lived up to your expectations," Grayling said slowly. "He is a good man. Society doesn't know the half of his character."

But Arabella did and that's what troubled her. Merrick had told her so much about his life, about his troubles with his family, and about his concerns for his half siblings' welfare that her feelings were torn. She was drowning in instances of his good deeds, yet she couldn't answer truthfully if she loved him in return. "I have seen enough instances of his kindness and generosity to believe you."

Grayling sat forward, elbows resting on his knees as he watched his young family at play. "I worry for him some days. When we were young, he flitted from woman to woman without ever looking back or leaving hard feelings in his wake. When passions cooled, he could move on to a new lover without regret."

"Some people are like that. They don't feel deeply."

"But he does." Grayling shook his head. "I simply think he hasn't found the woman who is meant for him yet while I've been blessed with love twice."

Tightness closed Arabella's throat. She had to clear it several times before she felt sure her words would not betray her. "Perhaps he'll marry this season."

"I hope so." He glanced over his shoulder. "Now, while my delightful wife is distracted by the children, will you please tell me what you asked her advice on last winter? It's driving me insane."

She grimaced. She'd hoped he might have forgotten that business. When she'd met Rosemary during the previous winter, she'd seized the chance to ask some frank questions she couldn't ask of anyone else. Grayling would never approve. "A personal matter."

"You were *my* friend first." He scowled. "At least I can be certain I'll learn what it is before Rothwell does."

Arabella faced the garden too. Merrick had been instrumental in seeing Lady Grayling's advice put into practice. With Rosemary's help, she'd been as well prepared as any new bride for what had happened in Merrick's bed, and it still hadn't been enough. She caught herself many times dwelling on what they'd done together. She'd been completely unprepared for how the experience had changed her. She could not stop thinking of Merrick today.

"Don't tell me *he* knows too?"

When she winced, Grayling stood and walked a few steps away. "For goodness sake, why on earth would you tell Rothwell?"

She stared at his broad back, feeling nothing but friendship for Grayling and mild irritation that he wasn't taking her silence well. "Because the matter wasn't something that concerned you."

He ran his hand through his hair. "Are you ill?"

"No."

"Penniless?"

Now that was a question for another day. She did not know exactly how her finances stood at the present moment. She would likely need Gray's assistance, or Merrick's if they continued as friends, to discover where she stood if she did not want to deal with Farnsworth directly. "Not quite."

He stared hard at her. "With child and the bastard won't offer to marry you?"

The terrace door banged behind them and Rosemary hurried out, one hand held protectively over her growing belly. "Grayling, do end your inquisition and lower your voice. Can you not see our dear Arabella's heart is already under siege?"

"What the devil!" He turned on his wife angrily. "You stay out of it. Don't give me the business of it not being my business. If not for your interference then I might have been able to solve Arabella's problem already."

Rosemary's lips firmed in a tight line, her eyes narrowed to slits. "Is that so?"

With no way now to deflect Grayling and a fight brewing between them over the misunderstanding, Arabella raised her hands to admit defeat. "Oh, for heaven's sake, this is ridiculous. I will not have the pair of you fight over who is the better friend. I went to London with the intention of finding a lover, Gray. You certainly would not have helped me with that. I asked Rosemary's advice on intimacy and she was kind enough to answer my questions. There, now you know almost every humiliating detail."

Grayling spun so fast to face her that he staggered a few steps. His mouth opened, then closed. He glanced between Arabella and his wife and then spun about again and left in a rush, heading for the stables.

Rosemary sighed heavily and sank onto the bench beside Arabella. "Maybe next time he will believe me when I say he doesn't need to know. From what I've gleaned, he sees you as a sister. One never wants to imagine one's siblings engaged in intimate acts."

"Perhaps." Arabella slumped. "What am I going to do?"

"I take it that Rothwell has turned your head around."

Rosemary just might be the most perceptive woman she'd ever met. "I never said it was him."

"My dear, you did not have to." Rosemary shifted closer. "I have eyes enough to see a hungry man staring at what he wants to devour. It surprises me that Gray hasn't guessed the two of you are involved. You have spent quite a few days with him, more or less alone, and I've never seen a man so reluctant to leave a lady, even in the care of his friends."

A smile tugged at Arabella's lips as she thought of Merrick's protracted leave taking. "He is protective."

"I think with good reason. What haven't you told Grayling about the season?"

"Quite a bit. I didn't want to worry him."

"Do you want to talk about it?"

"I don't know that it would do any good." She sighed. "I failed as a chaperone, was physically assaulted by my brother-in-law, almost forced into marriage with someone I barely knew and didn't care for, then slept with a man who should have been wicked except he claimed to love me."

Rosemary slipped an arm around her back and hugged her close. "A busy season."

She glanced sideways. "Far beyond anything I had anticipated."

"Life can be like that," Rosemary said and then sighed heavily. "I see now why you were reluctant to tell Gray the whole story and why Rothwell has become protective of you. Are you all right?"

Arabella was about to answer when a large hand clapped over her shoulder.

"Who the hell seduced you?" Grayling demanded.

Arabella sat up at the anger in his voice. A hot flush had

swept over his features and he looked fit to kill.

"When did you return?"

"Not soon enough," he growled. "Now answer me. Who do I have to kill?"

Rosemary clucked her tongue. "Really, darling, can you not guess who might have a claim on Arabella's affections?"

His gaze darted between them and then his eyes narrowed. "Rothwell? Damn him. I'll kill the bastard when he returns."

"Oh no, you will not." Arabella wasn't about to be bullied by Grayling. She was more than capable of managing her own intimate affairs. "Not when I was the one who asked him to."

His eyes widened, and then his stare became quite unnerving. Was this what it was like to have a brother to answer to? All of a sudden he grinned. "This is perfect. He'll marry you."

Rosemary shook her head sadly and stood. "I'll leave him to you, my dear, but if you need help banging some sense into his head, I'll do my best."

Although Arabella had never held back in prior conversations with Grayling, she wouldn't have minded having Rosemary at her side for this one. She glared at her friend. "Excuse me?"

Grayling tucked his hands behind his back and began to pace along the flagstone squares. "I should be furious, but there is an easy way out of this situation. I don't want to lose my best friend, but if he doesn't propose to you then I'm going to enjoy hurting him. The two of you will simply marry and that will be that."

"We'll do no such thing." Arabella sighed and collected her cup and saucer to put them on the tray for a servant to take. "I don't intend to marry. Excuse me, I'd like to visit with the children again before Merrick returns."

"Merrick now, is it?" Gray teased.

"Oh, keep quiet." She turned toward the house. "It's not like you've never been in a similar situation," she muttered.

"I'll remind you that I didn't expect to marry again either," Grayling reminded her as he blocked her escape. "But a very good friend threw the perfect woman at me and I had a second chance to have a fulfilling life. You deserve to be in love."

Rothwell had claimed her perfect, but she didn't think that true. There were many things she would change about herself if she could. "It's not the same. I don't have the faintest idea of whether I love him."

His eyes narrowed at her admission. "There's nothing to stop you being as happy as we are. You just have to be brave enough to jump."

She sank into a chair. "I'm not sure I am ready to marry again."

"Then that is an impediment only you can overcome. Rothwell has proven he's a man of honor by protecting you as he did. I'm not entirely happy about your affair, but only you can decide whether he's worth the risk of loving." Grayling leaned down and kissed the top of her head. "If he makes you happy, Bella, then tell me what have you got to lose? You have my blessing, if that helps. Augusta would approve, too, I think. She always had a soft spot for him."

The casual mention of Grayling's first wife, Augusta, once her best friend, brought tears to her eyes. She had missed Augusta desperately these past years and longed to hear her opinion. But Arabella was alone and had to make all decisions about her life without help. Only she could decide whether what she had with Rothwell was love or something far less.

When Stanton Harold Hall came into view, ice formed in the pit of his stomach. For the whole of the trip to collect his youngest half brother, he'd missed Arabella and now feared what she'd say to him about the addition to their outing. At his side sat his father's last mistake, a boy of eight years whose mother had recently passed and needed a home. The boy would live with him from now until he was old enough for schooling. He touched Danny's shoulder gently. "Dry your tears and be a good lad while I collect Lady Farnsworth."

Young Danny sniffed miserably but nodded. "I will, my lord."

"Good lad." He glanced at Holland's worried face. "Once the carriage and horses have been seen to, take him for a stroll about Grayling's gardens. Grayling won't mind and the boy won't be in the way there while you await us."

"An excellent idea." Holland ruffled the boy's hair as Merrick left the carriage. "We might even be able to rustle up a sweet cake or two if we ask nicely."

The pair had grown closer by the minute during their journey. He had hoped young Danny would bond with one of the others, but perhaps Holland was the best choice for a motherless boy. It would mean the child was about the town house more often rather than the stables, but at least there he could be kept watch over and would adopt the mannerisms of a gentleman more quickly.

He grinned at Grayling's butler, Cunningham, as he passed through the impressive double doors of Stanton Harold Hall and then glanced around the dim interior. Grayling strode forward to meet him at the door. "Grayling."

"Bastard," Gray muttered. "Come with me. We need to talk."

Merrick quickly looked for Arabella but didn't see her anywhere. Although he wouldn't be comfortable until he'd laid eyes on her again, he reluctantly followed Gray back outside and onto the lawns. When they stopped beside a shady tree, Merrick caught Gray's arm. "What's going on?"

"I should ask you the same thing." Grayling drew closer and Merrick was astonished to see his hands curl into fists. "I won't allow you to toy with Arabella's affections."

It was on the tip of his tongue to deny he was involved with Arabella, but this was his best friend. Her best friend too, and she'd clearly confided in him while Merrick was off on family business. "I won't pursue her if you're so set against us."

"But you'll ruin her."

"Not intentionally. Unfortunately, she's against marriage."

Grayling frowned. "I cannot understand why. Farnsworth treated her well from all I saw."

Farnsworth had neglected her, paying no attention to her opinions from what he could discern. Merrick would not make the mistake of doing the same. "I love her," he said simply. Being apart for the whole day and worrying about how she fared was a new experience for Merrick, though not entirely unpleasant.

"Then propose."

"I'd rather not have her think it's because you demanded it, if it's all the same to you." He shook his head. "I do have a special license at home."

"Then use it."

"I intend to. I was actually on the hunt for a bride while I was in London. I had whittled down my selection to three when Arabella sought my protection. Do you have any idea how fast a man can lose interest in other women once he sees an opportunity?"

"To seduce her? You bloody bastard."

"To get to know her without society watching." Merrick shrugged. "I don't know why you're so put out with me. It's not as if I'm trespassing on your territory. Oh, and did I criticize you for marrying your governess, who when I met her the first time went by an entirely different name?"

Merrick was well aware that the current Lady Grayling had an entirely murky past that no one ever brought up in conversation. Eventually he hoped Gray would confide in him.

Grayling scowled. "That was different."

"You're correct. The situations are as different as night and day. I will not rush Arabella with an offer of marriage when she is uncertain she wants more. When I do marry, I don't want to feel my bride chose me because she has not choice. Now, may we return to the house so I can say farewell properly to your charming wife and children? It will be dark soon and I want to deliver Arabella home to Winslette where she's happiest."

Gray pressed his lips together and then gestured toward the house. They returned without speaking. Merrick wasn't unduly surprised about Grayling finding out he'd slept with Arabella. It was reasonable that she'd confide in him. He just didn't like Grayling's assertion that they had to wed or else.

They found the ladies in the conservatory, children running around them and squealing. Arabella smiled shyly, fingers twisting at her waist. "You're back."

He nodded. Although he ached to touch her, Merrick concluded that being too forward in front of friends might embarrass her, so he reluctantly kept his distance. "A small difficulty. I'll explain in the carriage if I may."

"Of course." They chatted a bit longer and then it was

Arabella who claimed it was time to go. "I've been away so long and there is much to do."

Lady Grayling took her arm and led her toward the entrance hall. "There always is. Remember what I told you to do tonight. Come back and see us soon. Bring Rothwell with you for a longer visit if you like."

"I will." Arabella kissed her cheek, her cheeks burning quite red. "Until next time." She stole a glance at Merrick before rushing toward the carriage.

"Rosemary," Grayling growled. "Now what did you tell her to do?"

His wife looked anything but contrite. "An additional lesson. Nothing you've not had experience with."

Merrick glanced between them. "Have I missed something?"

Lady Grayling laughed as her husband followed Arabella out the door. "You did, but hopefully you won't feel so neglected after tonight is over. Good night, Rothwell. Please don't keep my friend waiting."

Puzzled, he joined Arabella in the carriage. Holland and young Danny were already seated with her. He quickly performed the introductions and then turned to Arabella. "What lesson did Lady Grayling have to share?"

"Later." Her face flamed. "Much later, in fact."

As the carriage left Grayling's estate, sniffling drew his attention. The boy was still upset, and Merrick was at a loss as to how to comfort him. Arabella suddenly leaned forward and took the child's hand in hers. "Partings are always hard, Danny."

The boy nodded, his weeping eyes locked on hers.

Arabella smiled. "When we get to Winslette, you must help me pick a room for you. You may have any unoccupied chamber for your own tonight as long as you are careful with my possessions."

Danny's eyes darted to Holland.

Arabella released him and sat back. "Even the one beside Holland's. I believe it is unoccupied too, so you are in luck."

The boy sat back as well and seemed much more at ease. Had he merely been worried he'd be left alone on his first night away from all he'd known? Merrick wouldn't do that to the boy.

Arabella caught his eye and he smiled at her. She truly was

good to comfort a boy she should never have paid notice to.

Holland cleared his throat. “Shall I inform the men we return to London tomorrow and have the carriage prepared for an early start?”

The return trip would take three days, and then he’d have nothing to look forward to but the boy’s care. Arabella made no protest and extended no invitation for him to stay. He studied her face, looking for signs she disagreed, and saw nothing to give him hope. He nodded but he wished he didn’t have to go. Arabella was all he could think about. He might very well need his brother’s stubborn nature to make him leave her and Winslette behind.

Chapter Twenty-Two

Arabella slipped inside Merrick's chamber and shut the door firmly behind her. She was confronted by his bare back, and her pulse raced as she discovered he was completely naked already. She licked her lips as her body reacted. "I had hoped to see you again."

He tossed the shirt he'd been holding across the room and sat on the edge of the bed. "I considered visiting your room."

She moved closer to see his face. He'd been silent and watchful at dinner and had only picked at his food. She hoped he wasn't annoyed with her for telling Gray and Rosemary about them. "Then why didn't you?"

He shook his head. "I wanted to."

She stopped at his side and lifted her hand to his hair. When she touched his head, he leaned into her palm. "I wanted you to, as well."

Finally, a smile. He caught her about her hips and drew her body between his knees. "I'm glad."

Between them, his length thickened and grew while she watched in wonder. Discovering just how easily he became aroused and how comfortable with it he seemed brought a smile to her lips. She'd learned much about pleasure from him and intended to thank him in a very personal way.

Slowly he toppled backward, taking Arabella with him so

they lay on the bed together. The heat of his body beneath her scorched her through two layers of nightclothes. She wore his banyan again over her nightgown, but the material was not thick enough to prevent awareness of every inch of him. When she was comfortable atop him, his hands danced over her covered bottom. "You're wearing my banyan again."

"I like it. It feels lovely against my skin."

He wriggled his hand between them and untied the belt. "I like you naked against me."

"I did notice that." She studied his face. "I wish you didn't have to go tomorrow."

He freed one of her arms from the robe and tugged the tie on her nightgown undone. "I wish I didn't need to go, too."

"I suppose you must have much to do for the boy?"

"I'm not going for that reason. The boy will live with me for a while before he eventually goes off to school." He forced her nightgown over her shoulder and kissed her bare skin. His lips, their startling caress, forced a moan from her throat in response. He chuckled softly, then continued, "I don't want to ruin your reputation. I'm not sure we'll avoid gossips as it is, but staying here any longer will only make the tongues wag worse."

Arabella at last understood how difficult it was to be good when you desperately wanted to touch someone. Doing without him today had been difficult. She was amazed at her restraint in not dragging him to a secluded corner every time he smiled her way since his return. "I know there is the risk of that, but I could never regret one moment spent in your arms."

He kissed her fiercely, tangling his tongue with hers and setting her senses on fire. Before she knew it, she was beneath him on the bed, her nightgown at her waist, his hands everywhere at once.

Remembering what she'd set out to do, Arabella pushed against his chest. "Lie down for me. Please."

He groaned and flipped to his back. "Woman, you're not going to make me beg, are you?"

"No." She rose onto her hands and knees as Rosemary had suggested and hovered at his side. Tonight she wanted to explore Rothwell with her lips and hands as he had done to her last night. Rosemary had explained as best she could, but the challenge she'd set herself was daunting. Merrick had likely had a lot of lovers, and they all might do this one thing better than she ever would. "I'd hate to make you beg for anything, but lie there and don't move."

She bent her head and kissed his shoulder, his chest, and then his flat nipple. He grunted as she licked it experimentally. When she attempted to draw the little bud into her mouth, he cursed. "Damn, now I know what Lady Grayling whispered to you."

She grinned. That wasn't *all* Rosemary had mentioned. Just the first in a series of suggestions that had made her eyes pop from her head. "You should thank her. If not for Rose, I'd have been even more clueless than I was."

He cupped her head and played with her hair. "I'd happily take over your education in passion, but the way you make me feel leads me to think you don't need the help."

She kissed the center of his chest and slowly worked her way down to his belly. "Are you sure? I imagine there are many things you like that escape me."

She kissed his hip, right where the bones protruded beneath his skin and he squirmed. "Believe me, you're already doing it."

She glanced up his body, noting he was breathing hard, and smiled. She moved ever so slowly until her face hovered above his cock and then met his gaze. The poor man looked about to throw her over and pounce. Tonight she would resist. Or at least try to. "Are you sure there isn't one thing you would want me to do?"

He swallowed. "I won't ask."

Rosemary's suggestion was perfect. He looked so astonished and she treasured that. She kissed him right on his shaft, paying attention to the strangeness of what she was doing and the ragged gasps her lover made. He fit in her hand like warm silk and as Rosemary had suggested, she was careful not to be too gentle nor too rough with him. She slid her fingers up and down his length, experimentally at first, and then with growing surety.

So far as she could tell, Rothwell wasn't unhappy about her attempt to please him. He rose to one elbow and his free hand caught her hair and twined it about his fist. She lifted his length away from his body and lowered her face again, intent on kissing him on the tip.

"Stop."

Rosemary had mentioned men tended to get bossy in bed, so she felt safe to ignore that particular command. She kissed the head as planned. His seed tasted salty and just the tiniest bit bitter when she licked her lips. There was more to do, she knew, so after a few more kisses she opened her mouth and ran her tongue around the head.

"Please," Merrick begged.

She smiled and repeated the movement, and when he begged her to stop again, she took the tip into her mouth as far as she could manage. It didn't seem very much at all, but Rothwell moaned as if she were torturing him.

She swallowed quickly before she licked her lips and tried again. She managed a bit more the next time and tightened her grip around him. Rothwell covered her hand and together they stroked his hot flesh.

Arabella did her best to bring him pleasure with her mouth, but Rothwell appeared much harder to please than she'd thought he'd be. Either she was doing wrong or he was resisting her efforts. She released him and sat back on her heels to study him. He'd taken his hand away too, and his breathing was fast and shallow. "You didn't like it."

"I loved it," he countered.

"It did not seem that way." She put her hands on her hips and glanced about the room. "I wanted to do something good for you before you left."

"Oh, believe me, you were. Too good." He scooted closer on the bed and brushed her hair back from her neck. "I'd like to last at least longer than a minute. We have all night."

Appeased somewhat, she took him in hand again and stroked him. Now that she saw his face, she noticed he was biting down on his lower lip in an effort to be silent. "So you liked what I did for you?"

His eyes darkened when, on the upstroke, she flicked her thumb across the head as Rosemary had suggested she could. "Everything and anything."

"Good. Because I could get used to seeing you like this." She quickened the movement of her hand, watching his face intently. It seemed to Arabella that it was taking all his control to resist her. She liked that about him, but she would have her way tonight. He would find pleasure first. As he'd said, they had all night. She knew he could become aroused again and in a remarkably short length of time.

Keeping her eyes on him, she rose to her knees and knelt between his spread legs. She kissed him quickly and then ran her tongue over his flushed lower lip. He groaned and his eyes fluttered shut. He caught her breast in one hand and squeezed feverishly, but Arabella was not about to be distracted by how he made her feel. It did not take long for the combination of daring kisses and touches to have him gasping. Determined to win, she brought her free hand to his chest and touched his nipple.

Merrick jerked and grunted as hot seed flowed from him and landed on his chest. Some of it spread over her knuckles, and when she released him, she raised her hand to stare at it.

Merrick pushed her hand away and kissed her hard. "What will I do without you when I return to London?"

Arabella didn't know and that bothered her. She liked Merrick touching her and she liked touching him in return. But would memories be enough for him? It might be a long time till she could come up to London again. Even when he tossed her onto her back and slithered down the bed between her parted legs, she decided it might be too long. In a month, Merrick might have moved on to someone else. Within the month, he was supposed to be married.

Dawn was touching the horizon with a gentle hand when Merrick woke from the doze that had finally claimed him. He glanced to his right and found Arabella awake and watching him. He turned to her and drew her against him, intending to make love to her one more time before he left.

She pushed him back, her face serious and unsmiling. "Good morning."

"Good morning to you, too."

Arabella jumped from the bed and collected her discarded

nightgown and his banyan. Disappointed to be denied one more intimate touch before he left, he shoved the pillows behind him and sat up to watch what she did.

To his delight, she appeared comfortable scooting around the room with her tempting bottom wiggling and her breasts bouncing with each movement. He hardened even more because each one of Arabella's curves suited him. "Aren't you going to kiss me today?"

A frown creased her brow. "I know you have to go and like an early start."

He quickly threw his legs over the side of the bed and stood. "Not this early."

Arabella paused with her nightgown half on. "I thought Holland said seven."

"How has Holland come to manage *our* schedules?" He shook his head. "He might have wished to depart that early, but I never agreed. Come back to me, my dear, so we might say good morning properly."

Her lips curved into a smile as her nightgown fell from her fingers. She slowly prowled toward him, running her gaze over his skin and making him break out into a sweat. His affair with Arabella had changed her nature. When alone, there was nothing she liked better than to torment him with her beauty. If he couldn't have her in his arms one last time, he might just go mad.

When she stopped before him, she set her hands on his arms and ran them up to his shoulders. He shuddered and embraced her. Never had a woman claimed his attention so thoroughly. If not for the need to protect her reputation and settle Danny in his new life, he'd never leave her.

He nuzzled her neck. "I love the way you touch me." He cupped her bottom, and brought them hard against each other.

Her lips curved into a wicked smile he'd like to think was for his eyes alone. "Likewise."

They were eye to eye. Her breasts rested against his. Their hearts beat close together. But not as one. After last night, he didn't want her to misunderstand his interest in her. If not for her dislike of marriage, he'd already have proposed. Arabella was the one for him and he would protect her. "I will ask my grandfather for assistance should word of our affair have any harmful effect on your reputation."

"Why would you need to do that?"

Merrick linked his fingers behind her back. "Farnsworth. He claimed he was set upon by thieves and you were abducted or ran off in terror. The story he painted is quite lurid and likely has caused much gossip because you've disappeared from London. However, should it become known that you were in fact alone with me, Farnsworth may have something very different to say about that night. I don't imagine he will be very kind in his accusations."

Arabella broke away, arms wrapping about her chest. "You saw what he did to me."

"I did, though only I did." Merrick followed her and wrapped his arms about her waist. "If he makes trouble for you, my grandfather might be of assistance."

"How?"

"We need to make sure your story is the one believed." He brushed his lips cross her shoulder, peeking at her breasts. "No one will question our story if the Duke of Rutherford is on your side. His aid usually comes with a price, though, and I will pay it if your reputation is saved in the process."

She turned in his arms. "I'm coming with you."

He let her go, stunned by her suggestion. He was trying to prevent further harm to her reputation, and she wanted to remain at his side, even when facing the duke. "Arabella, you are where you belong. Stay at Winslette until the dust settles."

Her face fell. "I don't know where I belong anymore, but I think I should be at your side when you plead for Rutherford's support. These are my troubles."

"Mine too, now." He caressed her cheek with the backs of his fingers. "If not for me the truth about Farnsworth would already be known."

"And I'd still be a virgin." She raised one eyebrow, as if daring him to suggest their affair was a mistake.

He bit his lip briefly. Could her insistence in accompanying him mean what he hoped? "Are you sure? It will not be a social call. My grandfather will require every detail of that night spelled out to him in full, and the decisions made in the days after. You may find it an uncomfortable experience, as we all do when called to account for our actions."

She nodded decisively. "Yes, I'm sure, Merrick. I will come with you and tell my side of the story. If I have lost society's good opinion and Farnsworth is believed before us, then I'm sure being with you is a much more comforting place to be. You and I know the truth."

"Have I ever mentioned how much I admire you?"

Her smile was sudden and somewhat smug. "Actually you have. Last night before you made love to me."

"I'd like to do so again."

She fluttered her lashes. "Make love to me or whisper sweet nothings in my ear?"

"I would gladly do both at the same time if I could keep my wits about me."

She laughed then and his excitement grew at the sweet sound. "They say that passion can confuse a body and the mind."

"Arabella, my dear, you were born for that."

A blush grew as she stared at him. Such large, trusting eyes. He smoothed a hand down her back, her lush curves beckoning his hands to explore, and put off his plans for yet another day. "The trip to Newberry Park should not be put off too long."

"A shame, but there is always tonight," she said firmly, her hands closing over his bottom and squeezing.

He laughed at her bold touch, then kissed the tip of her nose. "I'd better dress then and leave you alone to make whatever preparations you require."

Arabella giggled and released him. "Where will you be in an hour?"

"I thought I might survey the house to see where a conservatory might be built. The space you have is much too small."

"I've done so already," she said urgently. "Years ago now."

"You have? But that's wonderful."

"Farnsworth thought the plans excessive, but Mr. Piper can show you where the designs were stored."

"I'll go find him now." He kissed her again then hunted for fresh clothing. She was still watching him when he threaded a pin into his cravat. "I'll see you later. We could discuss the design as we travel instead of watching Holland smirk at his books."

She grinned and slipped his banyan around herself. "I'd like that."

As he headed for the door, hooves sounded on the drive outside. Puzzled, he doubled back and quickly checked the window to see who had come. Unfortunately, the carriage was already vacated and being turned around. Whoever it might be was already within Winslette House. He hurried for the door and wrenched it open.

Holland stood there, hand raised to knock. Merrick quickly blocked his view into the room where Arabella remained partially clothed. His brother's face was uncomfortably flushed, his eyes cast downward. "So sorry to disturb, my lord, but you have a visitor waiting in the drawing room."

"Grayling wasn't expected, was he?" Must be one of his new neighbors come to call on him. It was rude to send them away, but he wasn't truly the lord of the manor here. They must wait upon Arabella. He glanced at her. She couldn't meet anyone dressed like that, wearing only his banyan and a smile. She'd need at least an hour before facing visitors. "Let whoever it is know that Lady Farnsworth is otherwise engaged at this time."

Holland sighed. "Under normal circumstances I would have already done so, but this visitor is not a lady I have the power to send away. She asked for you specifically."

A sense of doom crashed over his previous good mood. There was only one lady Holland had ever failed to banish before. If Aunt Penelope was here, then there was no way to prevent scandal from blackening Arabella's name. He was too late to appeal to Rutherford. He took a deep breath. "My aunt?"

Holland inclined his head to confirm it. "She requested to see you first and then to have Lady Farnsworth join her at her earliest convenience. I've arranged a tea tray to be sent into the drawing room while she waited."

Aunt Penelope would interfere. He could feel his lips peeling back from his teeth at the snarl of anger building in him.

"Oh dear." Arabella fretted and then hurried around the room, frantically picking up her discarded nightgown. "I am not prepared for this."

Merrick quickly shut the door in Holland's face and pressed his head to the wood. He couldn't let Aunt Penelope influence Arabella now. He hadn't had enough time to convince her that their affair, and his love, was worth the risk of reconsidering her opinion on marriage but now he had no choice but to make his intentions very clear.

He crossed to Arabella's side and knelt at her feet. He had little time to plead his case before all hope was lost. "Marry me."

Chapter Twenty-Three

The nightgown tumbled from her fingers in the sudden silence. "I beg your pardon?"

Rothwell caught her hand and pressed it to his lips. "I asked you to marry me."

Arabella's mind ran in all directions at once, but none of them led to a suitable reply. She was pleased to know her suspicions were true. He was on the hunt for a bride, but he surely hadn't been courting her. One brief affair, a few nights in a rogue's bed, for a widow did not immediately result in an offer of marriage. And with his aunt waiting downstairs, one of the most frightening members of the *ton*, now was hardly the time to consider such an offer properly.

She tugged her hand free of his grip, but Merrick's intense expression stirred a long dormant need deep inside. Arabella might have been married before, but this was her first proposal. She wasn't even dressed for such an important occasion.

She searched Merrick's face and he met her gaze steadily. He was serious about the proposal, but it was all too sudden for Arabella. Everything about him had taken her by surprise. Despite her conversation yesterday with Grayling, she was no closer to knowing how she felt about Merrick. She liked him. She liked the way he made her feel safe and attractive. But what she wasn't sure about was what loving him might feel like. "I cannot think now. Your aunt is here and I need time."

His throat worked as he swallowed. "Very well."

He stood slowly, straightening his waistcoat and sleeves with a heavy sigh that made her feel terrible for not having an answer. She set her hand on his sleeve. "I'm sorry, Merrick."

An odd smile flittered across his face before disappearing into a calm mask. "I must leave to deal with my aunt."

"I cannot understand why she has come. She received no invitation from me."

"My aunt rarely waits on an invitation when it comes to family. This estate is mine now, so she's simply invited herself. How typical of her."

"You're angry with her."

"I am." His lips pursed and then he frowned. "She knows full well I'd never invite her. However, I have an idea that may turn this disaster around. We may not need to travel to Newberry Park at all if Aunt Penelope can be convinced to assist you."

Arabella nodded slowly. "If I had Lady Penelope's support, the *ton* would never reproach me should Farnsworth's stories have twisted and spread too far." Her stomach fluttered. If all went well and Lady Penelope accepted her story as the truth, Merrick would be free to leave believing no further obligation existed between them. He needn't have bothered with a rash marriage proposal. He could return to London with a clear conscience.

"I was more worried what she would say about us, but…" He shrugged and faced the door. "We'll deal with the Farnsworth problem first and the other can wait until she asks why we are together still."

He frowned and the look on his face hinted he was trying to hide his feelings. He turned his face away when she smiled at him. They were together because she wanted to be with him. She liked him very much. She covered his hand with hers, but he wouldn't look at her directly. Had she disappointed him so badly by not jumping on the chance to be his wife?

She'd just gotten used to knowing what was going through his mind. He didn't like anyone knowing his business, and she could help with that by keeping his secrets gladly. "I will join you soon and happily explain what she needs to know and not a word more."

He squeezed her fingers. "When she is gone, I'll be at your disposal should you wish to speak again. I'd like a chance to convince you of my sincerity."

He kissed each of her palms and the feel of his lips against her skin caused her to smile. If she married him, she'd never feel undesirable. He had a way of turning each and every caress into a moment of worship. That side of a marriage between them would not be a chore. But was she ready to have another's needs placed before her own?

She swallowed. She honestly didn't know. She wouldn't lie to him. She certainly wouldn't marry just because of lust. "Of course."

Merrick smiled quickly, kissed her cheek, and then hurried to the door to receive his visitor. He didn't meet her gaze again as he slipped out, his steps echoing through the house. Arabella folded to the nearest chair and put her head in her hands. "My life is mad."

How had she gone from hoping for a kind lover to teach her the intimate arts to disappointing a rogue?

The door opened again and when Arabella peeked up, a gray head of hair had poked through the gap. "An intriguing parting," Lady Penelope Ford mused as she locked the door behind her. "You may call me Pen if you like."

Arabella gasped as panic gripped her. Lady Penelope Ford was supposed to be in the drawing room, taking tea and waiting to meet Merrick. There was no way to avoid a scandal now. She'd have heard them talking. She would know Merrick had just proposed and received no answer.

Lady Penelope looked around curiously. "So this is the bedchamber all of London will talk of in the coming weeks. Hmm, quite ordinary really for so scandalous a situation."

Arabella held Merrick's banyan a little tighter about her nakedness. "Lady Penelope. What brings you to Winslette?"

"Rothwell disappeared from London without warning. You also were reported missing. Is that not reason enough to become curious?" The lady shrugged. "Rumors have a habit of altering when it comes to my nephew. For instance, it's been suggested he'd turned over a new leaf this season and become somewhat respectable. I see now the gossips were utterly wrong."

Some of Arabella's panic ebbed. She had to keep her wits about her. She was facing one of the most influential women of the *ton*. "Oh?"

"Hmm, yes. My nephew was known for his, well… there is no delicate way to put it. Merrick has always been considered something of a scoundrel around women, much as his father was in his day. He used them, and then he tossed them aside should they become too demanding of his affections." Lady Penelope inspected her nephew's room with a disdainful eye. "So many have thought an affair might lead to an offer of marriage, but he fooled them all. Now, of course, he's set his cap too high. Many in the family thought he'd simply run out of ways to scandalize the world, but it seems he set himself a challenge in you."

A tight pain filled Arabella's chest. Lady Penelope believed Merrick's past affairs had everything to do with her decision not to marry him. That wasn't the case. Arabella doubted her own feelings more than his. "He's nothing like what you suggest."

Lady Penelope grimaced. "My dear, I do know what I'm talking about. I'm here to keep you safe from scandal that will follow this unwise affair. Why else would I come so far out of my way? We will say you were with me the entire time and no one need know my nephew seduced you."

Arabella moved slowly toward the door and unlocked it. Lady Penelope's behavior disappointed her. She'd condemned her nephew without cause and believed him a heartless seducer. Of course he had enjoyed many women before her, but he wasn't a cruel man. What sort of rogue bedded a widow, found her a virgin, and then proposed marriage? Merrick was the best of men. It was Arabella who had been the disappointment and she couldn't help it. "I have little desire for your help when you think so meanly of your own family. Why would I want your aid?"

Lady Penelope's smile grew brittle. "I have always been eager to help *you*. Merrick is a man and has made it very clear that he can take care of himself. As they all will do. Being an unwilling party to the scandals my family has engaged in makes me aware of the value of a reputation and what it costs to have lost one."

Arabella folded her arms across her chest. "Forgive me, but

we are strangers to one another. I don't know you."

Penelope smiled briefly. "We are similar creatures. We accept the restrictions of our society but still suffer from them. I hesitated to offer my support in London when I came to Merrick's town house, because I was not entirely sure he had you enthralled. I apologize for that. If you would dress in a more appropriate fashion, we can be underway."

"I am dressed as appropriately as I wish to be in my own bedchamber. You are the uninvited interloper."

"This is my nephew's bedchamber, is it not, and you are wearing a man's banyan, my dear." Lady Penelope came closer and fingered the material of the sleeve. "I'm in a position to know it's Merrick's garment."

Arabella held her ground. It was time to stop this now. "I think you should leave my home."

The door flew open. "You meddling old sow," Merrick growled. "What the hell are you doing?"

When he faced the door to shut it, a brief smile crossed the older woman's face. "Not one of your best, boy. Cool your heels a little longer. Lady Farnsworth and I are negotiating."

Merrick made an angry, inarticulate sound.

"Always so stubborn and hot-tempered," Lady Penelope chided. "His mother was much calmer."

Merrick was not hot-tempered. The only people Arabella had ever heard him disagree with were other Fords and her brother-in-law. She didn't know everything about Merrick yet, but he seemed a reasonable man. He just wanted his family to leave him in peace. "There is nothing to negotiate besides the method of your leaving. As far as I can tell, you can leave under your own steam or with his help."

Merrick snorted. "I see you're employing your usual charm to win Arabella over."

Lady Penelope's eyes narrowed to slits as her gaze flickered between them. "So, you've decided to throw over good sense and discard propriety?"

It only took a moment to decide. "Yes, Merrick has shown me nothing but kindness. You are so wrong about him."

Lady Penelope smirked. "So you will accept his proposal and become his wife?" She shook her head. "That should be a crowded affair, considering Lady Mary and Miss Milne both expect an offer of marriage immediately on his return to London. He's been very plainly interested in both young ladies. So attentive to them both, but do remember he can choose only one to share his bed legally."

"Hold your tongue," Merrick snapped at his aunt, hands curling into fists at his side.

Arabella's mouth fell open as it became clear Merrick couldn't refute his aunt's claim that he'd been courting two specific young ladies in Town. Likely while she'd been under his very roof. He'd gone in and out so frequently, but she'd never suspected anything had progressed to the point where a proposal was expected.

Her stomach turned over. He'd never said a word and then had the bad taste to offer a proposal she should not accept. Arabella was stunned that he hadn't mentioned any of it. He'd had ample time and opportunity.

Lady Penelope smiled a little sadly. "It is always important to have all the facts. Don't you agree, Lady Farnsworth? But I am here now, and I will do what I can to stem the damage. London is so rushed at this time of year that hopefully few should connect you to him. Merrick has made a mess of this, but with my support any harm to your reputation can be restored."

Merrick crossed the room and stopped close to her side. "I'd like a chance to explain."

Arabella turned away, devastated that she'd blundered so badly into Merrick's life. She couldn't even blame him for seducing her when she'd thrown herself into his bed. "He did nothing. It's my fault."

Lady Penelope clucked her tongue. "Now, my dear, I'm sure that is simply not the case. I'm told kindness can often be mistaken for a deeper affection. You're not the first to be duped."

Arabella pressed her cold hand to her hot brow. "I was a fool."

"No, you were not," Merrick insisted, spinning her around to face him again. "Arabella, I never lied to you."

When she looked into his eyes, Arabella's confusion wavered. He seemed sincere, but how could he be? He'd led two young ladies on while dallying with her. He should have remained in London rather than escorting her here. Why hadn't he? They'd not been intimately involved in London, and now things were even more complicated.

"An omission is still a lie," Lady Penelope added. "Come to London with me for what remains of the season, Lady Farnsworth. If you remain here as his tenant, the scandal will never go away."

Arabella hesitated. She did not want to become a pawn in any disagreement, but if she stayed here then she would likely be in the thick of it.

Merrick raked his hands through his hair and glared at his aunt. "Damn you. Why couldn't you just stay away?"

Lady Penelope offered a wry smile. "Because you are family, and no matter what happens, the family always comes first," she said simply. "Lady Farnsworth is a little wiser now, and I'm content. I'll return below and wait for her."

She glided out, leaving them alone again.

Merrick hurried to squeeze her hands as if she might need comforting. "The situation is not exactly how she painted it."

"Then how is it *exactly*? You have a special license in your possession. You have raised the expectations of two young women to the point where they await a proposal. How could you think so little of their feelings that you begin with me?"

He grabbed her by the arms and steered her to the nearest chair. Although she disliked allowing him to push her about, she needed the chair and sat gratefully.

He knelt at her feet as he'd done the night she'd sought shelter in his home. Her throat closed at the memory. "I do have a special license. My grandfather sent it to me, as he sent one to every grandson he has. I have admired you from afar for a long time and never considered I'd have a chance to win your affections. Yes, I began the season looking for a bride. I had not settled on either of the women my aunt mentioned. Then I kissed you by mistake and then you needed me. I liked that better than finding myself a bride. I acted selfishly, I admit."

A little of her disappointment faded. He had been a friend when she'd needed one most and it was Arabella who had changed things between them. All she needed to do now was prepare to make as graceful an exit as possible. "It seems my friendship has come at a high price to you. You had plans that I've blundered into."

"I've not offered for anyone but you."

She nodded, but it made no difference. "But you should. Lady Mary is a lovely girl, very pretty and a great conversationalist, and young. Her father is well connected and her dowry is large. She would make an excellent countess."

He shook his head. "I asked you to marry me."

"I have not agreed." She gathered her strength, stood, and faced the window. "You would do better with Lady Mary. Your family expects the match and more importantly so does she."

Merrick was on his feet in an instant. He grabbed her arms and turned her to face him again. "I will not offer for Lady Mary or anyone else. I want to marry you and grow as close as two people in love could be. I hope you will place no faith in anything else my aunt may have said."

"No. I am capable of making up my own mind." Arabella met his gaze, her chest hurting badly for the end of their affair. She would not continue to see him when he had two women waiting for him to propose to them. "I thank you for your kind offer, sir, but I must decline."

When he ran his fingers through his hair, Arabella longed to straighten it again. "I feared it was too soon."

"No, Merrick, it is far too late." She sighed deeply. "Your aunt has invited me to spend some time with her and I feel that is a sensible decision."

"Well, I do not." He took a deep breath and drew her into the circle of his arms. "I am in love with you, Arabella, and I will prove my worth. Wait and see."

His kiss was urgent and left Arabella breathless. When he left with no further mention of marriage, Arabella's throat closed. A surge of unfamiliar longing swept her.

Was it because he was a good man that she refused? She would not be the cause of his loss of honor. He had raised a young woman's expectations past the point of turning back. He should marry Lady Mary or Miss Milne. He should make either one love him. It would be easy.

She tightened his banyan about her body and rubbed her

hands over the rich material. She would never have his arms about her again and already she missed that. Merrick had given Arabella everything she needed to be happy and safe. She owed him for his protection and for overlooking her omission of her virginity. But with all he'd done, all he'd promised and delivered, that did not mean a marriage between them was in his best interests.

Chapter Twenty-Four

Merrick did his best to keep a civil tongue in his head, but his aunt's continued references to Lady Mary and Miss Milne before Arabella set his teeth on edge. Arabella was much too pale, much too timid now. She would not meet his eye, and if Aunt Pen kept bringing up the misunderstanding, she might never look at him again.

Luckily, Grayling and his wife had arrived unannounced and ended any plans to travel that day. Merrick had already had the carriage put away again and was biding his time until he could speak to Arabella alone. He was not going to marry Miss Milne or Lady Mary. Neither of them were Arabella, but there were two other reasons he wouldn't change his mind.

First, Arabella had accepted his half brothers' existence with not even a ripple of distress. She'd even guessed about Holland. Then there was her kindness to young Danny to consider. There was no reason for the boy to be lodged in the house. He would be perfectly comfortable in the stables with Jimmy and the others. Placing young Danny beside Holland in Winslette House had won his brothers over completely.

Second, until presented with the omitted details of his hunt for a bride, she'd stood up to Aunt Penelope. The first woman he'd ever witnessed doing so and that moment had been glorious. She might not have answered his proposal of marriage the way he'd hoped, but she wouldn't listen to false criticism. But then the tables had turned against him, and he'd been battling just to have her look at him.

He should not have rushed his proposal. He should have waited, as he'd suspected was the right course from the beginning. He tried to catch her eye one more time, but she turned toward her visitors instead.

"Gray, I need to speak with you in private," he whispered.

Grayling frowned. "About Miss Milne or Lady Mary?"

He scowled at his aunt. She'd done her work well if even Grayling had picked up on those names. "Neither."

Grayling's wife had a talent for deflecting discussion to the three little girls surrounding her—the apples of their father's eye and also their new mother's. The middle child, Maisy, wasn't so docile as to sit still. She climbed onto Arabella's lap and snuggled against her. His heart skipped a beat at the expression of tenderness on Arabella's face. She appeared completely enthralled by the little girl, her eyes growing soft and full of love. Merrick wanted that for Arabella so badly his heart ached. To make her part of *his* family so she would never be alone again and might, if they were lucky, have a daughter of their own. "Would you come with me?"

He led Grayling into the quieter library and shut the door. "Arabella refused my offer of marriage, thanks, I believe, in no small part to my aunt's presence and her accusations that I'd raised hopes in those two young ladies she keeps mentioning."

Suddenly, Grayling was before him, his hand fisted in his cravat, his expression furious. "I don't care what your aunt has to say. That isn't good enough for Arabella. Ask again."

Merrick fought to free himself and put distance between them. "Believe me, I have not changed my mind about wanting to marry her. I'm just not certain that what I say is getting through. She believes my aunt's accusations that I led those women on. I paid little more interest than any man considering marriage. Let me explain how things began, and perhaps you can suggest a way forward."

He told Grayling almost everything that had occurred over the past weeks, leaving out nothing of what he'd done in his search for a bride and why he believed Arabella was the better choice. They were good together. He did leave off mention of Arabella's virginity and the recent loss of it when they became lovers. That was private and would remain between them alone. "My aunt has managed to turn Arabella's trust from me and has convinced her to leave Winslette. I had not meant for that to happen. When I bought the estate, it was with the understanding that this would always be her home."

Grayling settled against a desktop, arms folded across his chest. "Arabella has always trod her own path. It seems my fears of a few months ago were accurate. How did you convince her to stay with you?"

He shrugged. "I did nothing. She seemed determined to hide, and I simply never suggested she leave. If not for my aunt, it's possible we would both still be in my London town house. As of a few days ago, she'd only just regained her confidence around others."

"I would never have guessed her to have been injured and afraid. She didn't confess the extent of the situation yesterday." Gray tilted his head. "Thank you for looking after her so well. For a scoundrel who can have almost any woman he wants, I'm rather proud of your restraint."

"Past tense." He shook his head. "I did what you suggested. I asked Arabella to be my wife this morning, well before the timing was right, and have been refused. I don't know what to say to convince her I don't want anyone else. She knew about the special license already. Found it herself and pretended not to until this morning. I fear the existence of the damn thing has convinced her I'm in a hurry."

Grayling's gaze grew shrewd. "She grows more reserved when troubled. She looks about to weep every time your aunt speaks. I take those two things as a very good sign. She's conflicted about what to do. Augusta used to worry when Arabella tried so hard to be agreeable. Rosemary has voiced the same concerns in different ways. The only thing I can suggest is patience. Destroying the license or allowing the license to lapse might ease her tension. How patient are you prepared to be?"

"I'd wait an eternity just to see her smile again." Hearing his own conclusions from Grayling's lips brought relief. He might still have a chance to change her mind, but revisiting the subject today wouldn't help. He'd have to give her time. He could do that. "The license is still in London, so I can do nothing there. Let's return to the ladies."

Merrick stepped back into the drawing room and glanced around without seeing Arabella. Lady Grayling was still trading subtle barbs with his aunt, the three children lolling on the thick carpet between them. Although Merrick listened for her footsteps, Arabella appeared nowhere nearby. He glanced at his pocket watch, wondering how soon after his departure she'd slipped away. He and Gray had spoken perhaps a quarter hour. It was unlike a hostess to desert her guests for that length of time.

When the ladies paused in their conversation, Merrick cleared his throat to interrupt. "When and where did Lady Farnsworth go?"

The pair glanced at each other, then at the clock. His aunt's expression grew disapproving. "Close on a quarter hour. She did not say what she needed to do, either."

Lady Grayling rose from her chair. "She excused herself soon after you left. I assumed she needed a private moment or was coming to speak with you."

"We did not see her. If you'll excuse me, I will check on her."

Merrick left them quickly, took the stairs two at a time, and barged into Arabella's bedchamber. The room was empty, as were all rooms above stairs when he inspected them. Sure that he'd overlooked no smaller chambers, he headed below and poked his head into every room he remembered from his tour of the house. In the small room where Arabella's fledgling greenhouse resided, Merrick found his half brother sprawled on the floor untidily, unresponsive when his name was called.

Merrick rushed to him and shook his shoulder. "Holland. Wake up, brother."

Holland stirred slowly, blinking at the room as he turned over. Blood oozed from a nasty head wound and Merrick quickly pressed a clean handkerchief to the injury. "What happened to you?"

"I don't remember." Holland slowly sat up and rested against him a long moment, one hand held to his head. "I heard a sound in here and thought to inquire if Lady Arabella needed my help."

Relief coursed through him. "Did she?"

"She wasn't here. I never saw her." Holland fumbled for his pocket watch and stared at the time. "I don't remember anything beyond that moment. I think it was a little after the hour when I must have come in."

Merrick peeled the cloth from the wound as Holland put his pocket watch away. The bleeding didn't seem too bad, but he wasn't used to such matters. He'd need help with his brother. "Someone else must have been here though."

He put his arm about his brother and lifted him carefully to his feet.

"The way my head hurts, I'm not surprised." Holland groaned. "Do you think Farnsworth returned?"

Cold fury filled him. "He better not have. I'll get you settled to rest, then search for Arabella."

Holland waved his hand. "Find your lady first. I can rest here as well as anywhere."

"Don't be absurd. I'll not leave you alone." Merrick bore the bulk of Holland's weight and shuffled him from the room. By the time they reached the drawing room doorway, Holland was passing in and out of awareness. Merrick was terrified. "I need some help," he shouted.

Aunt Penelope turned as he came through the door and then fainted clean away, settling to the floor with a sob. *Some use she would be.* Grayling reached them first and helped settle his brother on the fine damask sofa, and then Merrick checked on his aunt.

"She's only fainted," Lady Grayling said as she fanned the older woman's face briskly. "I'm sure she'll recover."

Merrick shrugged and then put his aunt back in her chair. "So much for her reputed strong stomach. I never imagined a little blood could upset her so badly."

Grayling helped his wife stand and then glanced at his brother. "What happened to Holland? Did you find Arabella?"

"I don't know and no, I haven't located her yet. She is not upstairs and while looking for her I found Holland out cold on the floor of Arabella's green tiny greenhouse. He thought she was there but said he saw no one in the room."

Holland groaned, his eyes fluttering open again. When he made to rise, Merrick pressed his hand to the man's chest. "Rest. You've taken quite a blow."

"I need to help you find your bride," he insisted. "Don't let her get away."

Merrick patted Holland's chest. It seemed at least his brother agreed with his decision to marry Arabella. Holland's approval meant a lot to him. "Not a chance. You must promise to remain here until I return. If you cannot, I'll have young Danny come sit on your chest to hold you still."

Holland's eyes flickered across the room and an embarrassed expression flickered across his face. When Merrick lifted his gaze in that direction, his aunt watched them, a strange, almost wistful expression evident.

"Are you well now, Aunt Pen?"

"Of course. Go find Lady Farnsworth," his aunt croaked, tears filling her eyes as she stared at them. "I can watch over him."

An odd look passed between her and his brother, and though unwilling to leave him in the dubious care of his maiden aunt, he was comforted by the knowledge that Lady Grayling would be there too. She certainly would send word to him if Holland worsened.

Merrick approached his aunt as she continued to stare at Holland. "Promise me you will take good care of him while I am gone. He is more important to me than you'll ever understand."

"I see that. I'm sure that between us we can manage his requirements." She drew in a deep breath, then stood and crossed the room, pulling up a footstool to sit beside Holland. Although rather shocked by her actions, he walked away. He had bigger problems than Aunt Pen's sudden compliance to deal with.

Together with Grayling he searched the main floor and, on the off chance that Arabella had returned abovestairs in the interim, sent a servant up to her room to check again. She wasn't found and no one remembered seeing her.

Merrick returned to the green room and studied the space. A faint breeze stirred through the room, rustling the leaves of the delicate orchids Arabella kept here. Merrick approached the tall windows and tested the latches. One was unlocked, and as he paid closer attention, he saw a thread caught on the window frame. One the same color as Arabella's gown.

His blood ran cold as he surveyed the view from the window. With all the trees studding the grounds, it was impossible to see far outside in any direction. Arabella could be anywhere, and he very much feared that Farnsworth had returned to take her away.

His hands curled into fists. If Farnsworth had harmed her again, he'd kill him this time.

Chapter Twenty-Five

The ties on Arabella's wrists had long since burned tender marks onto her skin as she'd tried to free herself again through the endless day that had just passed. She stared at her throbbing wrists helplessly. It was no use. Despite her best efforts, the knot remained firmly tied. She was hobbled—hands tied to her feet by a short rope between—denied any freedom of movement or any hope of escape from Winslette's ruins.

As the sun lowered in the sky, tendrils of fog rose from the nearby river, gradually cocooning her and her brother-in-law in a private world. She shivered as a chill swept over her skin. Cut off from everything and everyone she held dear, she'd no idea what plans Farnsworth had made, but she was sure she wasn't going to like them.

She hunched forward, attempting to reach her chilled legs and rub some warmth into them while scanning the view available to her for a means of escape. There were one or two rough-looking men outside the ruins, but they didn't look her way once.

Across the ruins, Farnsworth stared intently into the thickening fog, looking not at Winslette House but away from it. When he'd taken her from the house, he had spoken only a few words, threatening to hurt Merrick if she didn't come quietly. He'd already killed Holland simply for being in the wrong place at the wrong time. Once she'd glimpsed the rough company he now kept, she'd agreed to go quietly as there were three little girls, Rosemary, and Lady Penelope in the house.

Arabella bit her lip to hold back tears.

"Won't be long now," Farnsworth said with a terse nod in the direction of the disused road.

"What was that?" Arabella had kept up a constant stream of questions but had received little by way of response. All Farnsworth had said about his intentions so far was that he was waiting and then everything would be well again.

"The solution is at hand." He smiled and the sight chilled her to the core.

She swallowed the hard lump forming in her throat. She considered asking him to explain but decided against it. "May I have a drink?"

She might need to scream or to plead for help from whomever was on their way to meet them. Her mouth tasted of ashes. Surprisingly, Farnsworth revealed a travel case and produced a fine crystal goblet and bottle of red wine. He poured her a glass as if they were on a picnic and held it to her lips as a lover would. She attempted to sip, but his hand rose, forcing too much into her mouth at once. She swallowed quickly, only to regret it. The wine was rancid. Bitter.

She turned her face away, but his fingers dug into her hair, tugging her head around painfully until she held still. He forced her to drink the rest.

"You'd best learn to do what you're told now or come to regret it later." A cruel smile twisted Farnsworth's lips. "He won't like disobedience from you."

Arabella blinked as a wave of tiredness swept her. "Who?"

"The man you were too stupid to marry." He shrugged. "Now who knows what his intentions are? It's none of my business. All debts will be paid and I'll be free of the yoke about my neck. It's a shame you had to be so disobliging to your family."

In the failing light, she studied her brother-in-law critically, determined not to give in to fear and fall to pieces at the news that he was again using her as a means to cover his debts. Farnsworth appeared disheveled and weary. He was desperate.

"There," he said suddenly.

Arabella jerked her head up as he stepped from the ruins and strode a few yards farther away. Arabella watched him carefully for signs he would turn back to check on her and then tried to stand. Pain exploded as sharp needles of pain lanced her feet. She sat with a thump, realizing that her feet were utterly numb from being bound for so long. She couldn't run if she tried. She bit her lip as the world swayed just enough to make her feel she could fall.

When she raised her head, the rough fellows Farnsworth had employed had come closer and were laughing at her. Their images danced in her vision and her stomach rolled disconcertingly.

Farnsworth stopped at the edge of the old roadway and set his hands to his hips. Arabella caught the sound of movement beyond him and fought to focus her eyes. She heard horses, tack jingling in the distance, and then men carrying lanterns appeared.

"This is the devil of a place to meet, Farnsworth. I thought Winslette would offer a finer welcome than this. You'd better have delivered what your invitation promised."

A dark shape joined Farnsworth, though she could not identify who it might be immediately. He was tall. His voice held a demanding edge to it that nagged her memory.

"She's waiting. Exactly as I believe you like your women."

"Good."

Farnsworth turned and gestured to where she sat. "There she is. As you can see, Parker, she's docile enough for your plans."

Lord Parker came closer, his smile showing his delight and his greatcoat sweeping back from his body like the giant wings of death. "My dear lady. How well you look this evening."

"Help me," she begged, her words slurring. She lifted her heavy, bound wrists for him to inspect. It was growing harder to focus. "Farnsworth stole me away."

She shook her head, hoping to clear her foggy mind.

Lord Parker came close enough that he could inspect her bound hands. His fingers caressed the rough ropes and the reddened skin beneath, but he did not untie her. "You've done well, Farnsworth. How long ago was she drugged?"

Arabella gaped when Farnsworth smiled. "Not long. A double dose since you've a ways to travel."

It must have been the wine. She forced herself to relax as Parker untied the rope between her hands and feet. Her feet tingled a little as she shuffled them. Given how they felt, she wasn't sure she'd be able to walk.

Parker turned his back on her. "The gag will solve any difficulties when the potion wears off on the journey. I'd rather not be disturbed by busybodies. The dose you gave will serve. Too little and she might cry out an alarm and draw attention. Too much..."

He left the rest unsaid and she shivered.

A gag? What sort of a fiend was he that he needed to resort to such measures? She swallowed hard as tears sprung to her eyes. Parker was strong, and if he didn't release her of his own accord, she didn't think she could get away without help. He would have no trouble subduing her if she tried to flee. She didn't like to think about what might happen after that.

"You're sure no one will look for her?"

"Not after the tales I've spread. She has no family to speak of besides me." Farnsworth nodded. "Are we square now?"

Parker circled back to leer at her. "She's more leggy than I usually like, but all women are the same in the end I suppose. You just have to teach them to behave."

Arabella stared. She should be scared by that promise. She should be terrified. But it was becoming so hard to think. She was on the verge of sleep when a voice cut through her stupor.

"Oh, I don't think you'll have the chance to teach her much of anything."

Arabella's heart thudded in response to Merrick's voice. She fought to turn her head to see if she'd imagined his arrival and saw him a short distance away on the edge of the ruins in the company of his servants, half-brothers, and Grayling. She smiled happily. Her Merrick, though shrouded in fog, would make everything all right again. He would take her home to Winslette where they both belonged together.

Chapter Twenty-Six

Merrick could not look upon Arabella without his rage rising. Seeing her barely aware of her surroundings and bound like a dog by this pair was beyond all understanding. "Untie her."

Farnsworth turned, his eyes widening with shock. At his side, Parker grinned as if they were meeting at their club. "What the devil are you doing here, Rothwell? This is a private matter and does not concern you."

Farnsworth had the sense to shrink a little. "Yes, a private matter."

Merrick shook his head and flexed his fingers. "This is my land now, and there is no matter so private where Arabella is concerned that I do not want to know where she is and that she is well. I said untie her."

Parker placed himself next to Arabella and petted her head like she was his favorite hound. Her head lolled to the side. "She's mine, Rothwell. Promised, in fact. Can you not see how perfect she will be?"

When Arabella swayed away from his touch so far that she might fall, Parker grabbed her by the hair and then hauled her to her feet. She couldn't seem to stand on her own, and he took a step forward.

"Pretty, isn't she?" Parker boasted. "I'll beat any disobedience out of her and make her perfect."

Farnsworth shrank back, placing himself behind Parker and Arabella.

Merrick continued forward but stopped as Arabella smiled. "She's already perfect."

Parker yanked on her hair harder and she whimpered. He drew her against him. "Go back where you came from, Rothwell."

Around him, Merrick's half brothers backed away, disappearing into the fog like ghosts. He quickly determined their intent when a man grunted somewhere in the fog, and then another. He kept his attention on Parker and Farnsworth, although the latter appeared distracted by what his brothers might be doing out of sight.

Grayling stepped forward and held out his hands. "Now, steady on. There's no need for this. Let Arabella choose for herself."

Parker spun Arabella around to face him, caught her jaw in the palm of his hand, and pressed his fingers into her cheeks. After a moment, her mouth gaped, lips pursing in an obscene imitation of a kiss. "Experience has taught me that women are too weak to make decisions. She's not protesting, is she?"

"She's drugged," Merrick reminded him. He counted to ten as Parker's hand caressed her throat.

"Not got sense enough to protect herself, even from a harmless devil like Farnsworth." Parker's free hand stroked down her back and rested on her bottom. He squeezed. "Besides, you took what I planned to have for my very own, Grayling, and now I will take what I want. Farnsworth made it so convenient to come to an arrangement."

Merrick spared a glance for Grayling, but he appeared just as confused. "What the devil are you talking about?"

"Married women are no challenge, but a woman unattached is much easier to persuade when their family wants nothing to do with her and cannot pay their debts." Parker smiled mockingly over Arabella's shoulder. "I've seen your wife, Grayling. I know what she once was. The whore was to be mine, but you stole her away from her world and married her instead. What will society have to say about that scandalous tidbit?

"Arabella will take her place or I'll ruin Farnsworth and his precious daughter, and you'll wish you'd never laid eyes on your talented wife too, because the tales I could tell about her proficiency in the bedroom would turn society against you and all you hold dear."

"This is between you and me. Leave Arabella out of this," Grayling argued, face turning a deathly shade that hinted Parker's accusations might just be based in truth. Merrick didn't know much of Rosemary's past, but if Parker did not stop touching Arabella's ass soon, he would kill him.

"But I do have someone who cares where I am," Arabella said suddenly, her voice slurring under the effects of the drug. Her head fell back as she stared at Parker, brow creased in thought. "We will be married soon."

Merrick's heart leapt at her words, a ruse that might just work to win her freedom from Parker's clutches without resorting to violence. Unfortunately, he didn't think Parker believing her was likely. She was not in her right mind.

Parker's attention flickered to her and back to them quickly. He began to move toward the waiting horses. Yet right at that moment, men whooped and hollered, causing the horses to rear and, once free, to scatter. The carriage lurched forward as the hitched horses took off across the field.

Farnsworth bellowed. "Go after them, you fools."

Parker's men were eager to do Farnsworth's bidding and quickly disappeared, leaving just Farnsworth and Parker to deal with. From the corner of his eye, he saw his brothers reappear, spread in a loose circle about Parker and Arabella.

He stepped forward. "Release Arabella to me now before blood is spilled."

Parker began to laugh. "Why do you care? She's not yours. It's all arranged with Farnsworth to cover his debts."

"I am Rothwell's, actually," Arabella said loudly. "It's all arranged. He loves me," she whispered, although it was likely everyone heard her. Her head turned in his direction, her expression blissfully happy.

"No." Parker looked to Farnsworth for confirmation, but the other man backed up a few steps instead.

Merrick strolled forward. "Where do you think she's been the past few days? My arms, my bed. She's made me the happiest man that ever lived. So you see, she does have someone who is not taking your treatment of her very well. Give her back to me."

Parker looked down at Arabella's dreamy expression and then glared at Farnsworth. "Farnsworth said she was visiting relatives and couldn't wait for her new life with me."

"The only relations Arabella has is Farnsworth and his daughter. The daughter eloped."

Beside him, Grayling stirred. "That's surprising."

"Our first collaboration. I'll share the details later." He smiled tightly, then turned his attention to Parker. "Let her go before I break your hands. I haven't any patience for seeing women mauled by animals."

Parker flung Arabella at him and stepped back. "I didn't know how things stood between you."

Merrick caught Arabella against him, embraced her, and then handed her into Grayling's care. "Try to keep her awake if you can."

His brothers formed a protective barrier before Arabella. Merrick stripped off his coat and tossed it to one of them. "Now you do. Oh, and to be clear, since Arabella cannot speak for herself at this moment, she does not like being tied up, gags, or anything to do with riding crops, except perhaps with horses. Not like a mutual acquaintance of ours does."

"Wait. I was misled." Parker looked for support and came up empty. "He said she had an open mind and wanted it this way: a little danger at the beginning to heat her blood. I would never have arranged it if I hadn't been assured of her inclinations."

"You know, Parker, I find myself uncaring of that fact. You both deserve to be punished for the way you treat women as property and, you know, even just for breathing. Beating one of you to a pulp seems the only choice I have."

He caught Parker by the cravat and hauled him close. Parker, being taller, was at an advantage, but Merrick was beyond caring about the level of the playing field in a fight. He protected his own.

Out of the corner of his eye, Farnsworth turned tail and ran off into the fog.

Parker's gaze darted to the men around him. "I'll pay you handsomely to get this oaf off me."

Jimmy stepped forward. "How much?"

Merrick rolled his eyes. Damn family. Always willing to get in the middle of a good disagreement.

Parker licked his lips. "Enough to set you up as a wealthy man."

Jimmy tipped his head to the side as he considered. "Can I live with you?"

"No." Parker appeared shocked by that idea.

"I'm in charge of Rothwell's stable in London." Jimmy folded his arms over his chest. "Can I pick your horses for you?"

"Don't be absurd."

Jimmy shook his head, smirked at Merrick, and return to the line behind him. "Another stiff-necked toff who thinks money is all that matters to a man."

His brothers muttered amongst themselves, some laughed, and no others came forward. Trust Jimmy to find a way to break the tension.

Merrick shook his head and released Parker. He wasn't worth the effort. A hard shove sent him crashing to the ground. "Don't come anywhere near Arabella again. Don't speak to her. Don't even tip your hat in her direction. Collect your debts from the man who owes you, not defenseless women and dependents. So help me God, I'm tempted to have every member of my family chase you down just to teach you a lesson."

Parker might be older, but he took the threat to heart. He scrambled to his feet with all the appearance of a fugitive. No one survived with their dignity intact when the Fords united against them. "That won't be necessary."

"I hope not, for your sake." Merrick smiled. "Remember, there is no port distant enough that my Ford cousins couldn't find you and ruin your life, too. They like my wife-to-be almost as much as my servants do."

He signaled to his brothers. "Drive him and his men from the estate. Use whips if need be. Parker should like that."

Jimmy grinned and slapped his short club across the palm of his hand menacingly. "Don't have one handy at the moment, my lord, but this and whatever else comes to hand will do in a pinch. It's our absolute pleasure to serve you."

Chapter Twenty-Seven

Arabella blinked as Merrick suddenly appeared before her. She sobbed in relief as he held her tightly against him. His hands cradled her firmly against his body, and he kissed her cheek. He held her as if he'd never let her go, and Arabella was content to stay like this for a very long time. She was so weary.

"I don't know what I would have done if I had lost you," he whispered, his voice rough with emotion.

"I don't know what I would have done if you hadn't come," she confessed, swallowing the taste of the dosed wine she'd been forced to consume. "I feared you would look for me on the roads and not the ruins."

His arms loosened and a battered cup filled with water appeared. She drained it quickly.

"I have a half brother to thank for that. One of them followed you all the way to the ruins and reported back to me that you'd gone off with Farnsworth and his dubious friends. I didn't believe it likely you'd had a choice in the matter."

She tipped her head to look up at the sky, noting the fog had lifted and the heavens were filled with a thousand twinkling stars. "What time is it?"

"Late. I've delayed returning till now." His fingers caressed her throat softly until she sighed. "The unfortunate effects appear to have worn off now, so we should be able to return."

She brought her gaze back to his. "Effects?"

He kissed her cheek lightly, then laughed. "You've been telling everyone I love you for the past half hour."

She covered her face. "I'm sorry. I don't remember doing that."

He helped her stand, retaining her hands in his. "Don't be. I'm not at all embarrassed by the truth. We only remained here because I didn't want my aunt to see you this way. Who knows what you might have told her?"

Just then, the half brothers returned and Arabella studied them. There were six men, all who bore a degree of similarity to the man holding her. "Which one followed me?"

"Archie. He's the youngest in my employ."

She spotted a shy, skinny fellow wearing a ridiculous grin as he stood about with the others. Even though she hadn't ever been introduced, his face when their eyes met was very familiar to her. She'd spoken with him before. "He was in Green Park the day after my niece ran away. After I spoke to you, I dropped a handkerchief and that young man returned it to me without a word. Thank you," she said to Archie. "I am forever in your debt."

He ducked his head in acknowledgement and then the others started teasing him. She smiled at their antics. Merrick had such an interesting family. They turned for Winslette House and led the way home.

Merrick curled his arm about her waist. "He's a quiet one. I left him behind that day to watch over you. You were preoccupied with worry about Cecily and the loss of your home and I knew it was not far, but I wanted assurance you'd made it home safely."

Arabella pressed her head to Merrick's shoulder and closed her eyes. She couldn't help but be surprised that he'd set his half brothers to watch over her even then. It was a sweet and protective gesture, like every kindness he'd showered her with, but at the time they had been barely acquainted. Arabella wasn't sure how she felt about his presumption, but she couldn't help but be grateful for it now.

They walked on in silence until Grayling, returning from the house, found them.

He frowned. "What's kept you?"

Merrick stroked her back slowly. "Can a gentleman not stroll about his own land with a pretty woman on his arm?"

Grayling's brow rose at Merrick's behavior and then he winked at Arabella. "I suppose, but as sweet as it is to see my friends express their affection so openly, it is growing rather late. My wife is growing anxious and I cannot explain the level of anxiety your Holland is unable to hide. Lady Penelope had to order him to sit down. He would have come after you in person if she hadn't just bellowed at him."

Arabella stopped and held her hand to her chest. "He's alive. I was so certain he'd…"

"Takes a hard blow to stop one of us," Merrick whispered for her ears alone. "Sounds as if he'll be fine in no time at all if he's fussing already. Not that I've ever known him to stop. We should return, though. I left Aunt Pen to watch over him and who can say what ill will come of that."

Arabella buried her face in Merrick's shoulder as tears filled her eyes. She hadn't thought of much of anything once he'd had pulled her into his arms, and the shock of what had passed before finally caught up with her.

"Everything will be all right, love," he whispered as he held her close while she cried. "Have faith in that."

She curled her arms about his shoulders and held on. "If not for you… I'd be lost."

He kissed her brow. "I was thinking the same thing. Let's get you back home and into bed."

When Merrick slipped his arm around her back again, she snuggled closer to him as they walked back to find every window in her home filled with faces. The servants who'd remained behind were waiting on her safe return.

She waved to them, but in going back, she had to face the immediate future. Merrick loved her and wanted her to marry him. Lady Penelope insisted she must consider her reputation and leave Winslette with her, putting her affair with Merrick behind.

She couldn't do either.

Merrick shifted to take her elbow as they ascended the short flight of stairs and then released her. When she glanced at him, his face was a perfect mask of patience and understanding. She didn't know if she love him, not yet, but he was dear to her.

When Grayling swept inside, she held Merrick back. "What do I tell your aunt?"

"About your abduction? I'd recommend the truth. She will find out of her own accord either way, and she'll know what to do to spare your reputation any harm."

"Do you think she will still want me to stay with her now?"

His hand fell away. "You don't want to stay at Winslette?"

"No. Not alone. I do not feel comfortable here anymore. I doubt when you are gone back to London I would sleep a wink."

Merrick shook his head. "I would stay with you, but my presence would not be in your best interests. My aunt has said very plainly that she likes you, and she is not one to change her mind so quickly. She won't hold you accountable for recent events, so I believe her offer will stand. She is also in the best position to help you regain your possessions from Farnsworth's town house and quash any rumors he started."

A small portrait of her parents, her few jewels, and many letters were all important to her. She had forgotten them. "I would indeed like some possessions returned."

Merrick smiled. "Then I will wish you luck now and hope you have an enjoyable season. My aunt is a busy woman, so you should have no end of entertainments to occupy your time."

"Will you call on me at your aunt's house?"

He shook his head. "Arabella, you know how I feel about my aunt."

"Yes, but will you still see me?"

He drew close, took her hand in his, and raised it to his lips. His breath beat across her skin, warm and soft, setting her senses on fire. "Every chance I get. I have grown used to seeing you every day, and I won't deny myself that luxury."

He peered at her a long time before he kissed her knuckles, her palm, and the inside of her wrist where she'd been bound. Her pulse leapt with joy and arousal, but he released her, a regretful smile on his lips. "I will miss you."

"I will miss you too."

He smiled suddenly. "You'd best go in and see to your guests. Grayling has a tendency to grumble when bored. I'd like to take a stroll around the house to cool my temper and see that all is well."

"Do you suspect Farnsworth or Parker will come back?"

"No. But I won't take any chances where you are concerned anymore." He turned away and started his trek to the darker side of the house.

Arabella's stomach lurched, and her palms grew sweaty. She had hoped to have more time with Merrick before necessity separated them. Her throat tightened as doubts plagued her. She didn't want her decision *not* to marry him to be the end of them. "Merrick," she called and ran after him.

He turned back immediately, and when she reached him, she threw her arms about him and kissed him urgently. This couldn't be all there was to their affair. She twisted her fingers in his hair, holding his lips to hers as she drew upon every limited skill she possessed to enthrall him. He groaned as her tongue swept into his mouth and teased him.

A door rattled and he broke away, shoving her behind him protectively. In the shadow of the house, two figures moved, disappearing behind trees and a sheltered corner not easily observed from where they stood. Arabella held on to Merrick's arm as he set off in pursuit of the pair. Whoever they were, they were leaving the house rather than creeping closer to it. "Who is that?"

"I cannot tell from this distance," he whispered. "Return to the house and I'll find out."

She grabbed his hand and held him tightly. "I'm not going anywhere without you."

Although he didn't look happy about it, Merrick didn't insist she go. He nodded and together they crept quietly across the lawn. The pair stopped a short distance from the house in a spill of bright moonlight that revealed Lady Penelope speaking with a man. The hand holding Arabella's tightened.

Ahead, the pair laughed and then Lady Penelope leaned forward to press a kiss to the man's forehead. After another few words were spoken, Lady Penelope retreated to the house alone and disappeared inside. The man she'd met turned, revealing his identity as Mr. Holland, Merrick's half brother.

Merrick cursed and strode forward, dragging Arabella with him. "What the hell do you think you're doing?"

Holland jumped clear out of his skin, and then he glanced around the clearing, guilt writ large in his every movement. "Just taking some air."

"Bollocks. What were you doing with my aunt?"

"I wasn't with Lady Penelope."

"I saw you talking to her in this very spot just now." Merrick stepped closer to hiss, "She kissed you."

"She did no such thing."

Although Holland tried to appear shocked, Arabella could see it was an act.

Merrick drew in a several deep breaths, his body tensing with anger. "Does she bribe you to spy on me? What price did you name?"

"It's not like that."

"Really, then what exactly is it like?" Merrick faced his brother, fury evident in every move he made. "How did she know Arabella was under my roof? You must have told her. Did you send a note to arrange an urgent assignation one night?"

"I would never." Holland pulled a face as if disgusted. "It's nothing at all like that."

"Then what the hell is she to you?" Merrick's free hand rose and he stabbed Holland in the chest with his fingers. "What did you talk about just now?"

Holland licked his lips, glancing left and right as if looking for rescue. "Many things. The season. The weather."

Merrick drew in a shaky breath and his fingers curled into a fist. "You and our half brothers are the only family I have, and I trusted you completely. What a fool I've been to confide in you, the very person feeding the Fords information about my life. No wonder grandfather sent a special license. I thought it less calculated than the delivery actually was."

"I do not tell her about you or Lady Farnsworth."

"You are dismissed, Holland."

Merrick turned and Arabella caught his expression at last. He was devastated by Holland's betrayal. Unshed tears filled his eyes, turning them glassy. He set his arm about Arabella's back to urge her away, and the tremble that shook him broke her heart.

They had gone barely three steps before Holland ran around

them to halt their progress. "Will you just stop and listen to me a moment? I can explain, but only if you keep an open mind and promise no harm to Lady Penelope's reputation."

"Why should I do anything you ask now? Why?"

Holland clutched his hands together before his waist, looking every bit guilty. "Of course I speak to her," he whispered. "She's my mother."

Merrick froze, clenching Arabella against him so tightly his fingertips hurt where they dug into her waist. "Never. My aunt is a spinster. She's never even considered marriage."

"It's true. I've always known."

Arabella turned in Merrick's arms, loosening his grip in the process, and held her hand to his chest to comfort him. Beneath her palm, Merrick's chest heaved. His eyes widened.

"Lies," he whispered.

"I couldn't tell you. No one knows about our connection."

"She never married, and I've never heard mention of suitors. There is nothing in her manner to suggest she'd ever been disappointed in love. How could you be her son?"

Arabella glanced over her shoulder in time to see Holland bowed his head. "She will not speak of that time, but from what she has said, I can only conclude that the experience was not pleasant. A trick perhaps to gain her dowry and Rutherford's favor?" Holland wrung his hands, eyes averted at his confession, and Arabella believed he was telling the truth.

Unfortunately, Merrick required more information to be convinced. "Go on."

"She has expressed strong views on the evils of gentlemen who engage in affairs before they marry and the natural consequences of such. That is likely why she has been so hard on you. What I do know for a certainty is that my mother left Newberry Park for several years around the time of my birth, and when she returned her sister had married Father. They never got along, as you may recall."

Merrick shook his head and released Arabella. When he paced away a few steps, Arabella held her breath. Such a situation made every difference to the revelation. If Lady Penelope had been forced and didn't want to marry the fiend, then Arabella could understand Holland's reluctance to mention the connection. Merrick's father had been truly evil.

"Aunt Pen might have nursed an older relation through the last years of her life," Merrick said at last. "But she never had a child. Rutherford would have disowned her."

"It does seem unlikely that she managed to hide my birth from him, but she was his favorite out of all his children. I cannot explain that. What I remember most were many moments when she laughed and played with me. I must have been very young for that to have happened.

"When she left to return to Newberry Park, she placed me in the care of her maid and new husband. I was already known as the servant's son to all who knew us and no one suspected subterfuge. But I remembered the truth and I cried for my real mother. Eventually, my new parents brought me to Essex and took up work in the tavern where we first met. I saw my mother but once a week when she came to the village. I was forbidden to call her mama except when no one could hear."

"You should have been the earl," Rothwell said suddenly, his posture stiffening at the idea.

Holland shook his head. "If that were so, then you would have been me; the bastard son of a man with absolutely no morals. Nothing would have changed his character even if he'd married my mother. He'd have taken his pleasure regardless with the same careless disregard. You may not be a saint where it comes to women, but you have been careful and kind to your lovers as he never was. She is proud of the man you've become, and will be even more so as soon as she realizes how deeply you care for Lady Farnsworth. I am proud of you, brother."

Merrick stared into the shadows instead of looking at Holland. "You should have told me."

Holland winced. "I could not. From the start you have suffered the weight of Father's misdeeds very badly. When they told you I was likely his child and should be sent away to prevent any scandal, you cut all ties with the Fords. I couldn't add another, worse, indiscretion to the burden. I kept the secret to protect you and my mother."

Merrick growled suddenly and stalked off, leaving Arabella and Holland alone. Arabella wasn't sure what to do or say, but when it became clear that Merrick might not return immediately, she smiled kindly at Holland. What a burden to bear in silence—caught between a brother and a mother, both of whom you love but who were at odds with one another, with no way to make it right.

Holland sighed loudly and gestured to the house. "If you would be so good as to return to the house, my lady. I have a lot to do before I depart in the morning."

Arabella approached and saw silvery tears slide unchecked down Holland's cheeks. She patted his sleeve. "Shouldn't you wait to see if he will change his mind?"

He smiled sadly. "I betrayed him. He has every right to be angry."

"Did you confide in Lady Penelope about me?"

"No. Not intentionally." He shook his head. "I have been thinking on my previous conversations with my mother. When she came to call on Merrick shortly after your arrival, she remarked that she hoped he hurried up and married, preferably to someone *pure of heart*."

"Pure of heart?" Arabella stared in astonishment. She'd never label herself that way. "Why ever would she think that meant I was there?"

"You must know my mother thinks very well of you. She never wastes her breath on someone she finds fault with. Merrick is not wrong about my mother's meddling tendencies." He pressed his lips together briefly, as if choosing his next words carefully. "She is an extremely observant woman and possesses a keen eye for inconsistencies in behavior. I must have glanced up at the ceiling and not known I'd done so. I would advise you never to play cards against her."

"Thank you for the warning."

"Please believe me, Lady Farnsworth, I never intentionally said anything about your presence. I should have been even more guarded than I usually am around her, a mistake I do regret very much. He turned his back on his family because of me. Since then I have tried my best to look out for him."

Arabella squeezed his arm to offer what comfort she could. Surely Merrick would change his mind. If he didn't, Arabella would talk to him about it herself and force him to at least reconsider. "Where will you go?"

"I've no idea, but I will think of something eventually." Holland gestured to the house. "Please, he would not like you left alone out of doors tonight after all that has happened. As I am sure you've discovered, he's very protective of those he loves."

Chapter Twenty-Eight

Merrick poured himself a drink to steady his conflicting emotions and drained it in one gulp. Although Arabella and his half brother had not realized he was there, he had lingered and heard their whole conversation. Despite the betrayal, he was concerned for Holland's future and where he might end up. His older brother had been with him since he'd come of age. They were friends as well as family.

"There you are, Rothwell. I was just about to come searching for you," Grayling grumbled as he drew close. "Rosemary would like to return home. The children are half asleep and wanting their beds."

"I'm sorry. I had a few matters on my mind."

"Well, I am not surprised." Gray leaned against the sideboard. "Do you want to talk about it?"

He glanced toward the entrance hall where Lady Grayling, the children, and Aunt Pen and Arabella had gathered, saying their farewells. Gray's carriage must have been called while his mind was elsewhere. The girls were leaning heavily against their stepmother and grumbling to her. Any moment there could be tears. He knew Grayling's daughters well enough to know sleep was what they needed.

Aunt Pen appeared as she always did—aloof and unimpressed by the tired children's interruptions. He would never be able to tell she'd ever been a mother and had harbored such a secret all these years. He could barely believe his aunt was Holland's mother, or anyone's, for that matter. It was unfathomable that his half brother would make up such an outlandish and potentially damaging story if it were not true. Holland worried just as much for the family's reputation as he did—if not more at times.

Merrick couldn't confide in Grayling about what troubled him. He would have to grow accustomed to the idea on his own. "Not this time."

Grayling slapped him on the shoulder. "Come see us tomorrow, or are you going back to London?"

Tomorrow he *should* return to London. Arabella would not marry him, and the longer he stayed, the more damage would be done to her reputation. Yet he couldn't bear to leave. If Arabella went to London in Aunt Penelope's company, he would have difficulty seeing her. His aunt was sure to get in the way even if he attempted a proper courtship. "I'll remain with Arabella and follow her back to London when she goes."

"Good man," Grayling murmured. "What's decided with her by the way? I know she told everyone the depth of your feelings when we were at the ruins, but what of hers? Have they changed in any way?"

"I don't believe they have. She's made it very plain that she doesn't want to marry again."

Merrick glanced past Grayling to where Arabella stood, speaking with Lady Grayling in hushed tones. The pair seemed firm friends and confidantes, even if Parker had hinted that Lady Grayling had a scandalous past. Gray hadn't offered up an explanation and there wasn't time now. One day he would ask Arabella where exactly she had met Rosemary, but not today. He had enough surprises to grapple with already.

Grayling tapped his arm, drawing his attention. "You can barely take your eyes from her. I would not have thought a proper lady would suit you, but you seem enthralled. Are you going to let her get away so easily?"

"I want her to want to marry me, Gray. Whatever she decides is best is what I'll have to accept. Wherever she goes, I will too, and we will see what develops."

"And if nothing changes?"

Merrick pushed his glass away decisively. "I'd rather not think on that, but I suppose I'll have little choice but to bury what I feel for her and attempt to start over."

"That might not be as easy as you think."

He stared at the beautiful woman who'd claimed him body and soul. She was unique and dear to him. She'd smoothly become a part of his life, and when they parted, he didn't think he'd be whole. "Nothing in life is ever easy. I'd hoped finding a bride might have been somewhat simpler than this."

"Then I'll hope that Arabella sees sense soon."

Merrick followed Grayling to the door, pausing at Arabella's side to wave them off. When the carriage had drawn sufficiently far away, he ushered her inside and made sure the doors were securely locked. He met his aunt's gaze several times, but in the end decided to hold his tongue and not say a word about recent revelations.

"Good night, ladies. I think I'll turn in."

Arabella's face fell. "As you wish."

He nodded. His aunt's expression grew puzzled and he turned away. He did not want to argue with her tonight. He did not want to hear her side of the story or her denial. The only opinion he wanted to hear was from his brother.

He made his way upstairs and found where his half brother rested his head. A light shone beneath the door and when he drew closer, Holland's baggage was the first thing he noticed. Already packed, standing beside the door in wait for the morning. Holland intended to leave as he could. Anxiety filled him and he pushed the door fully open. The room was neat and orderly. It would be easy to believe the room hadn't been in use except that Holland lay on top of the bed, dressed to leave, as if he couldn't wait to get away. "I always wondered if you slept fully dressed."

A brief smile flickered over Holland's face and disappeared again just as quickly. He did not rise as he usually would, but then again, Merrick had dismissed him. He wasn't a servant anymore.

"I cannot imagine why my habits are of any interest to you," Holland said in a dull voice lacking any interest in what he was doing visiting him at that hour.

He turned his face away and winced suddenly. He didn't complain. He expressed no outrage that he'd been injured. Merrick pulled a chair close to the bed and sat on it backward, folding his arms across the carved back.

He lowered his chin to his forearms and studied his brother, looking for signs of Aunt Penelope in his features. He noticed nothing different from what he'd always seen—a man of his father's making. "How is your head feeling now? Any better?"

"Does it matter?" Holland sighed heavily. "I will be gone in the morning, never fear."

Merrick chewed his bottom lip. A servant's life was often a great deal harder than it would be for one employed in his household. At Holland's age, without a reference to show another employer or connections he could admit to, he would have a difficult future ahead. "About that. I heard what you said to Arabella. Where are you going?"

Holland closed his eyes, his skin turning a distinct shade of red. "Away. It doesn't matter," he ground out. "I've never been wanted anywhere."

When Holland put it like that, Merrick's chest tightened painfully. Merrick would have drowned in his responsibilities long ago if not for Holland. Their half brothers, too, would have suffered and might never have come to his attention. Holland was the glue that bound their odd family together. "You were wanted, you *are* wanted, brother, but I could have done with the whole truth too."

Holland opened his eyes and slowly turned his head to stare. "You would never have wanted me around if you knew who my mother was. Admit it, you despise her."

He had and still did not want that woman involved in his life. Aunt Pen would meddle and pry and report his business to Rutherford. Who liked to be spied upon? He doubted she would change her habits for anyone. For years she'd ruled the family with the same opinions as her father. Family first—family meant legitimate *Fords*. She was not happy he chose to support so many of his father's mistakes. "Despite that, you are my brother. I must know where you are."

A strange smile flittered across Holland's face. "That is what my mother said to me when I entered your service. She wanted to know where you were so she knew where I would be. Her spying on you is merely a ruse to cover her real motives. She cannot write to me, but I can write to her because anyone would think I'm helping her keep you out of trouble."

Merrick gaped. It wasn't him under the microscope, but Holland. *Her son.* If that were true, then he hadn't one leg to stand on with his complaints. He sat back in the chair as he reconsidered his decision. The only thing he'd done by dismissing Holland in a fit of temper was upset them both.

Without Holland, he would have to advance another half brother to assist him. He didn't want to think of the chaos that would accompany that situation. Holland worked without his supervision or instruction most days. Since Merrick had become the earl, he had never once countermanded one of Holland's decisions when it came to the family and estate. He could easily have been the earl instead of Merrick.

Holland was sensible, thrifty, and fair. The Rothwell estates ran smoothly because Merrick had Holland at his side. He couldn't afford to lose him over this, and more importantly, he didn't need to.

He met Holland's gaze decisively. "We'll be in London for the rest of the season unless Arabella marries me, and then our plans may change to suit what she wants. Please ask your mother not to push the issue of marriage while Arabella is under her roof. I want her to change her own mind, not have it decided for her."

His brother sat up, apparently too quickly because his hand rose to his head to hold it. "You're taking me back?"

Merrick nodded. "If you want to stay, that is." He stood and swung the chair back into place beside the wall, leaving the room neat, the way Holland liked it. When he glanced around, his brother had risen to his feet, his expression stunned. "Of course I want to stay."

"The London town house is home, isn't it? Where else should you be but there?" When Holland said nothing to that, Merrick decided he'd done the right thing. Home wouldn't be the same without his family about him. His odd scrambled family of misfits that no one wanted. And to prove he harbored no ill feeling, he pulled his brother into a rough hug and held him tight. "No wonder we look so damn similar. Could use each other as bloody shaving mirrors, couldn't we?"

Holland's hand touched his head lightly as he tousled his hair. "I've thought so too on many occasions."

Merrick released him, overcome by emotions that threatened to unman him. "Get some sleep. The old sow likes to travel early." He winced at the insult he'd unthinkingly uttered before Holland.

Holland's brow rose.

"Forgive me," he begged quickly. "Old habits are often hard to break. But I will overcome this and behave in the future."

"Thank you." Holland nodded. "She's called the carriage for seven."

"In the morning? I gather you inherited the curse of rising early from her." Merrick rolled his eyes as he opened the door to let himself out. "Damn Fords, never let a man sleep till a decent hour."

"Mother can be a taskmaster about punctuality." Holland grinned widely. "The Fords never let a man have any peace. It's not in their nature."

Holland had just described their entire family, even the illegitimate ones. "Nor ours. Sleep well, brother."

Chapter Twenty-Nine

Arabella closed the door behind her softly and turned the key in the lock so no one would disturb her. Across the room, Merrick sat hunched on the side of his bed. She hadn't heard more than a few words from him all night, and she had been concerned about his disappearance. "I missed you tonight. Where did you go after Gray left?"

Merrick glanced around, unsmiling and serious for a change. "I wasn't particularly good company, and I wanted to speak with Holland again."

She approached him and discovered he'd begun undressing for bed, getting only so far as one boot off. "You couldn't have known."

He dragged a hand through his hair, looking confused and uncertain when he'd never been that way before. "Well, I know now and believe me, it will take some getting used to."

Arabella moved closer and laid a hand on his shoulder. "Did you speak to your aunt about it?"

He shook his head, gaze falling to the floor. "No. I don't think I ever shall have the courage to do that. In truth, I don't believe she would confirm or deny the accusation. I'd rather not stir the pot at all if that is all right with you."

"I think silence in this matter is definitely the right decision."

She rubbed her hand over his broad shoulders and then curled her fingers around his neck, slipping them beneath his shirt and pressing them against his muscles. He rumbled his approval. The heat of Merrick's skin soaked through his shirt and brought her pulse to life in the most disconcerting way.

"What will become of your brother? Would you like him to join the staff here?"

"No, but thank you, Arabella. That's a very kind offer." He removed her hand from his neck and brought it to his lips. He kissed her knuckles and then held her hand to his face. "He is coming home with me. We've spoken and he's made me consider the matter in a different light. Apparently Aunt Pen likes to keep track of him too."

"Well, she is his mother." She relaxed, pleased by his change of heart. "I'm relieved to hear that. Holland was quite upset. I would have hated to have you estranged from him. You make a very good team."

"I realized that, too." He leaned into her touch as if he found comfort in her presence. "She's kept him secret all these years. Not even Rutherford knows, and he usually knows everything. My father. Dear God, there are no words strong enough to describe him properly. He truly was an evil, grasping man. My father likely seduced Aunt Pen for her dowry, but when she wouldn't agree to the match and went away to deliver Holland in secret, he turned his attention to my mother. Imagine Aunt Pen's horror on discovering her own sister had married the monster."

Alarmed by the horror in his voice, she caressed his face and neck with her fingertips. "The stress of keeping Holland's existence secret would have been unbearable. The disagreement you had when you brought him to Newberry, it must have been fear of discovery, not anger, that provoked it. You do look remarkably similar. If Holland had lingered too long, your grandfather and others might have been found out and the scandal that would have followed could have torn the family in two."

He covered his face suddenly. "Oh God, Arabella what have I done? The things I have said."

She held him close as a lump formed in her throat. Merrick had been rather harsh in speaking of Lady Penelope, regardless of being provoked. "You are referring to your manner of speaking to her?"

"I never hesitated to complain to Holland about her meddling." His hands fell and he gripped the bed beneath him. "He has had to listen to every hateful word I've ever spoken about her. She is his mother. Yet he listened and never once complained."

"I think I can set your mind at ease a little." She drew his head against her and smoothed his hair with her fingers. "Yesterday when you cursed Lady Penelope, I was surprised at her reaction, or lack of. She smiled. I don't think you can hurt her, not when Holland is under your roof and you hold him in such high esteem. As I mentioned before, you were under no obligation to provide for him, or for any of your father's illegitimate children. You are a good man. The very best, as far as I can see."

Merrick looked up suddenly, staring hard at her face. "God, you're easy on me. Most women would have run shrieking from the madness of my life."

"Well, you've let me see a side of you that few can claim to know, and I never shriek. So unladylike," she told him, tears forming in her eyes. "And I cannot claim to have a perfectly sensible life either. I'm not sure I will ever again trust people as much as I once did."

"That's a shame." He caressed her cheek softly. "If not for your trust, I'd never have gotten to know you so well."

She bit her lip—at the moment people she trusted could be counted on one hand. Merrick was at the top of the list because of all he'd done for her without expecting a thing in return. Her heart beat a little faster. If she thought him the best of all men, did that mean she loved him? She bit her lip as the idea took hold. Could this really be what love was?

She shook her head, delaying that line of thought. The night would soon be over. She needed to ponder love with a clearer head. "You do what you can to help others less fortunate than yourself. Even without Farnsworth, I still would have seen it. You did not have to help my niece marry your cousin. And I know you feel some guilt over your father's behavior. I honor you for sharing your efforts to make amends for what wasn't of your doing."

Eventually, a smile teased at the corners of his lips. "I don't have any more secrets left to tell, Arabella. You know everything unsavory about me and my family now. The good and the bad. It's all there."

She kissed his forehead, his nose, and at last his lips. "I have one secret I should have told you too."

"Really? Just the one?"

"In coming to London to see Cecily matched and wed, I had a plan for myself. I wanted a lover. Someone who would teach me what I'd missed from my marriage. As you've discovered, my marriage was rather unfulfilling."

He cupped her face, brushing his thumb forward to brush her lips. "It was a pleasure I will never forget, nor would I want to."

She had found the perfect man for an affair. Merrick's patience and understanding had helped her feel less like an ignorant fool. He had opened her eyes to what pleasures might be found with him and made her want even more. "Nor will I. You have been an excellent teacher."

He fumbled with the ribbons on her nightgown, smiling in his wicked way as it opened. "There are other lessons I could share with you before I return to London."

"I was hoping you might be agreeable." She frowned at the thought of him leaving, but it would be for the best. "When do you go?"

He smiled and continued undressing her. "When you do. At the ungodly hour of seven in the morning, if you still intend to stay with my aunt in London despite all you've heard about us."

She nodded. Lady Penelope had spoken to her right before she went to bed and was rather determined to have her pay a visit, insisting they leave together tomorrow. Now that Arabella knew her better, she found the woman a lot less terrifying. "I think that might be best for now."

Merrick pulled a face. "Then I will call on you there if I may."

She grinned. "If you would brave your aunt's hospitality to see me, then I will be available at any time. I will look forward to your visits very much."

But there was still one matter that troubled her greatly. She tugged on his shirt and drew it over his head. "What about your plans to marry? The special license must be expiring soon."

"Let it." He stood and finished undressing her. As her chemise sailed across the room, he continued, "I was never in any rush. I'd very much like a chance to court you properly."

She searched his face for signs of frustration and saw none. "You might be wasting your time."

"It won't be a waste." He pulled her into his arms and brushed her lips with his. "Surely you cannot believe that what exists between us happens every day."

"I don't know. I told you I've never been in love." She wrapped her arms about his neck and pressed her cheek to his. "I don't know when I would be certain, in fact," she whispered.

It wasn't fair to him to lead him to believe anything less than the truth.

"One day, you might be surprised to find you cannot live another day without me. But for now I am content make love to you while I can." He drew her down to the bed at his side and set his lips to her throat. "What comes after we return to London is for you to decide."

The soft kisses he peppered over her skin woke her body completely and she reached for him, eager to bring him closer.

Merrick dragged her flush against him, already aroused and needing her. "I must take pains to avoid getting a child on you. I cannot ever be careless."

"I trust you."

"In this you shouldn't." He dragged her upper leg over his and ran his hand down the expanse of bare flesh. "I lose all sense and caution when I'm with you. How do you do that?"

As he examined her leg, he lifted his head to stare at his actions and exposed his throat. Arabella darted out her tongue and tasted his skin quickly. Merrick groaned. "Yes, just like that. One touch and I'm beyond thinking of much beyond the moment."

"I have no idea what I'm doing, but I am glad you like it." Arabella chuckled as she leaned in to kiss him there too.

Merrick groaned again, arms tightening about her shoulders to hold her against him. "I love everything you do. I'm afraid I always will."

Chapter Thirty

"I tell you, Rothwell, you have missed your chance. You have wasted valuable time mending fences with Lady Penelope Ford, and for what, I ask you? The dubious pleasure of her company? Now you will have to wait until next season to make the match you need," Lady Harrison warned as Lady Mary swept by on the arm of her future husband. "She would have made you an excellent countess if you'd not dragged your feet."

"I am not concerned," Merrick told her, attempting to hide his amusement at her outrage. "Lady Mary is not always kind to her servants, and that is a mark against her in my book."

Lady Harrison gestured to Miss Milne, who stood between her protective parents and her suitor, Lord Bellows. "And what of that, I ask you. How could you ignore another gentleman poaching in your territory? It was very clear you were interested in the girl, too. Milne has remarked more than once that you went so far as to discuss pin money."

Ah, so that was where he'd gone wrong and led Aunt Penelope to assume he was about to make an offer for Miss Milne. He silently vowed never to discuss pin money again except with Arabella.

It was a relief to him that the two young women Aunt Pen claimed were waiting for his proposal of marriage had found other gentlemen more interested in them. Arabella would have no cause for concern if the pair soon made a match with someone other than him.

A new face twirled past and he studied Miss Hayes. She was, as he'd first thought her to be, the closest to mimicking Arabella's grace ever to waltz through London's ballrooms.

"I see Miss Hayes has caught your eye," Lady Harrison teased. "Good choice, Rothwell. Very good, in fact. I do feel she will be an easy wife for a man of your inclinations."

Miss Hayes was popular, she was kind, and she was approved of by his Aunt Penelope, too. Yet one thing he'd discovered, that didn't truly surprise him overmuch, was that Miss Hayes might be close to Arabella in nature, but she wasn't close enough. For him, his head had been completely turned. He didn't mind that one bit.

"My inclinations?"

"Why, yes." Lady Harrison languidly fanned her face, her eyes skimming his chest then lower. Her brow rose suggestively. "It is well known you have a roving eye. Marriage will be very hard on you if your wife makes a fuss about every one of your affairs."

Merrick pursed his lips as if considering his answer, but he needed no time to decide what response to give. "I intend no affairs as I plan to marry only for love, Lady Harrison. Surely you approve of that."

"Love? Sir, you are cruel to make such a jest." She laughed at the absurdity.

Her mistake only caused minor irritation for him. He had known what he wanted wasn't the done thing in their society. Many men did not love their wives when they married. Sometimes they could not even stand them. He hoped to be the exception and make a better match. If his patience bore fruit, he would be a very happy man one day.

"Not at all. You wanted to know my requirements in a wife once, and I don't mind telling you what they are now. I want a wife to provide a son of course, someone whom I can talk to and share common interests with. I intend to spend every night of our marriage together. But what I want most of all is for that woman to know everything about me and yet love me despite my many flaws. If you'd placed a lady like that in my path, I would have braved any scandal or strife to make her my wife."

Lady Harrison stared at him in astonishment. "A love like

that does not exist."

"I have reason to believe it does." Beyond Lady Harrison, Arabella swept into the ball beside his aunt. As usual, his heart skipped a beat, but he did his best to hide his excitement from his companion. "Do excuse me. I see my aunt has arrived and I must speak to her."

He sauntered away without regret or doubts. A woman like Lady Harrison would never find such a love if she didn't believe it existed in the first place. From across the room, he admired Arabella as she stood close beside his aunt, chatting with animation to her nearby companions. As it always did, his tension eased as he saw her. He didn't mind not being her husband if he had the good fortune to see her every day. Just being in her orbit, talking to her, and occasionally dancing when his aunt pretended to cajole him to do so, made every day better than the last.

He eased into their group to greet his aunt first so as to avoid arousing suspicions that might embarrass Arabella. She had not told him she'd changed her mind about marriage, but then she had not ever suggested he stop paying her attention.

"Lady Penelope. A pleasure." He bowed to her but did not draw closer.

Her gaze raked him from head to toe and she smiled, offering up the one he normally did not like. "Rothwell. I hope all is well with you."

It had taken some time to reflect on their relationship and how it could or should change. Nothing had altered in any material way. He still did not trust her, but he was learning not to be so guarded about his life where it concerned Holland. "I am well, but my household has the sniffles. I hope for an improvement by the end of the week."

Holland was miserable in his sickbed. Merrick had forced his half brother back to bed that morning and only the threat of staying in himself to tend the man had gained obedience. The threat of Merrick missing a planned rendezvous with Arabella had kept Holland in his bedchamber throughout the day.

A frown grew on Aunt Pen's face, and then she bit her lip, a clear sign that she was more than a little concerned. "'Tis a shame when servants cannot perform their duties properly."

"True." He nodded, rather amazed that she worried over

Holland's health at all. "I know you were interested in the glasshouse for Winslette. The plans have just been delivered and feature the alterations we discussed last week. I'd invite you for luncheon so you might inspect them at leisure, but with sickness in the house..."

Since all of London knew of their long-standing estrangement but not the cause, a few breaths caught at his invitation. Aunt Pen saw her cue to interrupt and took it. "Dr. Pinkerton is always very good for a dripping nose. I shall deliver him to you in the morning and give my verdict on the plans after that. I am sure Lady Farnsworth would like to comment on the changes you propose to her former home too."

Aunt Pen cast a sly glance in Arabella's direction.

"I'd appreciate that very much." It was a struggle to keep the smile off his face as she turned away to speak to a newcomer. Aunt Pen had not the slightest interest in the greenhouse project, but Arabella had been the force behind the design of the greenhouse in the first place and surely would like to see the minor suggestions he'd asked to be included. He sincerely hoped she would accompany Aunt Pen tomorrow because he was aching to hold her in his arms again. It had been far too long since they'd had any time alone.

Chatter rose around them and he let it wash over him. He met Arabella's gaze and smiled a greeting. Her eyes glowed with approval, but she was encircled now by others and he couldn't reach her to tell her the latest development for her home.

"Excuse me, my lord," a footman whispered at his elbow. "There's an urgent message for your attention."

Merrick took the note from the servant's silver tray and ripped it open. He read it quickly and then hastily folded it again before anyone noticed what it really was. For a horrifying moment, he had feared the note had come from home with news that Holland's condition had worsened in his absence.

But it was only another special license, courtesy of his grandfather to replace the one that expired just yesterday. The Duke of Rutherford truly was a menace.

Finally free of a conversation that had grown tedious the moment it had begun, Arabella joined Merrick and glanced at the paper he kept tapping against the palm of his hand. Its size seemed familiar. "That looks important."

"It is. The Fords are meddling again." He passed it to her. "Read it if you like."

Arabella took the note and read it twice, just to make sure she hadn't imagined the missive might be what she'd been hoping for. "That was considerate and rather well timed. The other has just expired, hasn't it?"

"Yes." He took the paper from her and slipped it into his pocket. "Did you notice my grandfather's gift was even more presumptuous than his last?"

The duke had added Arabella's name this time. She hadn't met him as he remained at Newberry Park, but she judged it a sign of his approval and hope. "Oh, I don't know. It does save us some time."

"Arabella." His gaze snapped to hers, concern plain in his eyes. He eased back a step and Arabella followed so they might speak privately away from the other guests. "Are you increasing?" he whispered urgently.

She shook her head. "No. Not that."

Merrick had been very concerned about her conceiving a child, and she wanted to reassure him that he was nothing like his father. She knew if she became pregnant, he would marry her immediately. Yet to her surprise, she was disappointed not to fall pregnant after all. If she had, then Merrick would have proposed to her again immediately she was sure. The more time they spent apart, the more she wanted to be with him. She had come tonight in the hope he would ask again. This time round she knew what her answer would be.

"Good." His shoulders eased as the tension left him. "I am relieved beyond a doubt. I must admit I have lost more than a few hours of sleep in worry. I can never get enough of you when we are together. And when we are apart, I am a changed man. Holland is beside himself over my sleeplessness and the other servants are walking around as if on eggshells."

Arabella's cheeks grew hot. She hadn't imaged he'd miss her

as much as she'd missed him. She stared at the side of his handsome face, noticing he'd returned his gaze to the ballroom's occupants. She liked it better when she had his whole attention. "Ask me again."

Merrick turned swiftly and took her hand. "Marry me."

"Yes."

He lifted her hand and pressed a lingering kiss to her knuckles. When he lowered her hand from his lips, he was beaming so happily her heart filled with all the love she'd discovered she felt for him. "Tomorrow?" he asked impudently.

Tomorrow was too far away. She slipped the paper from his pocket herself and read it again. "A pity it cannot be tonight. This is a *special* license. We could be married at any time and any place of our choosing."

He squeezed her hand tightly. "I was trying to be patient."

"You have been more than patient." She touched his face, aware that everyone around them had a front-row seat to their discussion and did not care. In the past, she would have been concerned for the rules and hidden what she was feeling. But not now. Not today. She wanted to prove to Merrick that his understanding and patience had borne results. They belonged together. "I have one last confession to make. I love you."

"And I love you." He drew her against him, holding her gaze as if there was no one else in the room. He grinned. "Holland will dance a jig tonight, even with his sniffles."

"A match at last." His aunt smacked her fan against Merrick's shoulder, startling them both enough to look at her instead of each other. "Rothwell, it's about time you proposed. I've never seen such long faces as I have these past weeks. And you, Arabella, all this pretending you needed time to discover if you were in love. You should have married a month ago and saved us all the aggravation of waiting for the wedding."

Arabella met Merrick's gaze and couldn't help the laugh that bubbled from her throat. Merrick's relationship with his aunt was mending slowly day by day, but Lady Penelope simply couldn't help but tell them what must be done.

Merrick shrugged and kept his arms about her. "Arabella deserved to have her wishes respected, Aunt. I have enjoyed our time together immensely and harbor no regrets at all about the need to conduct a discreet courtship. Do stay out of my affairs. I want to talk to my dearest Arabella."

"Talk later. A marriage and nothing less," Aunt Pen insisted, then spun about to search the room. The next instant she did the most astonishing thing Arabella had ever seen. She raised her arm and madly waved it about in the air. "Mr. Gibbs! This way. Tonight will do. It's rather fortunate that I just so happen to have a vicar with me," she said to them with a straight face when she turned back, but her eyes twinkled with excitement.

Merrick took the folded special license from Arabella's fingers and studied it. "Why am I not surprised that the arrival of this coincided with a vicar's presence at a ball where a vicar is hardly ever needed?"

Arabella leaned close to his ear so she could whisper. "Can I describe to you the flurry of letters that have been passing from your aunt to Newberry Park for the past weeks? I've never seen such correspondence. It's been vastly entertaining listening to Aunt Pen extol the virtues of a swift and decisive marriage. My ears have been cruelly assaulted."

"I'm glad you were so well entertained and I'm equally glad her opinions had no bearing on your decision. All I had were Holland's glum face greeting me each evening when I came back empty-handed without you. Not a pleasant prospect either." He laughed good-naturedly. "Thank you."

Arabella set her hands to his face. He was such a dear, sweet man to be so patient. He was the most astonishing man for thanking her for loving him. "Aunt Pen, do excuse us a moment. There is something I've been longing to do these past weeks."

Aunt Pen beamed at Arabella's informal mode of address. "My dear, you may have him as soon as may be, and with my blessing of course, but get married to him first."

"Oh, all in due course." Arabella smiled at Merrick, excitement making her giddy and restless. She caught his coat in her hands and held tight. "I'm ready for my next lesson in love."

"And I'm ready for my first lesson in marriage." He winked. "I've never done it before, you know."

Arabella turned her face to Merrick's, and then she kissed him in the way he'd shown her on the night their accidental affair had first begun, right before the entire *ton* and Aunt Pen.

When the noise around them grew deafening, she rested her cheek against his so she could whisper in his ear. "And if I have my way, you'll never need to again."

Epilogue

Arabella snuggled closer to Merrick on the divan, the centerpiece of their new greenhouse at Winslette. The simple affair she'd hoped for had been expanded until the space was large enough for Merrick's collection and hers, along with enough comfortable chairs they could spend all day in if they had guests. Despite her contentment, she peeked through the frosted glass at the scene unfolding a few yards away to check on her latest matchmaking project. "I think it's sweet."

"You would." Merrick grumbled and then tossed the book he'd been reading onto a nearby table. "You're much too tender hearted. That girl will be the ruin of him."

Arabella's new maid, the first female, non-relation employee in Merrick's household for the past eight years, had developed an affection for Merrick's half brother that was impossible to miss. To Arabella, those feelings were certainly reciprocated. Holland couldn't keep his eyes from the girl, but so far he'd been entirely proper. "Lady Penelope doesn't seem to mind. She said Lisette knew *how to style hair*."

"Such a compliment. You call that smile at tea earlier happiness?" He stood to stare out the window at his half brother and Lisette, showing her his broad back, his long legs, and stirring wicked ideas in her mind again. "Bet he hasn't the courage to kiss her. He's going too slow."

Merrick wore everything very well. She liked him both in and out of his clothing. Right now, she wished he was out of it and they were upstairs in their bed. She shifted on the couch, suddenly disappointed that she must have luncheon with Aunt Pen soon. At the moment she would much rather tempt Merrick back to bed than entertain his family. "Well, you know she cannot show too much interest in the romance without drawing unwanted attention."

He looked at her curiously. "Why did you invite her then?"

Why had she? Simple kindness had certainly played a large part in her decision. "I didn't want to deny Aunt Pen the chance to meet Lisette. If the relationship develops as I hope, she will see her son made a happy man. Aunt Pen may never get to spend much time with him or any children they may have unless we invite her to stay with us. It is sad to imagine she might never be known as a doting grandmother. I think she would have been wonderful and spoiled them."

"I think your pregnancy has run amok with your imagination." Merrick rejoined her on the divan and pressed a kiss to the rounding of her belly where their child lay. "Do you hear that, sir or little miss? Your mama thinks well of everyone. We are very fortunate indeed to have her to love us."

"Not everyone." There were two who deserved to be ignored and distrusted. Her former brother-in-law, Lord Farnsworth, she'd given the cut direct several months ago and had enjoyed doing so, especially with Lady Penelope firmly entrenched at her side. The last she'd heard of him, his creditors had been carting his possessions from Hinkley to pay his debts when he'd suddenly disappeared. He hadn't only owed Lord Parker, he'd apparently run up debts everywhere.

She threaded her fingers through Merrick's hair as he rained kisses over her belly. "I may never speak to Lady Harrison again."

Merrick glanced up, frowning at the reminder of a recent encounter with the woman. "Louisa was informed I would be faithful to my wife. Have I given you reason to doubt me?"

"No. But..." Arabella scowled and struggled to sit up. So late in the pregnancy, she had little more grace than a whale and that made her even more irritated with Merrick's former lover. "She had no right to run her hands all over you as if she was allowed to eat you at the Fairweather ball."

Merrick pushed pillows behind her back to help her get into a more comfortable position. He didn't reply as footsteps approached.

When Merrick's youngest half brother, Danny, appeared at her side, papers in hand, she forced a smile to her face. The boy usually had a smile for her too, but today, coming direct from the schoolroom, he wasn't a happy fellow. He thrust them out. "I finished."

"Already?" She smiled as she took them, then caught Merrick's eye. "I think this young man might have the makings of a scholar one day."

Danny's penmanship had improved considerably these past weeks with extra attention given to that area of study. She no longer had to squint at some words now, and she was pleased. She wanted only the best for the boy.

Danny fidgeted, his steps soft as he crossed the room to peer out the windows while Arabella glanced over the papers. "Can I go now? The others are waiting for me by the stables."

Merrick raised a brow. "Or he'll make an eager fisherman. Yes, lad. But"—he held up one finger—"no matter what the others plan to do with their evening, you must come back to Winslette well before nightfall, or Holland will worry and come in search of you."

"Huzzah! I will. I promise," he called as he rushed for the nearest door.

They both laughed at his haste and excitement. Merrick faced her when the boy was out of sight and they could no longer hear him. "I think *that* brother might require an active profession rather than an idle one."

"Whatever you choose, he still needs to write legibly. I will certainly expect letters from him when he goes off to school." Although her heart ached that Danny would leave them soon, Arabella slipped the papers onto a side table and returned to their former topic of conversation. "We're not done talking about Lady Harrison."

"She said she stumbled."

Arabella did not believe that for one moment. Merrick did not give credence to how women of their circle viewed their marriage. Everyone whispered he would soon grow bored and betray her. She rubbed her hands over her belly, feeling uncertain and round and altogether unappealing. "The woman has surer feet that any cat. She was testing you out to see if you could be tempted away from me."

He took her hand in his and kissed her palm, her wrist, and the back of her hand. "Never. I am not a fool to risk losing you. Trust me, Bella darling. I love you. I love our life together. There is no one in the world that could tempt me away from what we have. Do you think any one of them could take your place as my wife?"

She squirmed a little more. His kisses only added to her agitation. "Well, I don't think they plan to marry you. Seducing you is probably more in line with their thinking."

"Not mine." He brushed his fingers over her cheeks. "You're matchmaking my illegitimate brother and I've a suspicion you're secretly planning his wedding day in your head. I knew what I was committing myself to the moment I let you into my life. My greatest fear is that you might grow tired of us."

"I'd never. It's just…"

"Darling." He kissed her lips softly and drew back. "You really are out of sorts today. What can I do to make you happier? Rub your feet, your back? Have a bath drawn and touch you everywhere?"

That last sounded divine. Arabella fell into his eyes, hoping that no matter what happened, or how much rounder his child grew in her belly, he would always be her best friend and confidant. Waiting for the baby to come was making her irritable, despite her efforts not to be. "Well, maybe a kiss or two more could turn my mood around."

His lips lifted in a smile that never failed to make her heart skip a beat and her body awaken. "Just one or two?"

"Maybe more," she confessed as he kissed the tip of her nose.

"For as long as you'll have me?"

She bit her lip as his warm hands slid beneath her gown and caressed her knee. More of that would be heaven. "The rest of our lives might just be long enough," she whispered as he drew her to her feet, escorted her upstairs with a wicked smile that sent her body into a pleasant hum, and showed her beyond a doubt just what their love meant to him.

If you enjoyed An Accidental Affair
Don't Miss the
next distinguished Rogue in

Keepsake

Discovering passion is easy. Keeping love, however, proves a challenge for the Distinguished Rogue in this fifth exciting installment to the series.

Chapter One

The Season,
June 1814

When a man settles on a new course for his life, it's necessary to relinquish the old and learn from his mistakes. When a marquess, disappointed, requires a replacement bride, it becomes absolutely certain that his next choice will live up to his expectations. Kit Reed, Marquess of Taverham, might not understand why his first wife had disappeared without so much as leaving a note, but that departure hadn't been anything to do with him.

He focused on the stage of the Theatre Royal, but his mind was distracted by what he needed to do tomorrow. He had to convince those who mattered that his marriage should be set aside and soon.

He had last seen *The Beggar's Opera* with Miranda, his first and fleeting bride, a few months before their marriage. He thought it fitting to see it one last time before he took the first steps on the path to have her declared legally dead after a ten-year absence.

He drew in a deep breath. There was no possibility she was coming back. He'd searched and hoped for so long after he could have had her declared legally dead that his friends were looking upon him with pity. He was done with the past.

He was done dancing to Miranda's tune

He might not have loved her, but she was his wife and he owed her for the dowry she'd brought to him through their marriage. A fortune that had saved him and their home from the tumbledown ruin it had been on their wedding day.

She should have stayed to see the good their marriage had brought to those connected to the estate. Because of her, every situation had improved greatly over the years.

His gaze flickered across the theatre briefly to where his married friends sat in their own box. Lovers surely, their hands linked, their eyes meeting and soft smiles twisting their lips. He looked down at his clenched fist and forced himself to relax.

There was nothing Miranda had liked better than theatricals, even badly performed ones that made her laugh uproariously and earned her so many disapproving looks. Miranda had been so different in her manner than anyone he knew that he could only conclude he'd been so blinded by her zest for life that he'd proposed before he'd thought the matter through properly. He knew better now.

He turned to Lady Brighthurst to whisper, "How goes plans for this year's hunt?"

A longtime friend and confidant, the recently widowed Emily knew only a portion of his reasons for attending this play. Emily wasn't as enthusiastic about the opera as Miranda had once been, but since she'd come up to town for the season to discuss their arrangement and had no other engagements tonight, she'd humored him by accepting an invitation so he wouldn't have to sit alone.

"It is well in hand, although"—she eased closer—"we have a great many more acceptances than usual this year. I cannot account for the increase in numbers."

Kit smiled, noticing a few familiar faces watching them closely rather than the performance on stage. When he frowned, they quickly turned their attention elsewhere. To Emily he said, "They come this year for the pleasure of your company and because of your renown for designing the most elaborate feasts. Acton's warm and gracious hospitality has always drawn the most avid hunters north, but you are the icing on the cake my dear."

"Thank you." Yet her brow creased into lines of deep concern. "I fear the number of guests this time around may be even too great for us to host."

Kit patted her hand soothingly. "Nonsense, the more the merrier is Acton's motto, and I'm sure with the continued help of staff and funds from Twilit Hill the event will be a merry one. Acton would sulk if I offered my estate as an alternative location for the hunt."

Besides, Kit hadn't hosted a gathering since his wedding day.

"Acton loves you as a brother," Emily continued with considerable feeling. "He would give way should you ask and particularly if doing so made me happy, too."

Kit shook his head. "But I will not ask. I will continue to support the event in my own quiet way. It's worked this way since I inherited the title and there's no need to change anything about our arrangement in the foreseeable future."

Emily laughed softly. "If only you let others see your generous heart and home more often, they would know how truly worthy a gentleman and dear friend you are."

"Thank you," he murmured while thinking he'd been a failure as a husband. Miranda had not thought him worthy in the end.

"She's seated in my place," Miranda's soft voice complained in his mind as if she'd the right to tell him what to do after all these years.

Kit closed his eyes and willed the voice of his wife to leave him in peace. *Miranda's place* at his side had been empty for so long. He had at last reconciled to never seeing her or hearing her voice again. *It's too late now.*

Emily jostled against his sleeve. "I beg your pardon?"

Kit opened his eyes quickly. Had he spoken out loud? He'd been a poor escort so far, burdened by a heavy heart in the face of his decision. "Forgive me, my dear," he murmured to Emily. "My mind wandered and I spoke out of turn."

Emily turned fully to look behind him. "Madam, you are in the wrong box."

Oh. There was always someone blundering into a box in search of friends and vacant seats so he took no notice. He pinched the bridge of his nose and left Emily to shoo them away.

Emily had been a great comfort to him over the years. She alone out of all his friends had counseled patience when taking his next step to secure a wife and heir, especially since his first attempt had been thwarted by Miranda's sudden and shocking disappearance.

She'd understood and accepted his hesitation in seeking to declare her dead. He could have taken these steps three years ago. No one had heard news of her, but with no body found there still seemed a chance she lived, so he'd continued to delay. The problem was Kit—he was having the devil of a time letting go of her memory. Miranda had made a lasting impression on him, despite their short time together.

Married a day. Not even the wedding night spent together.

It was the two dozen nights spent in her bed before the wedding that made Miranda impossible to forget.

"Unfortunately not." A feminine sigh sounded behind him, one edged with irritation. "I'll allow you to lay claim to the chair in Taverham's box for the night, but the man you cling to so firmly is certainly taken."

The hair on the back of Kit's neck prickled with awareness, but he dared not turn around. It was only a waking dream of Miranda. He had chased after shadows for a very long time.

Emily's fingers tightened over his sleeve in a startlingly strong grip. She gasped suddenly. "Why have you returned to haunt us?"

"Haunt you?" the voice taunted. "I'm not a shade of times past. I merely intend to make sure you understand that he cannot offer for you, even if he wished to."

Kit's heart raced as he stood. He recognized that voice, even after so long apart. Miranda's voice had never failed to send shivers down his spine with just a few words.

The comedic actress on stage faltered and fell silent, her gaze turning to his box. She lifted one arm to point and then used the other to cover her mouth as if she were stunned. With the performance so suddenly halted, the audience followed the actress' direction to stare at his box too. By his estimation, several thousand sets of eyes turned to discover the source of her distress. It was not a pleasant feeling by any stretch of the imagination to be the focus of such widespread scrutiny.

Lady Brighthurst stroked his arm. "I can assure you I am wanted here tonight."

"Tonight perhaps, but come morning the whole of London shall know your efforts to win yourself a marquess will amount to exactly nothing," Miranda's voice said mockingly. "Enjoy the theater, my dear. *The Beggar's Opera* was always my favorite. I am sorry the dowager marchioness has led your hopes on a fool's errand. She was unbelievably blunt about the practicalities of marriage to her son before. I remember his guardians left me with no illusions of marital felicity thanks to your existence."

Unable to ignore what he was hearing, Kit spun around. His breath ceased in his lungs and he took an involuntary step forward when he saw the woman standing behind him.

Miranda!

This could not be real. Not now. How could his wife come back to him when he'd just made the decision to end their marriage?

Even though shadows cloaked her features, he recognized his wife. "Miranda?"

The lady had the audacity to drop into low curtsy and flutter her fan as if she were overcome. *A curtsy of all things!* She rose and stepped farther into the light and the crowd in the theater gasped loudly, the theatergoers beginning to mutter to each other.

The last time he'd seen Miranda, she'd just spoken her vows after a long night of making love to him. That had been ten years ago. Since then, little had changed of her looks except she had become even more beautiful. She was still as elegant as his memory remembered, still as desirable as his fantasies supplied. His eyes lowered slightly from her startlingly direct gaze, skimming along her flawless skin and dipping into the cleavage her scandalously low-cut gown revealed.

He still wanted everything he saw.

"Darling," she replied in a clear, strong voice that must have carried far in the unusually hushed theatre. Her gaze raked him from the top of his head to the tips of his boots with a bold, proprietary eye. "You're looking well, husband. The new fashions agree with you, but I'm the first to flatter you tonight, am I? Your good friend there was just complimenting you on your boundless generosity with my dowry."

He stared at the woman he'd married a decade before. Same dark hair curling around her ears and nape, same almond-shaped gray eyes that he could lose himself in. Her cheeks were flushed with hot color and her breath was quick, forcing her breasts to rise and fall seductively.

However, her smile wasn't the one he remembered from before their marriage, though that might stem from finding him attending the theatre with a pretty widow on his arm and secret plans in his mind to marry again.

Yet the fact that he was in such a position was entirely her doing. He was not in the wrong. He had finally convinced himself that Miranda must be dead and had made new plans for his life beginning tonight. He folded his arms across his chest and refused to feel guilty. "Where the devil have you been?"

Emily stood and laid a restraining hand on his arm. "Is this the best place for this discussion, Kit?"

He nodded decisively. Miranda might still hold a certain power over his body, but he wanted everyone to know that it was not *he* who had driven her away. He had chosen his wife poorly ten years ago, and he would not be that unguarded, reckless man ever again. He'd paid a high price for her abandonment. Some whispered he'd murdered her for her dowry, though he'd never been outright accused of any crime.

He stared Miranda down. He would not say another word until she answered him.

"Where I was wanted." Miranda's eyebrow quirked upward innocently, and when she glanced at his companion, her smile was full of pity. "I am sure you are overjoyed to be witness to our happy reunion after so many years apart. I regret spoiling your first season out of mourning with my return, Lady Brighthurst, but you still cannot have him."

As the crowd's mutterings rose higher, Emily stepped around him to advance on Miranda. "You turned your back on a great man."

"I'm sure you've been a sincere comfort to him over the years." Miranda smirked as she drew back. "And if he's as attached to you as clearly as you are to him, then you may continue in that vein and skulk about together in private as much as you like. But remember, you'll never be his marchioness now unless he divorces me or kills me."

Kit scowled at Miranda's flippant remarks. Divorce was abhorrent to him, and while her disappearance might have angered him, even worried him, he'd never once wished her dead. He'd had enough subtle accusations of that nature to find no amusement in it.

He slipped around Emily to grasp Miranda's arm, more to prove her not a figment of his imagination than to pull her close. One touch, however, and that same reckless attraction stirred his heart as it had when he'd first met her, as if her disappearance from his life and their estrangement had never happened. He had the unfathomable urge to pull her into his arms and kiss her right there and then before everyone. He glanced around to clear his head.

Emily was right that their conversation needed a more private location if his thoughts already ran to the precursors of intimacy.

Around them, the theatre patrons craned their necks to watch his marriage resume with a gasping splutter. Tomorrow, society would talk of nothing else but his wife's very public return, and it would hardly be favorable speculation as to where she'd been all these years. "Perhaps we should move our conversation elsewhere. We are drawing attention."

"That was precisely my intention." Miranda did not fight to loosen his hold but stared at him cynically. "I chose the venue for my return well. I wanted everyone to see that I was alive just in case an accident suddenly befell me."

"And I must say that the sight of you fills my heart with boundless joy, Lady Taverham." Lord Louth, a friend of Kit's, stepped into the box behind Miranda, a wide grin upon his face. "I am delighted to see you returned to society at last, fair lady."

"Martin," Miranda cried. "Oh, you darling man."

Miranda pulled free of Kit's grip and embraced Louth with a degree of familiarity Kit found alarming. He suddenly remembered Louth had exhibited a puppyish devotion to Miranda before the wedding, and it seemed the admiration was now mutual. But how could that be?

When she drew back to a proper distance, her grin was the first sincere one to cross her face since he'd seen her. "I was coming to see you."

A pleased smile passed over his face. "That does gladden my heart. Are you all right?"

"I am. Are you well?"

"The same." He squeezed her hand tightly. "I'm sitting across the theatre in Daventry's box. The poor man cannot believe you're alive. Do you know he's married?"

Miranda laughed, a sound that thudded through Kit's entire being. He remembered that laugh very well, but the last time he'd heard it they'd been making love, laughing through the whole affair as if the real world of responsibilities and duty hadn't existed.

"The whole of England has heard of his marriage and the good he's done for his wife," she said. "I am so happy for Lillian. Such a sweet and kind girl who deserved someone who would spoil her."

Kit moved toward Miranda. Lady Daventry had been a virtual recluse for so many years before her marriage that few even knew she was alive. "How the devil are you acquainted with Daventry's wife?"

"I am acquainted with many," Miranda answered with a shrug.

Louth hooked Miranda's arm about his and held her there. "I had no idea you'd met Lilly until a moment ago. She's very keen to renew her acquaintance with you."

"And I her. Why, this very moment, in fact." Miranda glanced over her shoulder, a smile of triumph on her face when she met Kit's gaze. "I think I've done all I needed to do here."

Then, before he could blink twice, Miranda swept from the box on Louth's arm.

A wild roaring filled Kit's ears and he glanced around, afraid that he'd dreamed his greatest wish. Emily was pale, almost stricken in appearance.

He swallowed quickly. "Given the circumstances, I feel it best to retire for the evening."

Emily's eyes closed. "Yes. I expect you should. Don't worry about me. I am sure I can find my brother to drive me home."

"I knew I could count on you to understand." Kit drew in a shuddering breath.

Miranda lived.

His wife lived.

Kit was still a married man!

His wife had been at his side and then promptly disappeared again. He stared across the theater at Daventry's box. There she sat, greeting Lady Daventry as if she hadn't a care in the world and was an old friend. But Miranda still hadn't given Kit an explanation for her ten-year absence from his life and Kit would have his answers tonight.

He stormed after her, skirting the malingerers in the corridor between his and Daventry's box in order to confront his wife. He cursed under his breath when he found the box now empty of Miranda, Lord Louth, and even the Daventrys. He charged for the theater entrance, determined to catch his wife before she got away. Outside, carriages clattered past but none stopped to take passengers or were pulling away with new ones.

He raked his fingers through his hair. Where the hell had his damn wife gone now?

More Regency Romance From Heather Boyd...

Saints and Sinners Series

Book 1: The Duke and I
Book 2: A Gentleman's Vow
Book 3: An Earl of Her Own

Rebel Hearts Series

Book 1: The Wedding Affair
Book 2: An Affair of Honor
Book 3: The Christmas Affair
Book 4: An Affair so Right

The Wild Randalls Series

Book 1: Engaging the Enemy
Book 2: Forsaking the Prize
Book 3: Guarding the Spoils
Book 4: Hunting the Hero

Miss Mayhem Series

Book 1: Miss Watson's First Scandal
Book 2: Miss George's Second Chance
Book 3: Miss Radley's Third Dare
Book 4: Miss Merton's Last Hope

And many more...

About Heather Boyd

Determined to escape the Aussie sun on a scorching camping holiday, Heather picked up a pen and notebook from a corner store and started writing her very first novel—Chills. Years later, she is the author of over thirty sexy regency historical romances. Addicted to all things tech (never again will Heather write a novel longhand) and fascinated by English society of the early 1800's, Heather spends her days getting her characters in and out of trouble and into bed together (if they make it that far). She lives on the edge of beautiful Lake Macquarie, Australia with her trio of mischievous rogues (husband and two sons) along with one rescued cat whose only interest in her career is that it provides him with food on demand and a new puppy that is proving a big distraction.

You can find details of her work and writing at
www.Heather-Boyd.com

Printed in Great Britain
by Amazon

40546981R00148